The
Shadow Dancer

❮ The ❯
Shadow Dancer

Margaret Coel

BERKLEY PRIME CRIME, NEW YORK

THE SHADOW DANCER

A Berkley Prime Crime Book
Published by The Berkley Publishing Group,
a division of Penguin Putnam Inc.,
375 Hudson Street, New York, New York 10014.

Visit our website at
www.penguinputnam.com

First edition: September 2002

Library of Congress Cataloging-in-Publication Data

Coel, Margaret, 1937–
    The shadow dancer / Margaret Coel.— 1st ed.
        p.   cm.
    ISBN 0-425-18640-7 (alk. paper)
    1. O'Malley, John (Fictitious character)—Fiction.   2. Holden, Vicky
(Fictitious character)—Fiction.   3. Wind River Indian Reservation
(Wyo.)—Fiction.   4. Arapaho Indians—Fiction.   5. Women lawyers—
Fiction.   6. Wyoming—Fiction.   7. Clergy—Fiction.   I. Title.

PS 3553.O347 S47 2002
813'.54—dc21
                                                            2002066525

PRINTED IN THE UNITED STATES OF AMERICA

10   9   8   7   6   5   4   3   2   1

Acknowledgments

Many people read all or parts of this manuscript and contributed the expertise and good judgment to make the story much better than it otherwise would have been. I am very grateful. My sincere thanks to:

Thomas D. Lustig, senior staff attorney, Rocky Mountain Natural Resources Clinic, National Wildlife Federation; Thomas Dougherty, senior advisor, office of the president, National Wildlife Federation; Mike Pease, bomb disposal officer, Boulder Police Department; J. David Love, Ph.D., retired research geologist, U.S. Geological Survey, and Jane Love, friends and excellent advisers, as are Swede Johnson, attorney, and Elizabeth Girard, M.D.; Elaine Long, author of *Jennie's Mountain*, a friend and writer whom I've long admired; Arthur Long, expert on many subjects, including dynamite; John Dix, my nephew and the best baseball player I know; Carl Starkloff, S.J., and Anthony Short, S.J., valued friends and consultants, both formerly of St. Stephen's Mission on the Wind River Reservation; Beverly Carrigan and Carl Schneider, also valued friends and sharp-eyed readers; Karen Gilleland, another excellent friend and gifted writer;

Virginia Sutter, Ph.D., member of the Arapaho tribe, long-time friend who has taught me much about the Arapaho Way; and Kristin Coel Henderson, my daughter, and George Coel, my husband, the best consultants and toughest critics of all.

Dedicated to

Eleanor Margaret Henderson

Father, the morning star!
Look on us. We have danced until daybreak.
We have danced until daybreak.
Take pity on us.
Take pity on us.
Hi'i'i'!

Stand ready!
Stand ready!
So that when the crow calls you,
You will see him.
You will see him.

— ARAPAHO SONGS

◀ 1 ▶

My relations, stand ready, stand ready. I bring you the words of the father himself, Hesuna'nin. The father sent the lightning that cleansed and burned me into the ground. He took me to the shadow land, where I saw the ancestors: Black Coal, Sharp Nose, Yellow Calf, Little Raven, Medicine Man, Left Hand. I saw the beautiful women standing tall and proud and the children running and playing with hoops and sticks. The father told me to tell you that the new world is coming. Already crow is flying on the clouds and bringing the ancestors back to us. They come with the mighty herds of buffalo, deer, and elk. Once again the white lodges will spread beneath the cottonwoods. Green grass will cover the plains. There will be wild fruits and vegetables, and the rivers will run clean. The father will keep his promise to us. The new world will slide over the old, like the right hand over the left.

From a half-mile down the road, Father John O'Malley could see the small, white house reflecting the late afternoon light, stark and solitary in the empty expanse of the plains. The second act of *Faust, "De l'enfer qui vient,"* rose from the tape player beside him and mixed with the sound of the wind over the half-opened windows of the Toyota pickup. It was the last Monday in May, the Moon When the Ponies Shed Their Shaggy Hair, in the Arapaho way of marking the passing time. For a week, the temperature had been setting record highs.

He turned into the bare-dirt yard and stopped next to the concrete stoop at the front door. The curtains in the front windows were half-closed against the sun, making the house seem inviting, a shady oasis. A twenty-year-old sedan with the rear bumper bent at one end was parked next to the house. He let the tape play a moment, then hit the off switch and got out, giving the door a hard slam that sounded like a rifle shot in the quiet. Anybody inside would know he'd arrived.

He leaned against the pickup and pulled his cowboy hat down against the sun. It was not polite to bang on the door and call attention to yourself. If someone wanted to see you, he'd come out and say so. Beyond the house, the plains ran into the dun-colored foothills of the Wind River mountains. The white peaks lay along the blue sky like a serrated knife.

In his eight years at St. Francis Mission on the Wind River Reservation, Father John had come to love the quiet vastness and the way the plains revealed their secrets when you happened upon them unexpectedly—the swell of a bluff, the cut of an arroyo, the patches of sagebrush and pink, blue, and yellow wildflowers. So different from Boston, where he'd spent most of his forty-eight years. He was an Irishman, from a long line of Boston Irish with the same red hair and blue eyes and white skin that always looked flushed in the sun.

He'd been a drunk in Boston, alone in his study, grading papers for his American history classes at the Jesuit prep school, sipping whiskey—a harmless relaxation after the long day, he'd told himself. He'd found so many ways, dozens of ways, to hide from the truth there, until the day the Superior had confronted him. He'd spent a year in Grace House, and afterward—still recovering, always recovering—no one had offered him a job. Except for Father Peter at an Indian mission in Wyoming that Father John had never heard of. Three years later, Father Peter had retired and Father John had become the Superior. You couldn't hide here, with the earth stretching into the sky. He was grateful for that. Your shadow was always alongside you.

"There you are, Father." Minnie Little Horse stood in the opened door, patting at the white apron draped over her pink housedress. The sound of her voice surprised him. When had the door opened? She was in her seventies, with tightly curled gray hair that matched the pinched look on her dark face. Squinting into the sunshine, she waved him inside.

"How are you, grandmother," he said, using the term of respect. He followed her into the L-shaped living room that extended into the kitchen in the rear. Another elderly woman—this would be Minnie's sister, although she looked frailer and more sunken into herself than the last time he'd seen her—sat on the sofa: needle in one hand, white thread dangling over a piece of tanned deerskin in her lap, an embroidered design of colored beads taking shape on the skin.

"You remember Louise," Minnie said.

"Yes, of course." Father John walked over, and the old woman slipped her free hand, small and rough as bark, into his. Her face was crosshatched with wrinkles, the thin hair only partially concealing patches of pink scalp. She looked up at him out of ancient eyes, like the eyes of grandmothers in the Old Time, staring out of the bronze-tinted photos.

"Eat, eat," Louise said, removing her hand. "We got cold chicken in the fridge. Minnie'll get you a plate." The other woman was already starting for the kitchen.

He had to laugh. The people were always trying to feed him. A habit from the Old Time, he knew, when Arapahos fed everybody who wandered into the villages.

He thanked the sisters and said he'd take a raincheck. The afternoon was wearing on, and Elena, the housekeeper at St. Francis, served dinner at six. It was Monday. That meant stew. Elena ran the residence like a drill sergeant. She expected promptness, and he was usually late. He would be late today, but his new assistant, Father George Reinhold, in all his German exactitude, would no doubt be on time, which, Father John knew, would only partially mollify Elena.

"Cup of coffee, then?" An impatient let's-get-this-over-with note seeped into Minnie's voice.

"Coffee would be fine," he said. He took the chair across from Louise, set his hat on the side table, and made small talk for a few moments: the hot weather, the wild grasses burned brown in the sun. The old woman smoothed the deerskin in her lap. What's it gonna be like in July, when the real summer heat comes on? They oughta move to Alaska, she said. Finally she laid the deerskin on the cushion beside her.

"I been saying to Minnie," she began again, and he knew this was what the sisters wanted to talk about, "we can't keep our worrying all bottled up. We gotta call Father John."

The call had come this morning. Minnie's voice, breathless and hurried. She didn't want to bother him, but she didn't know what to do, and he, being a white man . . . Could he come over? He'd glanced at his daytimer. A married couple due in for counseling in thirty minutes, social committee meeting this afternoon, parish council meeting tonight. And he wanted to finish writing the annual report for the board of directors meeting next weekend.

He dreaded the annual board meeting—the bishop himself from Cheyenne and seven Jesuits from around the country, all scrutinizing the financial and spiritual conditions of St. Francis Mission. And always the possibility that the board would decide the mission had outlived its purpose—a nineteenth-century anachronism adrift in the twenty-first century—and recommend to the Provincial that it be closed.

He'd told Minnie he'd try to swing by about four-thirty or five.

Minnie was back with two mugs of coffee—one for him, the other for her sister. She sank onto the far side of the sofa, clasped her hands over the white apron, and drew in a long breath, composing something inside her head. Finally she said, "Louise and me, well, we been real worried about my grandson, Dean." The words came in a torrent, as if a dam had burst.

"What's going on?" Father John could still see Dean Little Horse running around the bases after he'd hit the ball into left field, long legs stretching out to take him home. Another score for the Eagles, the baseball team Father John had started his first summer at St. Francis. Dean was fifteen then, tall and thin-limbed, with black hair that fell over his forehead and dark eyes lit with curiosity and intelligence. He'd gone off to college three years later, and the last Father

John had heard, he'd landed a job with a software company in Lander.

Minnie bit at her lower lip, then she said, "We can't find him, Father."

"What do you mean?" Father John set his mug on the table next to his chair. The house was stitched with tension.

"Four days now, since last Thursday. Ain't that right, Louise?" Minnie glanced over at her sister. "We been calling and calling. He don't answer the phone. I went to his apartment in Lander yesterday, but nobody was there."

"What about his office?"

"That's just it, Father." The woman sat perfectly still, frozen with anxiety. "I went to his office, and they said he didn't come to work Friday and didn't show up today."

Father John leaned forward. He set his elbows on his thighs and clasped his hands, trying to fit what the woman had said into some kind of logical context. Dean Little Horse might have decided to get away for a few days. Maybe he went fishing or decided to take a trek into the mountains.

He didn't believe it. No Arapaho would just leave without telling his family. And Minnie and Louise were Dean's family. They'd raised him from infancy, from the day after his father, Minnie's only child, had died in a car accident. Dean's mother, seventeen years old and terrified, had shown up at the front door. Twenty below zero outside, Minnie once told him, snow so deep that the girl's footprints across the yard looked like post holes, and she'd handed Minnie a bundle wound in blankets and said, "Your grandson. I can't take care of him."

Minnie had tried to get the girl to come inside, but she'd turned and run back through the post holes, hopping through the swirling snow on one leg, then the other. Minnie had begun unwrapping the hard, still bundle, shaking with fear that the baby—God! She hadn't known about the baby!—was already dead, frozen to death.

"Have you contacted the police?" he said finally.

Minnie was shaking her head, eyes closed against the possibility. "We don't want the police, Father." She opened her eyes and gave him a look that pleaded for understanding. "Dean's a good boy, never had trouble with the police. Louise and me, we don't want the police to know his name. Far as they're concerned, Dean Little Horse don't exist, and that's how we want to keep it. They hear he's missing, they're gonna classify him with the losers and drunks that hang out at the bars."

"Fort Indians," Louise said.

Father John understood. The drunken Indians who, a hundred years ago, had hung out at the forts, trading their buffalo robes and their women, everything they had, for another drink of whiskey. Oh, yes, he understood. He'd traded his career for whiskey.

"Dean was twenty-three last March." Minnie scooted to the edge of the sofa. "He's got himself a college degree, knows all about computers, You're a white man. You tell me where he might've gone off to."

Father John had to glance away from the raw fear in the women's eyes. They both knew that Dean Little Horse could have gotten into serious trouble—a reservation Indian, making his way in the outside world. There were people who'd run an Indian off the road if they saw him. He'd been in the backseat of a van once, on his way to speak at a luncheon for local businessmen. The Toyota had been sputtering, in need of new spark plugs, and they'd offered to pick him up. Four white men and the Indian priest, careening down the highway toward Riverton, and an Indian standing alongside the road, waiting to cross.

"Let's see how high he jumps," the driver called out.

"Yeah, go for it." The others whooped and hollered. The van veered toward the Indian, who jumped back, stumbled, and fell into the ditch.

"Stop!" Father John had shouted. Even the memory brought the heat into his face.

"Hey, Father." The driver's head had swirled around, as if he'd forgotten who was there. "No harm done. Just a little joke."

"Let me out," he'd said.

"Hey, what about your talk?" One of the businessmen seemed to realize what had happened. "Lots of people gonna be disappointed."

They were a quarter-mile down the highway when the van finally pulled over. He'd crawled past the brown-trousered legs, freed himself, and slammed the door. The van had squealed into the traffic and he'd run back to find the Indian, but the man was gone.

He felt his skin prickling. *Dean was like that Indian. He could be lying in a ditch somewhere.* He said, "I'll have a look around Lander."

"Oh, would you, Father?" The fear in Minnie's eyes dissolved into a look of such trust and expectation that he could almost feel the weight of it settling over his shoulders.

He said, "I'll need some information. Dean's apartment. The name of his company." He pulled out the small notepad and pencil he always carried in the pocket of his plaid shirt.

Minnie recited the addresses, telephone numbers, all from memory.

Father John wrote quickly. "What about his friends?"

"Friends?" Minnie was quiet, and he glanced up. Her dark eyes were like stones. "Kids he went to high school with on the res, lot of 'em moved away. Far as I know, Dean was making new friends. He never had trouble making friends. Everybody likes Dean."

"I think he had a girlfriend," Louise said, her voice small and tentative.

"Oh, Louise." Minnie gave the other woman an impatient look. This was well-trodden ground. "We don't know that for sure."

"Too busy to come for dinner last few Sundays," the other woman persisted. "Only normal a good boy like Dean would find himself a nice girl to spend Sundays with."

"Any idea of who she is?" Father John said.

Minnie squared her shoulders and drew in a long breath. "Dean never said anything about a girlfriend. I think . . . I really think he would have told us."

Father John slipped the notepad and pencil back into his pocket, then got to his feet. "Look," he said, taking in both women. "We'd better only give this one day. If I don't find him, I want you to promise to file a missing persons report."

Minnie pushed herself out of the sofa. "Louise and me, we feel a lot better already." She glanced around at her sister pressed against the cushions, as if to ward off a blow that only she saw coming.

"Tell Dean to call us right away, Father," Minnie said. "Tell him how we been awful worried."

Father John jammed down on the accelerator. The pickup thumped over the hard-packed dirt and onto the road. An uneasy feeling set like a rock in his stomach. Nobody dropped off the earth for four days. Something had happened. He should have insisted that Minnie go to the police immediately, but he knew it wouldn't have done any good. No amount of reasoning could break through the logjam in the woman's eyes. He was going to have to try to find her grandson. He had to get as much information about Dean Little Horse as he could, and he had to get it fast.

❮ 2 ❯

The sun had burned hot all day, and now the heat pressed down over the flat, open stretch of plains on either side of Blue Sky Highway. Vicky Holden eased up on the accelerator. Ahead a line of traffic waited to turn into the graveled parking lot in front of the Arapaho tribal headquarters. She stopped behind a white pickup, her turn signal clicking in rhythm with the flashing light on the pickup. The air seemed hotter than on the highway at sixty miles an hour with the breeze blowing through the Bronco.

She didn't mind the heat, the smell of dry sage in the air. Reminders that she was home again after four months at Howard and Fergus, her old law firm, trying to convince herself she belonged in a steel-and-glass skyscraper on Seventeenth Street in Denver. She belonged on the Wind River Reservation, where not every foot of earth had been paved over and there were still the open spaces and sky that had always sheltered and comforted her people.

The traffic inched forward. Vicky could see what was causing the bottleneck: a dozen men and women—all Indians—circling the entrance to the parking lot, waving placards and shoving baskets at the vehicles that slowed past. They looked young, early twenties, she guessed, with calm expressions that might have been painted on the dark faces. The women wore long, white gowns that brushed the tops of their moccasins; the men, white shirts and trousers with fringe dipping over the shoulders and running down the arms and legs.

A semi slowed past, the driver gawking out his window. Then the white pickup swung into the turn and Vicky followed, bouncing over the gravel past the Indians. The men's clothing was made of buckskin, like the clothing of the warriors in the Old Time. The women's dresses were muslin. Now she could make out the painted symbols on the clothing: blue bands for her people, whom the other plains tribes called the Blue Sky People; yellow circles and crosses for the sun and the morning star; red thunderbirds for the eagle, the messenger of the Creator, and squiggly lines radiating from the eyes, the symbol of lightning.

A placard thrust itself across the windshield and Vicky stomped on the brake. Red block letters said: HESUNA'NIN IS THE WAY. PREPARE FOR THE NEW WORLD.

The placard slid past, and for a second, she caught the eye of a tall, muscular man with black braids that hung over the designs painted on his shirt. His features—the knife-edged mouth, narrowed eyes, and fleshy nose—seemed to sink into his flat face. He thrust a basket into her opened window. A few coins lay in the bottom. She pushed the basket away.

The man—Pueblo, Ute, Cheyenne, Lakota, she wasn't sure, but he didn't have the sculptured face of the Arapaho—stepped back and glanced around, the narrowed eyes issuing orders to the others. Then he started across the parking lot toward a black truck, a hopping motion, as if his left leg worked independently from the rest of his body. The others moved out of the circle and marched behind him like a precision drill team. He waved the placard overhead and shook the basket in a slow, jerky rhythm.

Vicky had no idea who the Indians were, and the realization made her feel as if she'd happened into an alien place, not her own place at all. Even the moccasin telegraph had failed to reach her since she'd returned to Lander. Had she remained on the reservation, where she belonged, instead of living and working in town, she would know. She would be connected.

She tried to push away the sense of being adrift. She was back home, after all; Lander abutted the southern boundary of the reservation. She swung right and parked in front of the squat brick building, once a school, now the tribal offices. She grabbed her briefcase from the passenger seat and crossed the sidewalk to the glass door.

A blast of cool air rushed over her as she stepped into the dark-tiled entry: receptionist's desk against the opposite wall, plastic molded chairs along the side walls. Two elders had pulled their chairs forward and were staring out the door. One of them grinned at her. "We was bettin' on whether they was gonna let you pass," he said.

Vicky smiled at the elders, then walked over to the receptionist, a strikingly pretty young woman who leaned sideways around the computer monitor with the poise of an expert rider turning her pony. Vicky gave her name and said she had an appointment with Norm Weedly.

"He's waiting." The woman's eyes switched to the corridor on the right.

Vicky found the office: third door on the left, TRIBAL

WATER ENGINEER printed in black letters on the pebbly glass. She was about to knock when the door swung open. Weedly gripped the edge. Tall and wiry, with ropelike muscles in his neck and forearms, wearing blue jeans, yellow plaid shirt, and hiking boots. Arapaho, in his early forties, Vicky thought, close to her own age.

"Come on in." Weedly ushered her into an office not much larger than an outsized closet. Two chairs and a metal desk with papers and folders sloping across the top took up most of the space. Motes of dust hung in the column of sunshine that slanted through the window. Tacked on the walls were maps of the reservation and aerial photos of the major rivers—Wind River, Little Wind River, Popo Agie— that spilled out of the mountains and into a spidery system of irrigation canals. Other photos showed views of the main reservoirs: Diversion Dam up north and, to the west, Bull Lake Dam, an earthen wall paved with concrete that contained a lake the color of turquoise.

"How ya doing?" Weedly threw the question over one shoulder as he walked around the desk. He sank into the swivel chair, picked up a folder, and motioned for her to take the straight-back chair next to the door.

Vicky sat down, settled the briefcase on her lap, and fielded the small talk about the weather, the heat spell— early this year—all the polite preliminaries to the real purpose of the meeting.

Finally, the water engineer cleared his throat and said, "So, what's your opinion on our problem with the Wind River, counselor?"

Vicky felt a little flush of satisfaction. Her people had finally asked for her opinion on an important matter—the ongoing damage to the Wind River and to the fish and wildlife from the inadequate stream flow. There were a lot of lawyers in big-name firms with more experience on water issues and Native American rights than she had, and yet Weedly had called her—a fresh look at the problem, he'd said. Whatever she suggested, he'd promised to take to the JBC, the Joint Business Council, which represented the Arapahos and the Shoshones, the two tribes that shared the reservation.

Vicky raised the flap of her briefcase and extracted the clear-plastic-covered report she'd spent the last two weeks writing. "We have to go back to court. We don't have a choice." She handed the report across the desk.

Weedly flinched. She might have handed him a firecracker about to explode in his face. He stared at the plastic cover. "Not gonna happen, counselor. JBC's had decades of lawsuits over water, enough to satisfy anybody's litigious nature, and when it was all done, State Supreme Court gave the state the right to control the amount of water in the rivers."

"But the U.S. Supreme Court affirmed our treaty rights to the water." Vicky heard the stridency in her voice.

"All well and good, but the state still decides how that water can be used." The engineer jumped up and turned toward the photos behind his desk. "State has a lot to say about the amount of water in the reservoirs and irrigation canals," he said. He might have been talking to himself. "And every year, after the spring runoff piles up silt against the dam headworks, the local irrigation district decides to release walls of mud into the Wind River." He turned back to her, a mild look of surprise in his expression, as if he'd just remembered she was there.

"I was hoping you'd find some legal loophole for us to

keep the Wind River from dying." He shifted his gaze above her head, as if the river itself had suddenly come into view. "This summer . . ." He halted, then stumbled on: Hot weather. Silt. Evaporation. River dies, might never be able to reclaim it.

Vicky got to her feet—she always thought better on her feet—and walked over to the window. Outside, the black truck was gone. Only a few pickups and her Bronco stood in the lot. She felt shaky with a sense of futility and help-lessness. What had he expected of her? A miracle? Was she supposed to find a loophole that had just happened to slip by the scrutiny of other lawyers?

She turned back to the man standing ramrod straight behind the desk. "Bull Lake Dam is the key," she said, ges-turing toward the photo of the thick turquoise finger of water crooked into the green mountains. "One hundred and fifty thousand acre-feet of water. Everything below the dam"—she swept her hand over the map of the reserva-tion—"depends on the water stored here." She held the man's gaze. "I suggest we file a federal lawsuit based on our rights as a sovereign nation to regulate water quality in the rivers. We ask the feds to impose water quality standards, which would ensure a better stream flow and cleaner water. A limited lawsuit."

"No such thing. We'd be opening up the whole compli-cated water issue again. Last thing the state's gonna want to see." He leaned over his desk and flipped the edge of the plastic cover, as if he should open it but didn't want to, and Vicky wondered if he would ever read the report.

"You said yourself the river will die."

"JBC won't go for it." His fingers scratched at the report.

Vicky drew in a long breath. "I'd like to get on the agenda for the next JBC meeting."

"I'll give the council your report." Weedly pushed the plastic across the desk. "You lawyers," he said, a lighter tone now, "never give up hope the courts can settle everything. Problem is, Vicky, we have other issues with the state. We might be sovereign, but take a look." He gestured toward the map of Wyoming, the reservation a large block of red in the center. "We're surrounded. We depend on the state for maintenance on state roads across the res, money for schools, welfare programs. Let's say we file another lawsuit on the water issue and the federal court says, yeah, Indians got the right to regulate water quality in our rivers. You think the state won't make us pay in other ways?"

"That shouldn't happen."

"Yeah? Aren't you forgetting something? The Indians lost the war."

Vicky got to her feet. She gripped the briefcase hard; the leather felt flimsy and wrinkled in her hand. Did everything have to be filtered through a prism of the past? Would her people always be immobilized by the old fears?

She said, "What about the agenda?"

"Won't do any good."

"I'd like to try."

Weedly was quiet a moment. In his eyes, Vicky saw the smallest flicker of possibility. "I'll see what I can do," he said finally. Then he started around the desk and stretched out a sinewy hand for the tan cowboy hat on the coattree in the corner. "Past quitting time. I'll walk out with you."

Vicky led the way across the deserted lobby, the receptionist's chair pushed into the desk, the two plastic chairs angled toward the door. Outside, the late afternoon heat lay over the parking lot like an invisible ceiling. The sun was high above the mountains, a red-orange flare that cast blue shadows over the foothills in the distance. An engine thrummed out on the highway. Except for the Bronco and a green Ford pickup—Weedly's vehicle, she assumed—the parking lot was empty.

"The Indians took their placards and baskets and left," she said.

"Good news." Weedly kept in step across the sidewalk. "Last week they were up at Fort Washakie disrupting traffic. Did the same over at Arapaho. Mostly, people ignore them, so they go back up into the mountains to wait for the end of the world."

"What's it all about?"

The man threw her a sideways look. "Where you been?" There was a hint of amusement in his voice. He knew she'd been working in Denver.

"On another planet." She'd been back only a month, hardly enough time to settle into a new office in Lander and write the report Weedly had asked for. She still had a sense of displacement, as if she'd stepped out of herself for a while and now had to get used to her own skin. There was so much to catch up on.

"James Sherwood, you know him?" Weedly gestured with his head toward the entrance to the lot where the Indians had been circling about.

"Sherwood family used to run a ranch in the mountains west of Fort Washakie." Vicky walked around the Bronco, inserted the key, and opened the door. A blast of heat hit her.

"That's the family." Weedly remained on the sidewalk, hands jammed into the pockets of his blue jeans. "Old people died, rest of the family moved off the res. All that's left is James. Calls himself Orlando. Lives up at the ranch with his so-called followers, the shadow dancers. Every six weeks they put up what they call a shadow dance that lasts four days. Dancers claim they go into the shadow world and commune with the ancestors, who, they say, are on their way back to earth. Gonna be Indian heaven here soon. Maybe all our water problems'll solve themselves."

He gave a shout of laughter and shook his head.

"I didn't see Sherwood here," Vicky said.

"Never leaves the ranch. Too busy communing with the ancestors. Real sad, I'd say. James Sherwood was a bright kid at Indian High. One of the best and the brightest." Weedly stared across the empty lot. "God help us if that's what becomes of the best and brightest."

"What happened?" Vicky said.

"Heard he moved to Denver, went to college, got to be a computer whiz kid. Landed a good job, then bam! Went on a hike in the mountains one day and got hit by lightning. Spent time in a coma. Says he died and went into the shadow world. Met up with Wovoka himself."

"The Ghost Dance prophet," Vicky said, reaching into her memory for what she'd heard about Wovoka. Bits and pieces started to come: Paiute Indian, started the Ghost Dance religion sometime in the 1880s, gathered followers from tribes across the West, her own people among them. Now she had it: Grandmother had told stories about how the Ghost Dance had given the people hope in the bad time when they were sent to the reservation and the buffalo was gone and the children were crying with hunger. Father, was what Wovoka called himself. Hesuna'nin.

"Followers come from all over," Weedly was saying.

"Probably some Arapahos at the ranch." He let out a guffaw. "Orlando says the new world's coming on the last day of one of the dance sessions, just like Wovoka prophesied. All the followers got to do is keep dancing. If the new world doesn't get here after one dance session, they wait six weeks, then hold another. One of the Indians out here told me the dancing's gonna start up again tonight."

Vicky was quiet a moment. "What do the Four Old Men say about it?" The spiritual leaders had the final word on Arapaho beliefs, an authority that Sherwood, or Orlando, seemed to have taken to himself.

"I suspect the Four Old Men are thinking that sooner or later Orlando's followers are gonna give up, just like Wovoka's followers did when they kept dancing and dancing and the new world never came. Pretty soon Orlando's gonna be sitting up at his ranch all by himself, one lonely prophet."

Weedly shrugged. "Orlando's harmless. Big nuisance, sending the followers out to block traffic and make converts, but harmless."

The man gave her a little wave and started across the lot toward the green pickup. "I'll get back to you about the JBC," he called.

Vicky was already behind the steering wheel, pulling the door shut. She backed out, lowering the windows as she went, then shot forward onto the highway, the wind hot and scratchy on her face and hands. She checked her watch, conscious of her muscles tensing. She'd agreed to meet her ex-husband, Ben, for dinner at the Peppermill in Lander at six-thirty. She was going to be late. Ben hated it when she was late.

❮ 3 ❯

The sun seemed stuck in place over the mountains when Father John turned into the mission grounds and drove through the tunnel of cottonwoods, branches drooping in the heat. *"Gloire immortelle"* swelled around him. He swung onto Circle Drive beyond the trees, and the vistas opened up. White clouds shot through with reds and oranges hung motionless, like clouds painted on a blue canvas.

He checked his watch. Almost seven. The quiet interlude between the end of the day's activities and the beginning of the evening's. The buildings around Circle Drive had a vacant, abandoned look: the yellow stucco administration building with his office in the front corner; the church with the white steeple towering over the mission grounds; the old gray stone school, now the Arapaho museum; the two-story red-brick residence. Between the buildings he could see the faint shadows beginning to spiral onto the plains.

He parked in front of the residence, turned off the opera, and hurried up the sidewalk. From out on Seventeen-Mile Road came the scream of a truck taking the curve too fast.

The minute he let himself in the front door, the three-legged golden retriever, Walks-On-Three-Legs, bounded into the entry and stuck a wet nozzle into his hand. He patted the dog's head and promised they'd have a game of Frisbee soon. Then he set his cowboy hat on the bench next to the door. From the kitchen down the hall—past the stairs, the door to his study, the archway to the living room—came the odor of meat and vegetables simmering in tomato sauce.

" 'Bout time you got home." Elena stood at the end of the hall, a short, squared figure silhouetted in the white fluorescent light that shone through her cap of gray hair, electrifying the strands. She wore a shapeless dress cinched at the waist by a blue apron, which she smoothed across the middle, as if she were laying a tablecloth. Her face was in shadow, eyes black slits of irritation.

The old woman had been keeping house for the priests at St. Francis now for . . . nobody knew how long. Every time he'd asked, he'd gotten such answers as: since the snows piled up to the eaves, the pastor got a used blue Chevy, the grass dancers won the biggest prize in the powwow. He'd finally understood. The number of years wasn't important. The mission had been passed down to her from the ancestors, along with dark brown eyes, a caramel complexion, and a world infused with spirits and wonders, not always meant to be analyzed and counted. She lived in a tiny house two miles away with her husband and an assortment of grown kids and grandkids, but St. Francis Mission was also home.

Father John followed the squat figure into the kitchen, the golden retriever bounding beside him. Father George was at the table, elbows scrunching the red-checkered tablecloth, an empty bowl with traces of stew pushed to one side. The new priest had short, sandy hair above a prominent brow that made his gray eyes seem deep-set and shadowy. He wore a yellow polo shirt, and the opened collar spread around his thick neck. There was a solidity about the man, a certitude, Father John thought, that seemed to draw people to him, the way a shelter on the plains might draw people in a windstorm. Father John could imagine someone in trouble coming to Father George and going away comforted and assured, reined in against a wall of stone.

His assistant lifted a mug of coffee in greeting. "Missed a great feast," he said.

"Drove like Mario Andretti to get here." Father John walked over to the cabinet, took out a bag of dog food, and shook the kernels into the dish on the floor. It was a pattern they'd developed, he and Walks-On. When he came home, he fed the dog, even though, he knew, Elena had already fed him. He set the bag back on the shelf. "Turned down chicken dinner at Minnie and Louise Little Horse's."

"Good thing." Elena was ladling chunks of potatoes, carrots, and meat into a bowl. "Those old ladies don't know the first thing about cookin'. Could've poisoned you by mistake." She set the bowl down hard on the table. Thick brown liquid washed over the rim and dripped onto the tablecloth.

Father John sat at his place across from the other priest, said a silent prayer, then took a bite of stew. It was delicious, and Elena had kept it hot, the way his mother had kept dinner for him all those years ago when he was late coming home from baseball practice.

"Much better than chicken," he said, glancing up at the housekeeper standing next to the table, hands on hips, gray head tilted in an attitude of expectation.

"You got that right."

She gave him a dismissing wave, but he could see in her

expression that he'd worked his way back into her good graces. He smiled up at her, then took another spoonful of stew.

"As I was saying to Father George before you come in the door . . ." She was untying her apron, folding it in half, hanging it over the metal bar on the stove. "I got a baby shower for my granddaughter tonight." She started down the hallway. "Leave the dishes," she called. "I'll get to them tomorrow." The usual parting instruction, and usually he rinsed out the dishes and stacked them in the rack.

"Parish council meeting's been canceled," Father George said.

Father John held his spoon suspended over the bowl. The front door slammed shut, sending a tremor through the floorboards. He'd been counting on tonight's meeting, the last meeting with the Arapahos on the council before the board of directors arrived.

"Two guys with the flu. Three people out of town. One woman had a family emergency in Casper." The other priest shrugged. "Had no choice but to call the other members and cancel the meeting."

"Maybe we can reschedule before the weekend," Father John heard himself saying. He'd call the Arapahos on the parish council tomorrow. He wanted to go over the annual report with them before the board meeting this weekend.

What was it about the annual board meeting that had him so on edge? "Important matters on the agenda, John," the Provincial had said last week when he'd called. But there were always important matters on the agenda. It was what wasn't on the agenda that bothered him, followed him like a shadow—that this was the year the board would recommend that the Jesuits close St. Francis.

He ate some more stew and tried to ignore the uneasy feeling. It defied logic. The Jesuits had run St. Francis for more than a century. Why would the Society close the mission now?

"Don't count on the parish council having much influence on the board," Father George said, as if the man had seen into his head. "The board will look at data, John. Clear, quantified data. Types of liturgies and programs, numbers of participants, and most important, results."

"What's going on?" Father John pushed the bowl of stew aside. He was no longer hungry. This new man, his assistant, here only two weeks, seemed to know more about the agenda than he did.

The other priest gave a snort of laughter and set his mug down. Threads of coffee ran down the sides. "What makes you think I'm privy to the board's thinking?"

"You know the new members." There were seven directors, including the bishop. Three—still a minority, he reminded himself—were new: a philosopher, a college president, a former Provincial—all Father George's colleagues. His assistant had been a Provincial himself once—that was the year Father John had spent at Grace House. He winced at the memory, the juxtaposition of their careers.

Father George flattened both hands on the table. "Isn't it obvious that the board has to consider whether we're making the best use of our limited resources and manpower?"

Father John didn't say anything. This wasn't going to be the usual meeting, with black-suited, white-collared men nodding over the annual report, eager to get back to college classrooms and administration jobs and leave the management of an Indian mission to John O'Malley. The uneasy feeling churned inside him like an old engine trying to kick over.

"And another matter." Father George was just warming up. "You have to wonder—do you not?—about the depth of the people's Catholic faith, with a cult operating on the reservation. What does that cult leader call himself? Orlando!" The priest snorted. "Says he's a prophet. People can be taken in by such rubbish, you know. All it takes is some charismatic man and a lot of people—people who don't have anything else to believe in—will follow the leader into fire or flood. Don't forget what happened to the poor people who followed Jim Jones to Guyana. Cults can be very dangerous, John. We have to speak out against Orlando and the shadow dance from the pulpit."

Father John stared at the man across from him a moment. Somehow they'd veered off the subject. "You see the irony here, don't you?" he said finally.

"Irony?" Father George sat back in his chair, a relaxed air of expectation about him.

Father John hurried on. "The early Christians were also considered a cult. The Jesus followers were crucified and beheaded. Everybody thought they were mad. Some people still think we're mad, George. And priests like us are the maddest of all. We walk away from what everybody else considers normal." He threw his head back toward the hallway, the front door, and the world beyond. "We live far away from our families and everything else that other people hold dear, and we follow a charismatic leader."

"So now you're comparing Orlando to Jesus Christ?"

Father George raised his eyes to the ceiling and shook his head. Father John was quiet a moment. "I'm saying that the Indians at the shadow ranch are believers, George, just as we are, but we believe in a different messiah." His own belief, he was thinking, stabbed at him at times like a sharp knife and fixed him in place. He was always free to walk away, he knew, but then he would be left with the wound, open and gaping like a void.

"You're playing the role of devil's advocate," Father George said. "Frankly, John, we don't have the time to play intellectual games."

The other priest pushed himself to his feet, and Father John wondered if his assistant was referring to the shadow dancers or to St. Francis Mission. Which one was running out of time?

"The shadow dance is a cult," Father George went on, "and we must speak out against it."

Father John said, "I want to talk to the elders before we say anything about the dance."

"The elders? I can't imagine they'd have anything to do with a self-proclaimed prophet."

"The shadow dance is a revival of the old Ghost Dance religion . . ." Father John began to explain, but the other man had raised his hand, like a traffic cop.

"From the 1880s! Times were different then, John. Indians were drawn to the prophet, Wovoka, because he promised them a better life, which, incidently, never came about. The opposite occurred. The Seventh Calvary—Custer's regiment, I believe—killed the last of the Ghost Dancers at Wounded Knee in 1890. Custer's revenge, some historians call the massacre. Correct?"

Father John nodded. It didn't surprise him that Father George had already looked into the history. His new assistant was thorough, a stickler for detail. He took in a long breath and started again to explain: The Ghost Dance religion was part of Arapaho tradition, and the elders guarded the tradition. Since Orlando seemed to have patterned the shadow dance after the old religion, he didn't want to say anything about it until he'd spoken to the elders.

"The board's going to decide whether to continue the mission, isn't that right?" he said, steering the conversation back on track.

Father George looked away for a moment. Walks-On, snuggled on his rug in the corner, snored into the quiet. Finally the other priest brought his gaze back. "I wouldn't expect a peremptory decision, John. They're reasonable men. They'll discern the best option."

Father John got to his feet and started stacking the dishes in the sink. He turned on the hot water, squeezed the bottle of yellow detergent, and watched the liquid churn into suds. Behind him, the other priest's footsteps moved across the vinyl floor and into the hallway.

"Where do you stand, George?" Father John glanced over his shoulder at the other man's back.

"What?" Father George swung around. In the backward tilt of the sandy head, the thrust of the jaw, Father John saw the truth. The Provincial had sent George Reinhold here to gather information—quantified data—for the board of directors. George Reinhold was the Provincial's man on the scene, the objective observer.

"I doubt my opinion will matter."

"What is your opinion?" Father John picked up the towel flung over the drainboard and faced the man.

"My opinion? I think we should close this place, sell the land, and use the money to better advantage. Offer more college scholarships to Arapaho kids. My opinion? That would produce a greater benefit over time than fielding a baseball team and trying to sober up a bunch of alcoholics. There are other places Arapahos can go for those programs."

He started backing into the hall. "I'm sorry, John," his voice softer. "The directors are aware of your fondness for the mission, but we have to be practical." He turned and continued down the dimly lit hall, grabbed the knob on the bannister, and swung himself onto the stairs. Each step sent a muffled thud reverberating into the kitchen.

Father John tossed the towel onto the drainboard. So, he was unexpectedly free tonight after all. He walked down the hall and, scooping his cowboy hat off the bench, let himself out the door.

‹ 4 ›

No sign of Ben.

Most of the tables in the Peppermill were occupied. The subdued sounds of music and laughter floated from the bar that adjoined the dining room. Vicky waited inside the door while the hostess threaded her way past the tables toward the front: tall, attractive woman in her thirties, with brown hair pinned back into a bun, the ends sticking out like feathers around her head, and thick, black eyelashes that deposited little flakes of mascara on her cheeks. Below the collar of her black dress was a tiny white name tag: MARY SEELS. She reached for the menus stacked on a small table.

Vicky said she was meeting Ben Holden.

The woman's hand stopped over the menus. A barely concealed look of surprise came into her expression. She seemed to look at Vicky for the first time: the black hair parted on the side and smoothed slightly back; the blue linen dress and silver necklace; the high-heeled sandals. Finally she said, "Mr. Holden hasn't arrived yet, but your table is ready. Follow me." She turned abruptly and led the way through the dining room to a table with a stiff white cloth and places set for two.

Vicky wondered if the woman was another one of Ben's conquests. There had been many over the years. Indian, white, Hispanic. Ben's appeal was universal.

She pushed the thought away—it no longer mattered—and studied the menu. Then she stared through the plate-glass window at the pickups and sedans crawling down Main Street, the people hurrying along the sidewalk, dodging pieces of paper tossed in the breeze. The conversation with Weedly played over and over in her mind, like the cracked phonograph records in her grandmother's house when she was a child. Had he really expected her to come up with some strategy that hadn't occurred to any other tribal lawyer in the last decade?

She smiled at the idea, so typical of her people. The Sioux and Cheyenne, they had taken up guns and bows and arrows and hatchets and gone out to right the wrongs, but the Arapahos said: Let's eat and talk and smoke the pipe together. They would stay at the bargaining table, looking for some way out of an impasse, even when the soldiers were surrounding the villages.

Madness. You couldn't negotiate with people who didn't want to negotiate. You had to fight white people with their own laws. The federal courts, she was sure, would support the tribe's right to clean water in the Wind River. But before she could convince a federal court, she had to convince her own people.

She spread the white napkin across her lap, then took a drink of the ice water the waitress had poured. Laughter erupted over the buzz of conversation from the nearby tables.

Still no sign of Ben. She was beginning to wonder if she'd gotten the right day. He'd been calling since she'd returned to Lander. Morning and afternoon calls to her office, and she, training a new secretary, installing the fax machine— a thousand details. Calls in the evenings to her apartment. *I have to see you.*

He'd called this morning, his voice tense, rushed. He was going to be in town. Dinner at the Peppermill? Six-thirty? "Fine," she'd said, managing to squeeze the word past the tightness in her throat. Ben was the father of her children, Lucas and Susan. The ties between them, she knew, would never be completely severed.

He was striding through the restaurant now with the purpose and confidence of a warrior, tall, still-in-shape, dressed in blue jeans and a starched white shirt that she knew instinctively he'd worn for her. She recognized the bolo tie with the silver eagle clasped below the opened collar. She had given him the tie on their tenth anniversary. The sight of him—when had she seen him last? four months ago?—sent a shiver running through her.

"Sorry." He yanked the chair from the table so hard that it floated free from the floor, like a piece of driftwood in his hand. Then he squared it a couple of feet from the table and sat down, not taking his eyes from her.

Vicky felt her mouth go dry. The memories came, unasked for, unwanted: Ben slamming into the house, shouting at the kids, kicking at the dog. And the smell of whiskey permeating the air, and she in the kitchen, standing over the sink, retching with the odor and the fear.

She made herself take a sip of ice water and tried to detect the odor now. Only the slightest whiff of aftershave.

"It's okay, Ben," she said, falling back into that other time. *It's okay, honey. Take it easy.*

"Business problem. Took longer than I thought." He waved the waitress over, a short, slim woman probably in her thirties with the stooped shoulders of someone much older and black, curly hair that emphasized the lines of fatigue in her face.

"Couple juicy burgers and some coffee, Lucy," Ben said.

Vicky started to change her order—a bowl of soup and a salad had sounded good—then stopped. It was barely perceptible, the silent acknowledgment between Ben and the waitress, as if they shared some secret. The woman nodded, then moved away.

Ben took a drink of water. He was gripping the glass hard. She could see the white peaks of his knuckles poking through the brown skin, and she felt her own muscles tighten with the effort—curious how familiar it seemed—to position herself somewhere out of the line of his anger.

"Goddam busiest season." He spat out the words, as if they'd been talking for the last hour. She couldn't remember when they'd last talked. The hurried telephone calls—she'd been in a hurry to end them—hardly counted.

She tried to concentrate on what he was saying about the Arapaho Ranch, where he was the foreman: shorthanded as hell right now, moving the herds to the high pastures, blasting out new roads, a couple of ponds. "Hell of a time for two Lakota bastards to rip me off." He shifted his gaze to some point across the restaurant, as if he wanted to reel the words back in.

"Rip you off?" she said.

Ben jerked back against the chair. "Forget it." He locked eyes with her, and she felt herself becoming small. "Those slimy bastards didn't reckon on who they're dealing with. I caught up with them a couple hours ago. This time tomorrow, there's not going to be any problem."

A chorus of laughter and the sound of clinking glass floated over from the next table. Ben turned and glared at the two couples. "Jesus, what I wouldn't give for a drink right now," he said, locking eyes with her again. "That's over. You know that, don't you?"

"I'm glad for you," Vicky said after a moment.

The waitress set two mugs of coffee on the table, then delivered the plates of hamburgers with french fires piled on the side. "You and me, Vicky. We've got unfinished business," he said after the waitress had stepped away. He was shaking the ketchup bottle over the fries.

Vicky held her breath. She knew the rest of it. It was as familiar as a wound that refused to heal, always there, festering. "Listen, Ben . . ."

"First thing we have to do is get Susan home." Ben lifted his hamburger and took a bite.

"Susan?" Vicky hadn't anticipated a discussion about the kids. "What are you talking about?"

He swallowed quickly, his Adam's apple bobbing in his throat. "Eat." He nodded toward her untouched hamburger. "You don't eat enough. You're too thin. You need to get some meat on your bones."

Vicky took her knife and sawed the hamburger in two, then picked up the smaller piece. Going through the motions now. She had no appetite.

"Lucas is working in Denver," Ben went on. "Not the same as living here, but Denver's only seven hours away. You finally came to your senses and moved back. Now all we gotta do is get Susan here, and our family'll be together again."

Vicky set the hamburger down. There was no family to reclaim. There were only individuals trying to make their way, and Ben, determined to round them up into a corral, the way he rounded up the herd on the ranch. "Susan has a good job in Los Angeles," she heard herself saying. "She has friends. She has a nice apartment."

"She can work at the ranch. I need another bookkeeper, and she's good at computers."

"You expect Susan to live on the ranch? A hundred miles from anywhere, surrounded by a bunch of cowboys?"

"Any of the bozos touch her, he answers to me."

"Ben, for godssake."

"Listen to me, Vicky." He leaned over the table. "We gotta start somewhere, you and me."

"We're never going to start again."

"Lucas can drive up on weekends."

"My God, Ben."

"We'll be together," he went on, and Vicky realized he was talking to himself, repeating what he probably told himself in the middle of the night, like some madman, unhinged from reality. "We'll go to the celebrations and the powwows, like we used to. Remember? You and me and the kids. We had a great time. We'll go out to my brother's place for dinner. Get to know one another again."

Vicky threw her napkin on the table and got to her feet, aware of the other diners craning around to watch. "I'm going to call Susan and tell her to stay in Los Angeles where she's happy," she said. "I'm going to tell her she can't live out your fantasy of the perfect family that we never were."

The color drained from Ben's face, something changed

behind his eyes. He laid his hands flat on the table and pushed himself to his feet, rising toward her, his chest heaving with the gulps of breath. Instinctively she drew back, the restaurant swam around her. She felt sick.

"You don't care about the family." He drew out the words until they hung between them like black smoke. "All of us broken apart like these here dishes." He grabbed a fistful of the white tablecloth and yanked it off the table. Plates, mugs, glasses lifted into the air, then crashed onto the carpet in a crumpled heap of white cloth, hamburger, fries, ketchup, shards of glass. Coffee and water pooled over the table and gathered into creamy puddles on the chairs.

"You listen to me." He took hold of her shoulder. His fingers dug into her flesh. She was aware of the stunned silence around them, the diners leaning toward them. "I've had enough of people taking what belongs to me. Susan's coming home. Lucas is gonna come home sooner or later. We're gonna work everything out between us, Vicky. You and me."

He let go of her so abruptly that she staggered backward, groping for the edge of the table to steady herself. Ben was already heading toward the front, a sure and unhurried pace, as if the most serious negotiations had just been settled. The hostess moved sideways as he shouldered past, and then he was out the door. The restaurant was quiet.

Vicky fumbled in her bag for a couple of bills, which she tossed on the table—they fluttered into a pool of water— aware of the waitress frozen in place a few feet away, staring at the mess strewn over the carpet. Outside the window, Ben's brown truck screeched into the street, black clouds fuming from the exhaust pipe. Out of the corner of her eye, she saw a dark truck pull in behind.

"I'm sorry," she mumbled toward the adjacent tables. Then she made her feet carry her through the dining room. Outside she kept close to the brick building, her legs shaking beneath her. She turned the corner and crossed the parking lot to the Bronco. Gripping the keys in the bottom of her bag, unlocking the door. She sank gratefully into the front seat and made herself take a deep breath. She had to be calm. It was only a scene—there had been others. And she knew the next scene: the ringing phone, Ben's voice at the other end. He was so sorry. Didn't know what had gotten into him. Could she ever forgive him?

No, she could not. Whatever talent she'd had for forgiveness was gone.

She turned the ignition and drove out of the lot, aware of the other diners inside the restaurant, mannequin heads turned toward the street, eyes following the Bronco.

She continued north, then turned west, driving aimlessly, eating up the time until Ben was out of town before she returned to her apartment.

‹ 5 ›

My relations, the ancestors are crying for the pain you have endured. They stumble and fall with their tears as they walk through the clouds. They cry because the evil people want to stop our dancing and prevent the new world from coming, just like in the Old Time. I say to you, the evil ones must not prevail. We must dance on and on.

Father John parked in front of the apartment building, a flat-roofed, red-bricked, two-story affair with arched windows and a glass entrance that, with the exception of the enormous blue spruce over the front sidewalk, probably hadn't changed in fifty years. The sun had begun to slip behind the mountains, sending layers of red, orange, and violet through the sky. A few vehicles slowed past; a car door slammed down the street.

Father John let himself into the small entry. A bank of metal mailboxes lined the wall on the right. He found DEAN LITTLE HORSE among the typed names in the windows. Apartment 2D.

He took the stairs on the left two at a time, came out

through a steel fire door, and started down the corridor. The bronze fixtures dangling from the ceiling cast an eery shade of yellow over the beige walls and worn beige carpet. The black numbers were barely visible on the doors. New Age music, soft and melodious, drifted past one of the doors. A baby was crying behind another.

He knocked on 2D. Silence. He rapped again, louder this time.

He waited a moment, then rapped on the door across the hall. Another moment passed before the door opened. A stocky, blond-haired man in his mid-twenties with fish eyes that blinked at him from behind thick glasses, wedged himself next to the frame.

Father John said he was looking for Dean Little Horse.

"You got the wrong place, partner."

The door started to close, and Father John placed his hand against the panel. "Look," he said hurriedly. "I'm a priest at St. Francis Mission. I'm trying to find the man across the hall. How long have you been here?"

The door opened wider. Interest flashed in the fish eyes. "Honey?" he called without looking away. "When we move in? Thursday? Friday?"

"Thursday." A woman's voice came from inside. Beyond the man's thick legs, Father John could see the stacked cartons, the plastic bubble wrap scattered over the green carpet.

"Ain't seen nobody over there," the man said.

Father John felt a knot tighten in his stomach. Dean had been missing since Thursday.

Father John thanked the man and started back down the corridor. The door slammed behind him, creating a kind of vacuum that trapped the muffled sounds of flutes, the faint smell of onions.

He stopped at 2B and knocked. Beyond the door, the scrape of footsteps. Finally the door inched open, held in place by a brass chain that bisected the face of a tall, good-looking woman with curly red hair. The sound of flutes rose around her.

"What is it? She peered under the chain and ran her fingers through a tangle of curls.

He told her his name, and she leaned into the opening, her gaze traveling from his cowboy hat to his plaid shirt, blue jeans, and cowboy boots. "Priest?"

He ignored the skepticism in her tone—it wasn't the first time he'd encountered skepticism—and told her he was looking for Dean Little Horse, who lived down the hall.

"Indian guy."

That was right. Did she have any idea where he might be?

"He's an okay guy." The woman visibly relaxed against the edge of the door.

"When did you last see him?"

She shrugged. "Haven't seen them around for a while."

"Them? Who else lives there?"

The woman fastened her eyes on the chain for a moment. "Some Indian woman. Never got her name. She was weird, you ask me. Came and went around here like a shadow. Kept to herself. Wouldn't even say good morning. Not like Dean. He was real friendly. Helped me dig my car out of the snow last March."

"Any idea where she might have worked?"

The woman gave a little shrug and went back to pulling her fingers through her hair. "From the way she looked, I'd say check the bars."

Father John was quiet. Louise Little Horse was right. Dean had a girlfriend. He said, "Where can I find the manager?"

The woman pulled a red curl toward the stairway. "First floor, first door on the left."

Father John made his way back through the steel door and down the stairs. He tried the manager's door, waited a few seconds, then knocked again. A phone was ringing inside—four, five rings—and then it stopped.

He headed outside. A middle-aged man in blue jeans and a white T-shirt, with a thick chest and a stomach that bulged over his belt buckle, was looming up the sidewalk. "You lookin' for somebody?" he called.

"Dean Little Horse." Father John dodged around the branches of the Blue Spruce. "You the manager?"

"One and only." The man squared his massive shoulders. "What happened? Girlfriend couldn't find him, so she sent you around?"

"What are you talking about?"

"Who the hell are you?"

"Father O'Malley from the reservation."

"Oh." The man chewed on his lower lip a moment. "Heard'a you, the Indian priest. Well, I don't like them Indians around here. Nothing but trouble every time I rent to 'em. Got the correctness police now, swooping down if I say I ain't renting to Indians, so I got to be careful. Dean, he seemed like a good guy, so I took a chance on him. Bad mistake. He takes off last Thursday. Girlfriend comes around, gets hysterical. Says she's gotta find him."

"When exactly was she here?"

The man rolled his eyes to the sky. "Last night. Yeah, Sunday night."

"You know her name?"

"That's a problem I got with Little Horse." The manager kept his eyes on the sky. "Never told me there was gonna be two of 'em in the apartment a lotta times. I charge more for two people. More wear and tear on the building, you know what I mean? Took a while before I figured out the girl was staying over a lot. I told Dean, your rent just went up, buddy."

"Her name." Father John spoke through his teeth.

"How should I know? Wasn't like she was official here. Kept to herself. Didn't like nobody getting friendly with her, know what I mean?"

Father John wondered how friendly the manager had tried to get. He said, "If you hear from Dean, ask him to call me at St. Francis Mission."

The man shrugged, then shouldered past, stepping off the sidewalk into the dirt and throwing aside a branch as he went.

Father John got into the Toyota, took the notepad out of his shirt pocket, and wrote: *Last seen, Thursday. Girlfriend: Indian. Looking for Dean Sunday night.*

The manager had disappeared inside the entrance when Father John started the engine and pulled into the street, but he could feel the eyes watching him through the slats that covered the corner window on the first floor. He headed toward Main Street.

The streetlights had flashed on, and little circles of white light shone into the dusk dropping over the cars parked at the curbs. Father John eased on the brake, trying to make out the numbers on the flat-faced brick buildings. Finally he caught an address illuminated by a neon sign blinking in the plate-glass window.

He took the next intersection on the yellow light and pulled up in front of a white stucco building with a pair of plate-glass windows on either side of the blue paneled door. Painted across the top in large black letters were the words BLUE CROW SOFTWARE. He got out and walked to the door. Locked.

In the shadows beyond the windows, he could see the rows of cubicles, computer monitors, and keyboards on the desks. A cone of light shone over the center of the office, where a man in a white T-shirt with sleeves rolled to the shoulders, earphones clasped over his head, and hips swinging side to side, steered a vacuum cleaner about, as if the machine were a stiff, unwilling dance partner.

Father John waved, but the man kept pushing—pushing and dancing—lost in the rhythms probably blasting in his ears. He swung around in an awkward tango, and Father John waved again. This time, the man looked up, his round, pinkish face frozen in a mixture of surprise and fear. He let go of the vacuum, pointed to his wristwatch, and shook his head.

Father John gestured toward the closed doors in the shadows beyond the light. Some poor, overworked manager might still be in the office. But the man waved him away, then turned around and curled his back over the vacuum cleaner.

Back in the pickup, Father John made a sharp U-turn in front of a truck, which sent out a loud blast. The noise reverberated off the parked vehicles. He waved in the rearview mirror at the driver, who was giving him the finger. Five minutes later, he was on Highway 789 heading north, a profusion of stars popping like firecrackers in the sky. The spiky shadows of piñons passed outside the passenger window, and outside his window, the Popo Agie River reflected back the stars, like a long, narrow mirror.

He slowed past the steak houses in Hudson, then turned left into the shadows of Rendezvous Road, his thoughts still on Dean Little Horse. College degree, good job, grandmother and great-aunt, and a girlfriend looking for him as recently as last night. A man like that didn't just step off the earth. First thing tomorrow, he decided, he would pay another visit to the Blue Crow Software Company.

Ahead, around a wide bend, blue, red, and yellow lights flashed into the gray dusk. Father John could see the vehicles blocking the road, men moving in slow motion, flashlight beams crisscrossing the flashing lights. Shards of broken glass glistened on the blacktop.

He stopped next to a policeman in the navy blue uniform of the BIA and leaned out the window, craning to see past the vehicles. "Anyone hurt?" he said.

"That you, Father John?" The officer moved closer and shone a flashlight in his face. Colored balls of light exploded in his eyes for half a second. "Chief Banner'll want to talk to you." The policeman turned the flashlight on three officers standing next to the dark truck parked ahead of the police cars.

Father John inched ahead a short distance, set the gear in park, and got out. The breeze was warm, laced with the odor of manure and something he couldn't identify for certain. Smoke? Voices, subdued and serious, mixed with the crackle of police radios. In the lights swinging over the white cars, he saw Art Banner, the Wind River police chief, coming toward him.

"How'd you hear?" The chief was only a couple of feet away, but he sounded like he was shouting through a bull horn. The lights alternated over the round, dark face.

"Hear what? What's happened?" A single-vehicle accident, Father John was thinking. Besides the police cars, the only other vehicle was the dark truck.

It was then he saw the shattered windshield and the figure slumped over the steering wheel, as still as death. It hit him like a sledgehammer in the chest: he'd found Dean Little Horse.

"We got a homicide." The chief tilted his head toward the truck. "Looks like he might've stopped to help somebody. Trying to be a good Samaritan." He stared for a moment at the plains extending into the shadows beyond the road. "Took a bullet in the head for his trouble. Anonymous call came in from one of the steak houses in Hudson about forty minutes ago saying somebody was dead out here. That's a fact. He's dead, all right."

"Who, Banner? Who is he?"

For a moment, the chief stood motionless in the flashing lights. Then he took off his cap and drew a fist across his brow. "Thought you must've heard already, John. Thought that's why you showed up here." He took in a long breath, as if he were trying to get enough air to expel the name: "Ben Holden."

‹ 6 ›

Father John stepped past the police chief and walked over to the truck. He had a sense of unreality, as if he had stepped into a nightmare of darting lights and hushed, disembodied voices. The brown Ford truck was solid and clear, real. Inside, collapsed over the steering wheel, was Ben Holden: the humps of his shoulders beneath the blood-soaked shirt, the head falling against the steering wheel. His temple was smashed, bloody.

He couldn't remember when he had last seen Ben Holden, what they had talked about. It made no difference. The unspoken subject between them had always been Vicky.

A flashbulb went off behind him, suffusing the slumped body in the yellow light that exploded in the shattered windshield. The police photographer moved in closer and took a couple more shots, then backed away.

Father John reached inside the window and began tracing the sign of the cross over the man's head. "May God have mercy on your soul, Ben," he whispered. "May He take you to Himself and grant you peace." He was startled by the grief that hit him, like a cold blast out of nowhere. He and

Ben were alike—they might have been twins—battling the same demon, loving the same woman, in need of forgiveness and redemption. Redemption took time—a lifetime. Someone had robbed Ben of his time.

Out of the corner of his eye, Father John saw the shadowy figures converging on the truck. The breeze swept off the plains and swirled little bits of dust and twigs over the blacktop.

"This is gonna be the FBI's case." Banner's voice behind him. Father John turned slowly. "Agent Gianelli's on the way. Meantime we've got the weapon. Twenty-two-caliber pistol tossed in the barrow ditch over there." He gestured toward the ditch a few feet beyond the truck. "Lab'll pick up the fingerprints," he went on, a new confidence in his voice, as if his professional duties were the only thing of which he was sure. "Gianelli'll run a trace on the gun, see if he can identify the owner. My boys'll lift tire prints, if we find any."

Father John realized the chief had been hit by the same wave of grief that had hit him. Ben and Art Banner went back a long time. They'd grown up together, served in the Army at the same time, married the same year. There was the shock of it, the death of a man who had always been around.

The chief said, "Family's got to be notified."

"What about Vicky?"

"Just about to send White over to tell her." Banner glanced at an officer standing behind the truck. "I'd go myself, but the fed's . . ."

"I'll tell her," Father John said. His shirt felt moist against his back. This was the toughest part of being a priest, bearing the bad news that no one wanted, like a ragpicker appearing at the door with a burden of trash. And with the trash—words, that was all he had. Weak, indistinct, inexact words to try to convince the family that God would not desert them.

He started toward the pickup, then turned back. "You have her address?" They hadn't spoken, he and Vicky, since she'd returned to Lander. But she'd been on his mind. He'd picked up the phone—how many times?—wanting to know how she was, wanting to hear her voice. Each time he'd set the receiver down. There'd been no legitimate reason to call her: no parishioners thinking about divorce, no one picked up for selling pot or driving drunk. The moccasin telegraph kept up a running account of her new office, new apartment, but she hadn't called.

A faint look of surprise crossed the chief's face. There was an awkward beat of silence, and Father John wondered about the gossip on the moccasin telegraph that never reached St. Francis Mission, at least not his ears.

"Hold on." The chief nodded to the officer behind the truck, but the man was already thumbing through a notepad. He leaned into the flashing lights and read off an address.

Father John knew the place, a two-story apartment building with white railings around the second-floor balconies—a New Orleans building plunked down on the plains. He started for the pickup; the chief's voice trailed behind, ordering White and another officer to drive out to Spring Valley Drive and notify Ben's brother.

Father John backed across the road, then headed south the way he'd come, saying the same prayer over and over: "Lord, have mercy on the Holden family."

• • •

The apartment was warm and stuffy, and even though she'd stood in a hot shower for twenty minutes and wrapped herself in her white terry cloth robe, Vicky couldn't shake the cold that gripped her. What had she been thinking? That she could return to Lander and go on as before? That Ben would be on the other side of Blue Sky Hall at tribal get-togethers. Across the aisle at powwows. How was she doing? Oh, fine. And he? Just fine. A woman at his side, strikingly beautiful, clinging to him for her very breath. And Susan and Lucas on the phone: You hear what Dad's up to? They'd relate how Ben had increased the herd and accomplished other amazing feats to make the Arapaho Ranch the most successful in the state.

But he wouldn't be in her life.

She'd been wrong. Ben would never leave her alone. What did she have to do to be free? The iciness inside her, she knew, was anger as distilled and pure as crystal. She would be free when one of them was dead.

She sat down on the sofa, tucked her legs under her robe, and tried to concentrate on the report she'd given to Weedly this afternoon. She had to build a strong case, if she was going to convince the JBC to go back to court over the Wind River. It was important. The river was dying. They had no choice.

An insistent knock sounded at the door. She froze, her heart pounding in her ears, her breath trapped in her lungs. Some part of her had been waiting for Ben to come to the apartment. The Bronco in the parking lot, the light filtering at the edge of the drapes—he could see that she was here.

The knock came again. She got up, went to the door, and

peered through the peephole. On the other side: the tall, handsome man, the blue eyes, the red hair glinting under the ceiling light. A wave of warmth and surprise washed over her. Then she realized that John O'Malley would never come here unless something had happened. She yanked the chain free and opened the door, her hands shaking. Something terrible had happened.

"I have to talk to you."

"Susan?" she said as he stepped inside, his eyes never leaving hers. "Something's happened to Susan? Lucas? What? An accident? You've got to tell me." She was struggling not to scream. She knew how it went: An accident somewhere. The police called the mission, and Father John O'Malley drove out to deliver the horrible news.

"It's not your kids, Vicky," he said. Taking her hand, he led her to the sofa.

His voice had seemed to come from far away, the words seeping into her consciousness a half-second after he'd spoken them. She was still shaking, an involuntary motion that worked its way into the muscles of her arms and legs.

She took a deep breath and tried to calm herself. "Who, then?"

"It's Ben, Vicky. He's dead."

She stared at him, unable to summon a response. There were no words to contain the reality. Two hours ago, she and Ben were having dinner at the restaurant. They'd argued. He'd pulled off the tablecloth, sent their dinners flying over the floor, and stomped out. There must be some mistake. She could still see the wrinkled back of his white starched shirt.

"Accident?" Her voice sounded low and cracked in her

ears. She realized John O'Malley was holding both of her hands in his.

"He was shot on Rendezvous Road," he went on, his tone punctuated with sorrow. Something about Ben stopping to help someone. The police getting an anonymous call.

She couldn't understand. Nothing was making sense. She withdrew her hands and pulled back against the cushion. She was drowning, she thought. Wave after unfathomable wave of disbelief and confusion crashing over her.

She realized that John O'Malley had gone into the kitchen. There were the sounds of a faucet squeaking open and water splashing into the sink. How odd to be drowning, she thought, when the inside of her mouth was as dry as a bone.

He was standing over her, handing her a glass. She took a long sip of cool water. Then, steadying the glass in the folds of her robe, she looked up at him. "I'm responsible," she said.

"Vicky . . ." he began, but she put up one hand to silence him.

"We were supposed to have dinner this evening. Instead we had another argument. It was terrible. Ben . . ." She hesitated, blinking at the scene burned into the back of her eyes. "Ben stomped out, and I thought, *I thought,* the only way I would ever be free was if one of us was dead."

"No, Vicky." His voice cut through the fog in her head. He sat down beside her. "Whatever you thought, it didn't make it happen. It didn't kill Ben. That's magical thinking." She felt his hand covering hers again. "You must try to be rational."

She yanked her hand away. She knew all about white man's rationality. She'd sat through their logic classes and studied their laws. What did they mean? What the elders taught, that was the truth.

"You don't understand." How could he understand? "We must guard our thoughts. We must send only good thoughts into the world, because once they exist, they become real. They become *reality*. I'm responsible . . ." She dropped her head into one hand. The tears were coming, a dam bursting, for the man she'd once loved and for the way things should have been.

"I'm so sorry." He took her glass of water and set it on the coffee table. Then she felt his arms slipping around her, pulling her close. She leaned against his chest, feeling as if time had stopped. She could hear his heart beating. How fitting that John O'Malley was here. Of course he would come to her. Curious, she thought, that in the new world she'd tried to carve for herself since she'd divorced Ben, this white man had become so necessary.

There was a thud on the door. A second passed before John O'Malley settled her back against the cushion and got up. "Ted Gianelli," he said behind her. "He may have more information."

"Give me a minute." Vicky lifted herself to her feet. She made her way down the hall to the bedroom—shaky, dizzy. She untied her robe, tossed it over the bed, and pulled on a pair of blue jeans and a white cotton blouse, her fingers numb as they worked the tiny front buttons. The male voices floated from the living room like the low rumble of drums.

In the bathroom, she splashed cold water on her face, then stared at the woman in the mirror: mussed black hair; dull, black eyes; face blanched of color, like someone who had been ill a long time. Her ancestors would have chopped off their hair, slashed their arms and legs with knives—a fitting expression of the enormity of death.

She ran a brush through her hair and put on some lipstick. The woman in the mirror was transformed, a rational look about her, like an attorney, a white woman. She went back to the living room.

"Rotten news, Vicky. I'm very sorry." Ted Gianelli, the local FBI agent, was standing next to Father John, twin pillars of solemnity caught in the light from the table lamps. The agent was dressed in a dark sport coat and light trousers with knifepoint creases, a red paisley tie knotted at the collar of his light blue shirt, as if he'd dressed for the office and this was just a routine part of the day. His short black hair lay tightly against his head; his fleshy face remained as immobile as a mask.

"What happened?" Her voice sounded shaky. She dropped onto the sofa, and Father John walked over and sat down beside her.

"We don't have all the facts yet." The fed pulled a side chair over and perched on the edge. "Looks like Ben stopped voluntarily. There's no sign of skid marks. Could be somebody was in trouble."

Vicky nodded. That made sense. The reservation was Ben's place. He was perfectly at ease there. If someone needed help, Ben would stop. A chief was responsible for the welfare of his people.

"What was it? A robbery?"

Gianelli shook his head. "He had a hundred dollars in his wallet. Some very expensive tools in the lockbox in the truck bed. No sign that anyone tried to break in."

"The killer could have been scared away," Father John said. "Maybe he saw headlights coming down the road. Banner said somebody passed by and called the police."

Gianelli leaned forward, rested his elbows on his thighs, and clasped his hands between his knees, as if he were considering the possibility, his face still unreadable. Finally he said, "Police got an anonymous call from a pay phone in Hudson. Caller said he didn't see anything except a guy sloped inside the truck. But we've got the gun. Twenty-two-caliber pistol. Should tell us something." The agent turned toward her, anticipation working into his face muscles. "Ben Holden was a strong and powerful man. Men like that make enemies. What can you tell me, Vicky?"

She closed her eyes. The scene at the restaurant reeled through her mind in slow motion. She saw clearly now, all the details, nuances, and shadows she'd missed the first time. Ben wasn't angry with her. He was angry before he came to the restaurant. She was the catalyst that caused the explosion. She had always been the catalyst: the ranch equipment broke down, the kids misbehaved, she said something wrong, and the explosion burst forth.

She looked at the agent. "Ben was angry when I saw him."

"You saw him this evening?" Something changed behind Gianelli's eyes.

"We met at the Peppermill." Vicky paused, gathering the details. "He said two ranch hands—Lakotas—had ripped him off."

"Ripped him off? You mean stole something? Embezzled money?"

"He didn't say. He'd talked to them this afternoon. He said he'd straightened everything out."

"Where do I find the Lakotas?" The fed was jotting notes in a notepad he'd fished from the inside pocket of his sport coat.

Vicky shook her head.

"What time did he meet you?"

"About seven-fifteen."

"When did he leave?"

The scene was still rolling across her mind. She tried to calculate how long it had taken the waitress to deliver the hamburgers, how long they had argued. "It must have been close to eight." Then she added, "We had an argument."

"Mind telling me what it was about?"

"Come on, Ted," Father John said. She could hear the irritation in his tone. "What difference could it possibly make? You heard what Vicky said. Ben was angry at two Lakotas who ripped him off."

The fed tapped the pen against the notebook, the new element still in his eyes. Vicky said, "Ben thought we should be a family again."

Gianelli jotted something down. Then he said, "Eight-thirty, Ben would have been on Rendezvous Road. Did he say where he was going?"

Vicky shook her head. She'd feared Ben would stay in town and show up at her apartment. She'd thought it was Ben when John O'Malley had knocked. "He must have been on his way back to the ranch," she said.

The fed agreed that was possible. Then, as if he were talking to himself, he said, "Shouldn't be too difficult to get a line on the Lakotas. Stick out like sore thumbs. Every Arapaho and Shoshone on the res'll know where they're hanging out."

But they won't tell you. Vicky glanced at Father John and saw in his expression that he'd had the same thought.

The fed got to his feet, the quick, assured movement of the linebacker he'd once been for the New England Patriots.

"If you think of anything, Vicky, anything at all, call me. Oh, and Vicky . . ." He made it sound like an afterthought, a clumsy attempt. She clenched her fists and waited for the rest of it. "I probably don't have to tell you to stick around. Don't leave the area. I'll want to interview you again in the next couple days."

"What are you inferring?" Father John was on his feet. "You can't think Vicky had anything to do with Ben's murder."

"I'm not sure what to think at the moment. The investigation's just gotten started. Fact is, Vicky was the last one to see Ben alive."

"Wrong, Ted," Father John said. (It was if she wasn't in the room: strange, having her own life discussed.) "The killer was the last."

There was an awkward silence before the fed brought his eyes to hers. "Like I said, Vicky, stay where I can reach you." Then he walked across the room and let himself out, closing the door softly behind him.

Vicky felt as if she was going to be sick. She, a suspect in Ben's murder? It was ridiculous. Surely the fed didn't believe her capable of killing the father of her own children?

The realization came over her like a slow-moving fever. It was exactly what he believed. She was the last one to see Ben alive. And Gianelli *knew*. He knew about the past. He knew why she had left Ben all those years ago.

"My God," she said.

"Listen to me, Vicky." Father John leaned over and set a hand on her shoulder. "You're not guilty. You're not responsible. Gianelli'll trace the gun and find the killer."

Vicky struggled to control the panic leaping inside her. She set her own hand on his. A moment passed before she felt steady enough to get to her feet. "I have to call Susan and Lucas," she said.

"I'll get you the phone." Father John started toward the desk.

"Not from here." She couldn't call from here. She had to go home to her people where the spirits of the ancestors could strengthen her. Her mother had been dead five years now, but Aunt Rose was still alive. Her mother's sister, which meant, in the Arapaho Way, that Aunt Rose was also her mother.

"I have to go to Aunt Rose's."

"I'll take you." Father John's voice was soft and matter-of-fact. Rational. He understood. She always went to Aunt Rose's when the world shook beneath her and she couldn't get her balance.

"It's okay. I'll drive the Bronco," she said, starting toward the hall. She had to pack a few things; she didn't know how long she'd want to stay.

"I'll follow you, then," he said.

❖ 7 ❖

he screen door clacked into the silence that spread over the dirt yard behind the little white house. Vicky rearranged herself in the webbed chair and tried to shake off the sense of unreality that clung to her like a new skin. She watched Aunt Rose coming toward her: thick legs paddling forward, brown shoes raising little spitwads of dust. The morning sun blazing behind her made her pink housedress look as faded and gray as her hair. She held out a mug like an offering.

"You won't eat," she said. "Least you gotta drink something."

Vicky thanked the old woman and took the mug. The smell of fresh coffee came at her like an aroma breaking through a dream. She took a sip. She'd been sitting out in the yard since before dawn, watching the sun float up out of the darkness and turn the sky violet and red. Gradually the colors had melted into a crystalline blue. She had asked the spirits to guide the father of her children to the ancestors.

Aunt Rose unfolded the chair leaning against the house,

dragged it over, and sat down next to her. Vicky steeled herself for the urgent, well-meaning pleas for her to pull herself together, think of the kids. The old woman had been fussing over her since she'd knocked on the door last night.

She'd been expecting her, Aunt Rose had said. The moccasin telegraph was buzzing with the news. Vicky had waved at John O'Malley, his headlights washing over the Bronco, and stepped into Aunt Rose's arms. It was over now. She and Ben were over.

It had taken a while before she'd felt in control enough to call the kids. First Lucas. He was the strongest. He didn't speak for a moment. The sound of his breathing, irregular and forced, had filled the line. Finally the questions had begun, like the questions of a warrior trying to determine the cause of an ambush. How? Why? Who?

She told him what she knew, and he'd asked more questions. She didn't have the answers. After a while, the call had ended, and she'd rung Susan. Silence again, followed by screams that pulsed down the line. They'd talked only a few minutes, a breath of time, and there had been so much Vicky had wanted to say. But Susan had slammed down the phone, a punctuation, Vicky knew, to the anger her daughter harbored toward her—*she* was the one who had left the girl's father—anger that had exploded in an inarticulate blame for her father's death.

Susan was flying to Denver this morning, and she and Lucas would drive to the reservation. They'd be here this evening.

Aunt Rose's voice droned beside her, something about the old religion. "Do you good to hear the preaching," she said. "Take away some of the pain. Get your mind on the new world that's coming."

Vicky shifted sideways and gave the woman her full attention. "What are you talking about, Auntie? That cult in the mountains? Have you gone to the shadow dances?"

"Not the dances themselves." A defensive note crept into Aunt Rose's tone. "Only the Indians living up at the ranch take part in the dances. Every six weeks they dance for four days, like the Ghost Dancers in the Old Time. Wovoka gave Orlando all the instructions when he was in the shadow world. He promised that if the Indians dance, good things'll happen. We're gonna have our own land with plenty of trees and water and no whites telling us what to do. There's gonna be all Indians in the new world, like Wovoka said."

Vicky reached over and took the old woman's hand. "Surely you don't believe this nonsense."

Aunt Rose flinched. "Nonsense? The Creator give us the Ghost Dance a long time ago. Sent Wovoka to show us the new way of praying. Now Wovoka's sent Orlando. We gotta start praying again like in the Old Time, or the good things won't happen."

"Orlando is James Sherwood." Vicky kept her voice measured and calm. "The Sherwoods were always"—she hesitated—"different. Remember? James's father shot himself. His mother left the res and died in a mental hospital in Denver."

Aunt Rose was quiet a moment. "Orlando died, too," she said finally. "He stayed in the shadow world a long time. He was with Wovoka and the ancestors. He's a holy man."

"Oh, Auntie." Vicky stopped herself from saying that James Sherwood was crazy, *Nokooho*. She could still see the white-clothed dancers circling the parking lot, shoving collection baskets at motorists, and people dropping in coins. People like Aunt Rose, naive and trusting. She was always taking people into her home. How many times had Aunt Rose taken *her* in? No place to go? Rose White Plume always had room. The tribal social services, the police would drop off people for a few days. Nothing official. It was just that everyone on the res knew that Rose White Plume had a good heart.

"Promise me," Vicky said, "that you won't give the shadow dancers any money." She could imagine the old woman, entranced by the preaching, snapping open her pocketbook and dropping a few precious dollars into the baskets.

"Now, Vicky, I got enough. What I don't need . . ."

Vicky reached over and took the old woman's hand. "You already give away what you don't need. How many people have you fed in the last month?"

Aunt Rose tilted her head back and studied the sky. "Young couple with a baby drove up here from Oklahoma and got stranded. Couple kids fighting with their folks. Social services said they needed some cooling-off time." She paused, still searching the sky. The list was growing, Vicky thought. "Two, three girls stayed for a couple days."

"See what I mean, Auntie?" Vicky said, but she was talking to herself. Aunt Rose had shifted her attention toward the front of the house, and Vicky turned in her chair.

Her heart jumped.

For an instant, she'd thought the man coming toward them was Ben: tall and fit-looking, hair as black as slate, narrow sun-browned face, sharp, handsome features. And the same eyes, shining with anger. His boots kicked up swirls of dust. Vicky set her mug, still half-full, on the ground, stood up, and faced Hugh Holden.

"I want to talk to you, Vicky." He was a couple of yards away now.

"Hello, Hugh," Aunt Rose said, a scolding note ringing in her tone. The Arapaho had ignored the proprieties and launched immediately into business.

Hugh Holden glanced at the old woman, but there was no recognition in his eyes, no deviation from his purpose. He came closer. Vicky could smell the sour mixture of coffee and cigarettes on his breath.

"What happened last night between you and Ben?" The man stood with fists clenched at his sides, white knuckles straining against the brown skin. He was like Ben.

Vicky stepped backward, a reflexive motion. The chair wobbled against her leg. "I don't understand . . ."

"Bullshit. The fed says you and Ben had dinner. How come, Vicky? How come you were willing to have dinner with somebody you hated? Walked out on without so much as a go-to-hell. Broke up his family. Broke him up bad. Then, when he tried to get you to come back, all you could think about was some priest. That priest . . ." He drew in a long breath that flared his nostrils. "John O'Malley's the reason you turned against Ben. What'd you decide? To get Ben out of the way so you and the priest can have your little romance?"

"That's crazy, Hugh." Vicky tried to keep her voice calm. She'd had this conversation before, but it had been with Ben. Ben had believed the same, and she had never succeeded in convincing him that there was nothing between her and John O'Malley, except friendship. He was her closest friend, that was all. He was a priest.

"God knows I never understood what kind of spell you put on my brother," the man went on as if she hadn't spoken.

"Years he carried the torch for you, sure you were gonna come to your senses and go back to him. Even made plans to add rooms on the cabin up at the ranch. Room for Susan. Room for your office." He gave a snort of derision. "You being a lawyer were gonna want an office."

"Hugh, listen to me," Vicky began, struggling to wrap her mind around the magnitude of the fantasy world in which her ex-husband had lived. "Ben had trouble with a couple of ranch hands."

"You're the only trouble Ben had," he said, spraying her face with pinpricks of spittle. "Why a restaurant in Lander, Vicky? So he'd be sure to drive across Rendezvous Road? You knew he was gonna be out there alone. You set him up."

"What?" Vicky reared back. "How dare you!"

"I know what happened." The man's mouth twisted sideways. "You might fool everybody else, but you don't fool me. You hated my brother. You didn't want him bothering you, showing up in Lander, messing up your life. You wanted him dead."

Aunt Rose stood up. "You've said enough, Hugh Holden. You'd better go."

"How'd you arrange it, Vicky?" The man kept on. "Who'd you hire to shoot my brother? Skin? White man?"

"For godssakes, Hugh," Vicky said.

"I swear on my brother's grave you're not gonna get away with it. I'm gonna be all over that FBI agent until he gets you convicted, and if the law doesn't get you, Vicky, I swear I will."

"I said, get going, Hugh Holden," Aunt Rose shouted. "You ain't welcome at my house anymore."

Vicky made herself hold the man's eyes until he'd turned

away and started back along the side of the house. He was almost to the front when he stopped and looked back. "One more thing. The family's gonna make the funeral arrangements, you got that? We're gonna bury my brother like an Arapaho warrior. His kids are gonna be with the family where they belong, but you better not show your face. That's a warning."

Vicky felt as if her muscles and bones had fused together. She couldn't move. Her eyes stayed locked on the Indian until he'd disappeared around the house. She was barely aware of the warmth of Aunt Rose's hand on her frozen arm.

"You come inside now," the old woman said. "I'm gonna get you some more hot coffee." An engine growled into life, tires squealed. Vicky saw the blue pickup peel down the road ahead of a cloud of dust.

"He thinks I killed Ben," she said. *She had thought . . .*

"Man's crazy with grief. Don't know what he's saying." Aunt Rose lifted her chin and locked eyes with her. "You are my sister's daughter and you are my daughter. You had nothing to do with this terrible thing. You are not a murderer."

Vicky felt the tears coming. The contours of the old woman's face, the shape of her shoulders and arms blurred in the sun. She ran a hand over her cheeks.

"Let's go inside," she said, but Aunt Rose was staring toward the front of the house.

"Looks like we got another visitor."

Vicky followed the old woman's gaze. A white Blazer was slowing for a turn into the yard, a white man behind the wheel. The Blazer swung out of sight. She heard the engine cut off, the door slam shut.

"Well, it's to be expected," Aunt Rose said. "People

gonna be dropping by all day. You go on inside. I'll tell 'em you ain't up to seeing folks just yet."

"It's okay, Aunt," Vicky said. "It's the fed. He could have news." She started down the side of the house through the sunlight reflecting off the painted wood, aware of Aunt Rose hurrying behind her, gasping for air.

In the front yard, Gianelli was standing on the stoop, one fist in the air, as if he'd just knocked and was about to knock again. "Vicky," he said, glancing around. "We have to talk." Then, to Aunt Rose, "How are you, Mrs. White Plume?"

"You'd better come in." Aunt Rose made her way to the stoop, brushed past the agent, and pushed the door open. "Come on, come on," she said, beckoning the man inside.

Vicky followed. The living room was cool and smelled of coffee and the bacon and fried eggs that Aunt Rose had tried to get her to eat earlier.

"Sit down." The old woman kept moving toward the kitchen. "I'll get some coffee."

Vicky sat down on the sofa. "What have you found out, Ted?"

The agent didn't say anything for a moment. He was still standing, glancing around, the helplessness about him almost comical: white man in polished, tasseled shoes and blue sport coat, surrounded by a sofa and chairs that might collapse under his weight, a rabbit-eared TV, sunlight glinting on the glass that covered photos of the ancestors.

After a moment, he took one of the wood side chairs and fumbled for the notepad inside his blue sport coat.

"Not a whole lot," he said finally. "I want you to tell me again what happened last night."

Vicky felt the muscles in her throat constrict. What exactly had she told him? How would he compare what she'd said then with what she said now? How would he construe her words? This was how suspects felt, she thought. She went through the story again: Ben preoccupied and angry, arriving late. They argued. He stomped out.

The fed looked up from the notepad. "You didn't say anything last night about him throwing the dishes on the floor."

Vicky was quiet a moment. "Obviously you've talked to people at the restaurant."

"About a dozen witnesses saw the whole thing. All of them say Ben was out of control, but you didn't tell me how bad it was. Why didn't you?"

"We'd had similar scenes in the past." *God, she was on the witness stand. She was the defendant.* "You know about the beatings, Ted. You know why I left Ben fifteen years ago. Everybody on the res knows. What are you getting at?"

"Witnesses say something else, Vicky." The agent drew in a long breath and tapped his ballpoint on the notepad. "They say you were pretty angry, too. They say you followed Ben out of the restaurant. They say your Bronco followed his brown truck down Main Street. A good prosecutor might conclude that, over the years, you'd accumulated a lot of reasons to want Ben Holden out of your life permanently. A good prosecutor might think you followed him to Rendezvous Road."

Vicky jumped to her feet. "You've known me for five years, Ted. We've worked together on cases. Do you really believe I'm capable of shooting someone?" She stopped. She had shot a man last year to stop him from killing John O'Malley. She had been capable.

She rephrased the question: "Do you think I'm capable of premeditated murder?" Out of the corner of her eye, she saw

Aunt Rose in the doorway to the kitchen, eyes widened in fear, two mugs of coffee shaking in her hands.

"I think anybody might be capable, if they're pushed hard enough." The agent stood up and faced her. His eyes were as still and opaque as stone. "Do you own a pistol?"

Aunt Rose let out a little groan.

"Of course not." Vicky made her voice hard to match his eyes.

"Where did you go after you left the restaurant?"

"I drove around for a while and went home."

"Anyone see you? Friend? Neighbor?" He was shaking his head in answer to his own questions. "Look, Vicky, I want to help you. Give me someplace else to look."

"I told you, Ben'd had trouble with two Lakota ranch hands. He met with them just before he came to the restaurant."

"Roy He-Dog and Martin Crow Elk." The fed nodded. "Ben's assistant says the Lakotas left last week. They're probably at Pine Ridge by now."

"Ben said they were still here."

"He could've been mistaken, or . . ." The agent hesitated. "Maybe you misunderstood."

"I'm telling you the truth."

Gianelli let out a long sigh; his shoulders sloped forward. "I have to ask you again not to leave the area."

"You're saying I'm under suspicion for homicide."

"Everybody's under suspicion, this point."

"That's not true."

"Vicky—" he began, but she cut him off.

"From now on, if you want to talk to me, you'll have to contact my lawyer."

"You're a lawyer."

"Right. A fool has herself for a lawyer."

The fed pulled his lips into a thin line above his squared jaw. "That's the way you want it." He slipped the notepad back inside his sport coat, and walked to the door.

She turned away. The sound of the door closing came like a shot behind her.

"That white man's crazier than Hugh Holden." Aunt Rose sounded quiet and determined.

Hugh Holden. Vicky could feel her heart knocking. Ben's brother knew how persistent Ben had been. Hugh would confirm everything the fed already suspected. She had a motive to kill her ex-husband; she had no alibi.

She said, "I have to get back to Lander, Aunt."

‹ 8 ›

It was half past seven when Father John drove out of the mission grounds and turned onto Seventeen-Mile Road. Blue Crow Software opened at eight, and he wanted to be there. Before he'd left, he found Father George in his office at the rear of the administration building—down the corridor lined with the tinted pictures of past Jesuits at St. Francis Mission—and told the man he'd be back in a couple hours. The pale gray eyes had flickered up from the computer monitor. One hand rose in acknowledgment.

"There'll be a lot of phone calls." He'd tried to warn the other priest. Everyone on the res had probably heard about Ben Holden's murder by now. The moccasin telegraph was efficient. The phone would be ringing off the hook with people wanting to talk, trying to figure it out.

He'd offered Mass this morning for Ben Holden. *Lord, give him your peace.* He'd prayed for Vicky and for the family. *Give them your strength.* The few old people scattered about the pews had joined in the prayers, voices rumbling through the quiet. The early light streaming through the stained glass windows played over the wrinkled brown faces lifted toward him. They made him a priest, he'd thought, the people who needed him. Just as sick people made someone a doctor and people in need of justice made someone a lawyer. He drew his priesthood from the people.

Then let me be the kind of priest they need.

After Mass, he spent a half-hour at his desk going over the annual report, checking the quantified data that Father George and the new members on the board would be scrutinizing. He totaled the numbers of participants in the programs that Arapahos couldn't find elsewhere, at least easily: religious education, baptism, confirmation, marriage preparation. The numbers looked good. But good enough for reasonable men charged with recommending the best use of limited resources?

Dear God, he hoped so.

Just before he'd left, he'd dialed the number of Amos Walking Bear, the president of the parish council. The elder had answered, his voice clear and sharp. He'd probably been up for hours. They spent ten minutes talking about Ben Holden's murder, and Amos had broken the news: The family wanted an Arapaho ceremony. The funeral wouldn't be at the mission.

Father John had stopped himself from asking why the Holdens didn't want a Catholic funeral. The answer hovered at the edge of his mind. When Vicky hadn't gone back to Ben in the past, the man had blamed him. The Holdens probably also blamed him. He and Vicky were friends. Just friends. And yet, the truth was—he couldn't hide from the truth—she was important to him. He had never meant to love her; it had just happened. He had the odd feeling that Ben and the Holden family had seen a part of him that he'd tried to hide, but it was like his shadow. It was visible.

Father John realized that the elder had switched to the subject of the parish council. "Might get some of the members to a meeting tonight," Amos said.

That was great, he'd said. Then he'd told the elder that he'd see him at seven o'clock and pushed the disconnect button. For a moment, he thought about calling Vicky. She'd been on his mind all night—there in his dreams, small and vulnerable, looking at the fed with wide, questioning eyes, as if she were struggling to comprehend what the fed had just told her: Stay in the area.

He'd replaced the receiver. It was still early. Aunt Rose was probably up, but Vicky might still be asleep. He hoped so. She needed the rest, and Aunt Rose wouldn't want him disturbing her. He tried to ignore the unsettling feeling that always came over him when she went to her people on the reservation, as if she'd gone into another world through a door he couldn't enter.

Now he turned south on Rendezvous Road. The plains opened around him, a rough cut of brown bluffs and hidden arroyos that swallowed up the thin strip of blacktop stretching ahead. Scattered clumps of sagebrush bent sideways in the wind. In the far distance, the mountains emerged through the white haze.

He rewound the tape in the player beside him. The machine clicked and whined and finally spilled out the opening notes of *Faust*. After a few miles, he slowed around a wide bend. The road looked different in the daylight, but this was the spot where Ben Holden had been shot, no doubt about it. Tiny yellow and blue wildflowers poked through the brush in the barrow ditches on both sides of the road. There were no other vehicles in sight, no houses, no sign of human life, only the sweep of the plains and, on the west, the foothills striated yellow and blue in the sunshine.

The yellow police tape stretched down the other side. He hit the stop button on the tape player, pulled across the pavement, and got out. A bee was droning over the ditch, and somewhere a crow was cawing. The breeze was already hot, and the tape fluttered between the metal poles stuck in the dirt at the edge of the blacktop. Beyond the tape was a rectangle of flattened brush and wild grasses where the truck had been parked. A faint trace of tire tracks led to the flattened area. No sign of skid marks. Gianelli had been right. Ben had intended to stop.

Father John walked about thirty feet down the road to the end of the tape, his eyes hunting the ground for other patches of flattened grass. The breeze swept along the ditch. Nothing looked disturbed.

He crossed the road and hunted his way back. No indication of another vehicle off the road. He crossed back over to the pickup and slid behind the steering wheel, trying to form a picture in his mind of what had happened. Brown truck looming out of the dimness, headlights scraping the blacktop. The truck slows, pulls off the road, stops. No engine trouble, no flat tires, no reason to stop. Unless there was something up ahead, larger than a person standing by the road. A vehicle stopped in the road.

Father John started the pickup and turned back into the southbound lane. Vicky said that Ben had gone looking for two Lakotas yesterday. They'd ripped him off, and Ben Holden was the kind of man to take matters into his own hands. The Lakotas could have guessed he'd take the shortcut across the reservation on his way back to the Arapaho Ranch. They could have been waiting. A truck parked across the road could block both lanes.

Gianelli was a good investigator, Father John told himself, slowing down the main street of Hudson. The agent would put it all together. He'd probably found the Lakotas by now, taken them in for interviews. Unless . . .

He gripped the wheel hard. The Lakotas were in South Dakota, swallowed up in the emptiness of a reservation like Pine Ridge. The FBI might never find them, which meant that Ben's murder might never be solved and Vicky . . . Suspicion would cling to her like a black shadow the rest of her life. He swallowed back the dry knot of anger in his throat. He and Vicky had worked together to help so many people, and now she was the one who needed help. He had to find a way to help her.

He passed the semi on the straightaway outside of town and leaned onto the accelerator, eating up the miles into Lander. Twenty minutes later he found a parking space a half-block off Main Street and walked back to the office of Blue Crow Software.

At the desk inside the door was a young woman with a dusting of freckles across her pale cheeks and dark hair that fingered the shoulders of her blue blouse. He was looking for Dean Little Horse, he said.

The welcoming smile froze in the pale face. "Dean Little Horse." She enunciated each syllable as if she were testing a foreign language. Then she flattened her hands on the desk and levered herself to her feet.

"What'd you say your name is?"

He hadn't said. Now he told her his name and said he was the pastor at St. Francis Mission.

She nodded. That made sense. Indian priest looking for an Indian. "One moment." She sidled around the desk, then took off almost at a run across the green carpet, down an aisle between rows of cubicles. She knocked on a door in the rear and slipped inside.

Father John waited. The clack of keyboards sounded through the low electronic buzz that permeated the air. Two men in T-shirts and khakis emerged from one cubicle and crossed into another, heads bent together, voices hushed and tense.

Finally the woman came back across the office. "Tom can see you now." She nodded toward the door. Standing in the opening was a short, dark-haired man in a blue shirt with sleeves rolled up to his elbows and blue jeans.

Father John made his way down the aisle and took the man's extended hand.

"Tom Miller. People around here call me boss, but not to my face." He gave a forced laugh that ended on a high note. The man probably hadn't hit thirty yet. He ushered Father John into a small office with a desk perpendicular to a window that looked out on a parking lot next to an alley.

"Have a seat." Miller nodded toward the red plastic bucket chair in front of a filing cabinet. He sat down behind the desk, lifted one hand, and started rubbing his shoulder, the corners of his mouth turned up in discomfort. "Hardball. Pulled the deltoid. Thanks to spending way too much time in front of computers since I started the company. We make the software that keeps your water flowing out of the faucets." Pride seeped into the man's voice. "It's our software that opens the gates at Bull Lake Dam and lets out the right amount of water. So you're looking for Dean Little Horse."

Father John took the bucket chair. He removed his hat, hooked it over one knee, and said that was right. "When's the last time you saw him?"

"That would be . . ." Miller stopped rubbing his shoulder

a moment and stared at some invisible calendar behind his eyes. "Thursday. Left work early. About four, I'd say. Hasn't shown up since."

Father John took a couple of breaths. "Has he called? Offered an explanation?"

"Nada." The man's fingers carved a circle into his shoulder. "One day he's in his cubicle writing code, next day he doesn't show up. I figure it's some Indian thing. You know, somebody dies, so he has to go to the ceremonies, take care of family business."

"Has Dean not shown up for work before?"

Miller dropped his hand and settled back against the chair, forehead scrunched in concern. "Come to think of it, can't say that's the case. Dean's a reliable guy. When his grandmother started calling here, I decided he's got himself into trouble. Too bad. Dean's a genius at problem solving, and him taking a powder leaves us in the lurch. We're developing software for dams in five states. We gotta push the product out the door."

"What do you know about his girlfriend?"

"Girlfriend?" The man gave another snort of laughter. "Best advice my old man ever gave me—he ran a Fortune Five Hundred—was, stay out of your employees' personal lives. I don't ask, and they don't tell."

"Dean have friends around here?" Father John nodded toward the door.

Miller shrugged. "Shares cubicle space with Sam Harrison. Not in yet. You might catch him later."

Father John stood up and thanked the man, who had started to his feet before gripping his shoulder and sinking back. "Maybe you should see a doctor," Father John said.

"Doctors. What do they know?" He lifted a couple of fingers in farewell.

Father John let himself out and walked back down the aisle, aware of the eyes swiveling toward him from the cubicles. The receptionist's desk was vacant.

Outside, the street was nearly deserted. A couple of vehicles moving past, two businessmen making their way up the sidewalk, briefcases brushing the sides of their pressed blue jeans, a young woman pushing a stroller, hugging the shade under the store awnings. He turned the corner and jaywalked to the pickup across the street. He was about to get behind the steering wheel when a man darted out of the alley behind the software offices.

"Hey!" The man waited for a couple of pickups to pass, then started across the street. "You the guy looking for Dean Little Horse?"

Father John slammed the door and stepped into the lane. "You a friend?"

"Sam Harrison. Just drove into the parking lot out back. Boss said you wanted to see me." The man looked like a college kid, with curly brown hair, an eager, handsome face, and questioning eyes behind the round glasses with thin wires clipped behind his ears. He was dressed in khakis and a striped beige shirt. A gold chain glinted around his neck.

"What can you tell me about Dean?" Father John was thinking that Harrison must have come in the office from the back parking lot while he was exiting the front.

"You up for a cup of coffee?" The man glanced toward the corner. A pickup came down the street, honked, veered around them, honked again.

"Let's go." Father John led the way across the street. They walked in silence down the sidewalk and around the corner

to the coffee shop with the pink saucer and cup painted on
the plate-glass window, blue steam rising from the cup. The
man insisted upon paying for a couple of mugs of coffee at
the counter. They sat down on the metal ice cream chairs at
a round table with fake marble on the top.

" 'Bout time somebody got serious about finding Dean,"
Harrison said. Behind the round glasses, questions and concern mingled in the man's eyes.

"Where do you think he is?" Father John took a sip of
coffee.

The man shook his head and cradled his mug in both
hands. "I thought we were friends, you know? Dean and I
got along real good. First Indian I ever got to know. That's
something, isn't it? Lived next to the res all my life and
never got to know one of the Indians." He took a drink of
coffee and seemed to contemplate this. "Maybe I got it
wrong, about us being friends. Maybe he didn't trust me
after all. Me, being white. If he was in trouble . . ." He let
the words drift over the table.

Father John set his mug down. "You think Dean's in
some kind of trouble?"

"Maybe. He got real quiet the last few weeks. Real short
tempered, which wasn't like Dean. Bit my head off a couple
times. He was working on upgrades for the software at Bull
Lake Dam. Boss says I gotta take over the project now."

Father John worked at his own coffee again. Then he set
the mug down and pulled the notepad and pencil out of his
shirt pocket. "I hear Dean had a girlfriend. Any idea who
she is?"

"Janis some Indian name." The man shrugged.

"Arapaho?"

"Yeah, but not from around here. Oklahoma Indian, Dean

said. Came up here last winter. He met her at a party on the res. Man, she must've been something. Gorgeous, Dean said. A real fox, you know what I mean? Dean was in love for sure. Said she was real spiritual. I asked him once what he meant, and he said, 'Part of our tradition. You wouldn't understand.' "

"What do you think he meant?" Father John prodded. Something stirred in the back of his mind, remnants of gossip, and then he had it. Indians from other places were coming to the res to join the shadow dancers.

Harrison pushed his mug aside and stared out the painted window. "Come to think of it, Dean said something about some ranch in the mountains she went to live on. She'd come to town now and then, and he'd be real happy. Then she'd go back to the ranch, and he'd be a bear. Afraid he was never gonna get her back. Worrying all the time about Janis." He snapped his fingers. "Beaver, that's her name. Janis Beaver."

Father John jotted down the name, then slipped the notepad back into his pocket, drained the last of his coffee, and got to his feet. "If you hear from Dean," he said, sliding the metal chair into place, "ask him to call me. Doesn't matter what kind of trouble he's in."

Harrison tilted his head back and gave him the kind of solemn, focused look he used to get from the best students in his American history classes.

He walked quickly back to the pickup, checking his watch as he went. Almost ten. Time to drive up to the shadow ranch and make it back to the mission before the Eagles practiced at four. He slid behind the steering wheel, flipped open the glove compartment, and pulled out the cell phone a couple of his parishioners had given him a few weeks ago. He seldom used it, and when he tried, he found that, more often than not, it didn't work on the reservation.

Now he punched in the numbers for Information, then called Eldon Antelope, one of the dads who helped coach the baseball team. An answering machine picked up. "If I'm late for practice," he said. "Take over, will you?"

‹ 9 ›

L AW OFFICES OF VICKY HOLDEN.
The old-fashioned sign on the front lawn mimicked the house, with curlicue posts that matched the gingerbread trim on the eaves. Vicky parked at the curb and hurried up the sidewalk. After four months in a Denver skyscraper, she could hardly believe her good luck to find a bungalow zoned for offices on the corner of a quiet, residential street. On the front door, below the beveled glass, was a bronze plaque engraved with her name. She let herself inside.

"Oh, my!" Esther Sundell, the secretary she'd hired two weeks ago, rose from behind the desk in what had once been the living room. Her hands fluttered a moment, then clasped together. She was in her fifties, with light brown hair fading into gray, cut just below her ears. About her own height, Vicky guessed, five-foot-six, but stouter, with broad shoulders and a thick waist concealed under the oversized blouses that she favored.

The day Vicky opened the office, Esther had appeared at her door. She was related to Laola, she'd said, Vicky's former secretary, although Vicky still wasn't sure how she was related. She needed a job, and Laola had told her that Vicky needed a secretary. She'd hired the woman on the spot.

"I didn't think you were coming in," Esther said, a trace of anxiety in her voice. She was still nervous about getting everything just right.

"I'm not in." Vicky opened the French doors to her private office in the former dining room. She'd called early this morning and left a voice mail, knowing she wouldn't be able to concentrate on work. That was before she'd realized she was at the top of Gianelli's suspect list.

"Then I *did* get your message right?" There was obvious relief in the woman's voice. "You've had about twenty calls. I said you were out for the day. I canceled your appointments for this afternoon."

Vicky thanked the woman, dropped her bag on the desk that straddled the space between the window and the French doors—a dining table would have stood here—and adjusted the white, horizontal blinds. Slats of sunshine shot across the walls and gray carpet.

"I just wanted to say . . ." The secretary was standing in the opened doors, hands gripping the knobs. "Well, I heard about your ex-husband. It's all over the news. Radio, TV, big headline in the morning paper. If there's anything you need, all you have to do is ask."

Vicky perched on the leather chair she'd hauled from Lander to Denver and back to Lander again, under the impression that she could haul a piece of home around with her, and gave the secretary a smile that she hoped would end the conversation. She reached for the phone.

Esther remained between the doors. "Ben Holden must have been a wonderful man. Foreman at the Arapaho Ranch!

And my, so handsome in the newspaper picture. Like one of the Indians in the movies."

Vicky gestured with the receiver. "An important call," she said. *God, even in death, Ben could attract women.*

"Oh, of course." The hands fluttered upward like birds scared out of a nest. Then the woman backed into the front office, pulling the double doors with her until they clicked shut. Her shadow moved across the glass panes.

Vicky tapped out the number for Howard and Fergus, her former firm in Denver, and asked for Wes Nelson, the managing partner.

There was a brief silence, then the familiar voice at the other end. "Tell me you've had enough of small-town practice and you're ready to come back to the big time."

Vicky was struck by the irony. She'd wanted to come *home*, and yet, if she'd stayed in Denver, she wouldn't be a murder suspect now. "Something terrible has happened," she said. Then she told him about Ben, spilling out the details of the scene at the restaurant, the shooting on Rendezvous Road, the fact she did not have an alibi.

"Whoa, Vicky," he interrupted. "You telling me the feds think you had something to do with this?"

She said it looked that way and forced a little laugh.

"You need a good criminal lawyer, Vicky. We have the best in the region. Who do you want? I'll send anybody you name."

Vicky stared at the piles of papers on her desk. No Seventeenth Street criminal lawyer would want to set aside a mountain of work, drive three hundred miles to Lander, and hold her hand through a ridiculous investigation. She said, "I'm thinking about a couple of lawyers in the area." She gave him the names. Wes had connections throughout the region. "Who would you recommend?"

"You think one of the firm's lawyers wouldn't jump at the case?"

"There isn't a case," she said, striving for more confidence than she felt.

"Not yet, but it could go hard on you. I want to make sure the FBI agent plays by all the rules." Wes was quiet a moment. "What about an attorney who *used* to be at the firm? UCLA grad. Hated to lose him, but like you, he wasn't cut out for city life. Has firsthand experience dealing with federal agents on Indian reservations."

A memory stirred somewhere in the back of her mind. Indian lawyer at the firm two or three years ago. Substitute the University of Denver for UCLA and the lawyer's résumé sounded like her own.

"Adam Lone Eagle," Wes was saying. "Lakota. Hails from Pine Ridge."

Lakota! One of the seven branches of the Sioux Nation. The largest tribe on the plains, fierce, warlike. They couldn't be ignored. Her people had tried to stay out of their way, but there were times—after the massacre at Sand Creek for one—when Arapaho warriors had gone over to the Sioux to fight the whites.

"Curious," she said. "Ben had trouble with a couple of Lakota ranch hands before he was killed."

"Fed picked them up yet?"

"He thinks they've already gone back to Pine Ridge."

"All the more reason you're going to need Adam Lone Eagle. If they've gone into hiding, he might know how to smoke them out."

"Adam Lone Eagle." Vicky let the name roll over her tongue. "Where do I find this warrior?"

"Practically in your backyard. He's with Grant and Bovee in Casper now."

That Indian lawyer. Vicky vaguely remembered the news flashing across the moccasin telegraph a year ago. Another Indian lawyer in Wyoming. Lakota. She'd put it out of her mind. Her people weren't likely to hire a Lakota. She smiled at the irony. She was the one who was going to hire him.

"How soon can you get to Casper?" Wes asked.

Vicky glanced at her watch. Almost eleven. Casper was about a hundred and fifty miles away. "I can be there by two," she said.

The roofs of Casper twinkled in the sun ahead. She passed the turn to the airport and drove toward downtown through streets laid out more than a hundred years ago, wide enough in which to turn wagon trains. She found a parking place a block from the redbrick building with the white sign on the front: GRANT AND BOVEE, LAW OFFICES. Then she walked back, edging past a group of men in suits, two abreast, talking, laughing, gesturing, as if they owned the world, which they did, she was thinking. And Gianelli was like them.

She pushed open the heavy wooden door and stepped into the cool, spacious reception area, all marble floors and over-stuffed chairs and tables with bouquets of fresh flowers. A middle-aged woman with a head of tight black curls and thin black eyebrows penciled above her eyes glanced up from behind the half-moon desk. Vicky gave her name and said she had an appointment with Adam Lone Eagle.

"Oh, yes." The eyebrow's rose in two perfect arches. "Mr. Lone Eagle's expecting you."

❮ 10 ❯

Vicky followed the secretary down the corridor to the door with ADAM LONE EAGLE written in black letters on a wooden plaque. The door was half-opened, and the secretary ushered her inside. Standing by the desk across the room was a man probably in his forties, close to six feet tall, with muscular shoulders and chest that filled out his blue-striped dress shirt. His black hair was cut long and combed back, shiny in the light. He had a narrow face with prominent cheekbones, a long nose with a bump at the top, and a full mouth above the strong chin that curved into a little cleft. Handsome, she thought, with the golden brown complexion of a man who lived in the sun, like a warrior in the Old Time.

"Vicky Holden!" He seemed to rear back, the dark eyes appraising her. She saw the flash of approval in his expression. He started forward, took her hand, and led her into the office. "About time we met," he said, not letting go of her hand. His grip was warm and firm. She could feel the strength in the man, and it gave her a measure of comfort and security that she hadn't felt in so long, she'd almost forgotten they existed.

"Thanks for seeing me on such short notice," she managed, taking in the office around them: the soft gray carpeting and slatted blinds that blocked most of the sunlight, the polished desk that reflected the fluorescent ceiling lights.

The man directed her to the chair in front of the desk, then walked around, taking his time—a signal, she thought, that there was nothing to worry about—and settled into the brown leather chair on the other side.

"Funny thing," he began. (Ah, the polite preliminaries would be observed. It increased her feeling of comfort.) "Wes has often mentioned you. Said we should meet. I was planning to drive over to Lander one of these days and introduce myself. Couple of Indian lawyers oughtta know each other, don't you think?"

He pulled a yellow pad across the desk and plucked a gold pen from a holder. His fingers were long and well-shaped; his nails trimmed and neat. He wasn't wearing any rings. "Sorry to hear about your ex-husband." He held her eyes a moment. "Terrible thing. Must've been quite a shock. Wes tells me you and Ben had dinner together before he was murdered."

"It was an attempt to have dinner," she said. "It turned into a row."

"Not the first time, I take it." He left his eyes on hers, and she saw that Wes had filled him in.

"Now Ted Gianelli thinks you had something to do with the homicide."

Vicky relaxed into the chair. She was in competent hands. "He isn't the only one," she said. "Hugh, Ben's brother, thinks I hired someone to kill Ben." She paused. "I want you to know before we go any further. I did not murder my ex-husband."

"I didn't ask you." Adam was jotting something on the pad. "Frankly, it doesn't matter."

"Doesn't matter?"

"We don't have to prove your innocence. Gianelli and the U.S. attorney have to prove your guilt. That's their job. My job will be to make sure they stay within the legal boundaries while they look for evidence."

"There isn't any evidence, Adam." Vicky stood up and walked over to the window. She pulled the slats apart. A column of sunshine lay over the street and sidewalk. A businessman hurried past, and at the curb, a woman was lifting a child out of a car seat in a van. An ordinary day, Vicky thought, except that the earth was shifting beneath her.

"Why does that upset you?" There was a surprised note in the lawyer's voice. "You know how the system works. You know I have to shield you from an indictment."

Vicky made herself take several slow breaths before she turned back. Adam Long Eagle was on his feet, fingers tapping the desk, dark eyes on her. "So, do we go forward?"

She nodded and walked back to the chair.

"We both know innocent people can be indicted and prosecuted," he said. "All it takes is enough circumstantial evidence to put together a logical case. You're in a precarious position. Abused ex-wife. You spent ten years married to Ben Holden, ten years of abuse. You've been divorced for . . ."

"Fifteen years," she said.

"Wes said Ben wouldn't leave you alone, always wanted you back. That true?" The man hurried on without waiting for an answer. "You have no alibi for last night, and any dim-witted prosecutor can make the case that you had a motive."

Vicky walked back to the window. It was disconcerting hearing her own story from a stranger. "They found the weapon," she said, looking back. "A twenty-two-caliber pistol. There might be prints. The gun can be traced."

The lawyer sat down and filled a couple of lines on the notepad. "Don't count on it," he said finally. "Killers don't leave behind traceable guns with prints, unless they're certifiably stupid."

That was true. Vicky pushed open the slats again and stared at the pickups and sedans passing outside. The pistol would probably be a dead end.

"You own a gun?"

She whirled around. "No."

"What about access?"

"Access? I can buy a gun at any gun shop."

"Easy access. Anybody you know . . ."

"Ben owned guns. Every rancher on the res owns a gun. There are lots of people I know with guns. What are you getting at, Adam?"

The lawyer stood up and came around the desk. "I don't like it. Gun left at the scene." He shrugged, but there was something forced in the gesture. "It might be traceable," he said, a lack of conviction in his tone.

"Yes." Vicky heard the same tentativeness in her own voice. They both knew that whoever had waited for Ben on Rendezvous Road was clever and determined. Why, then, had the killer left the weapon?

"From now on," the lawyer was saying, "you do not talk to Ted Gianelli or any other fed, police officer, sheriff's deputy, or detective. You talk to nobody about the homicide. Got it? When Gianelli calls, and he will call, your secretary will tell him to call me. All communication goes through me. And another thing, you don't talk about the homicide to anybody else. Not friends or family. Nobody. I don't want Gianelli picking up random bits of information that he might use against you. Is all this clear?"

Vicky walked back to the chair, then to the window again. "So your strategy is to sit tight and act guilty," she said. "That's crazy. Ben argued with a couple of ranch hands. Lakotas." She stopped pacing and locked eyes with the man.

The lawyer reached back and dragged the yellow pad across the desk. "Names?" He gripped the pen and glanced up at her.

"Roy He-Dog. Martin Crow Elk." The names that Gianelli had given her were imprinted on her mind. "The fed claims they went back to Pine Ridge last week, but he's wrong. Ben met with them yesterday."

"I know the families." The gold pen moved over the notepad. "I'll make a few phone calls to Pine Ridge and tap into the news. If they're on the res, I'll hear about it." He looked up. "You think they shot your ex-husband?"

That was the problem. She'd been so sure. It *had* to be the Lakotas who followed Ben to Rendezvous Road. But she didn't have any evidence. And Gianelli was right about one thing. Ben was a powerful man; he could have made other enemies.

Vicky folded her arms and stared out the window. It was clear now—hadn't she known all along? No one could know whether the Lakotas were guilty or innocent until they were found. And if they were still on the res, she was the one who would have to find them.

She glanced back at the lawyer. "I'm going to ask around . . ."

"Haven't you heard a word I said?"

"We're talking about my life, Adam."

"Let Gianelli do the asking around."

The office was quiet. Outside a truck geared down.

"He won't find the Lakotas."

The lawyer slapped the notepad down hard on the desk. It made a sharp, crackling noise. "If you want me to advise you, you have to play by my rules. That's the first rule: Play by my rules." He allowed the words to fill the space between them. "I have to know everything about you. How you spend your days. Who your friends are. That's the way it has to be if I'm going to shield you from a murder indictment."

He reached back and withdrew a business card from a metal card holder. After jotting something on the card, he handed it to her. "My home number. You can call me anytime, day or night."

"In the meantime, what exactly am I supposed to do? Hibernate in a cave?"

"Do what you normally do. Go to the office. Take care of clients. You must have work to do."

She told him about the report on the Wind River for the JBC. God, how could she concentrate on the report?

"Good. Finish the report. See your friends and family. Go to Ben's services."

"I'm not invited."

He stared at her a moment, as if he had to bring a new image of her into focus. "So Ben's family really does think you're responsible." He drew in a long breath. "What they think doesn't matter. We'll stick to our plan."

Vicky slipped the card into her black bag. "What about your fee?"

"The fee's taken care of. Wes's instructions were: 'Don't worry about the tab, just keep her safe.' You're going to be all right, Vicky. Trust me."

◀ 11 ▶

Father John drove north out of Lander, the highway curving toward the foothills, then running straight into the parched, empty plains. Traffic was light: a couple of RVs with out-of-state plates, pickups with two or three Indians in the front seat. Father John squinted past the sunlight reflecting off the hood. *"A moi les plaisirs"* blared over the thrum of the tires on the road, the noise of the wind. He'd been drawn to *Faust* lately, the soaring, plaintive music and the story of a man who gave up his soul—and for what? What could be more important than your soul?

He turned west out of Fort Washakie and started winding up a narrow ribbon of concrete. Below, the reservation crept toward the horizon, golden in the sun and peaceful, with small houses scattered about and roads that carved the land into large squares. Cottonwoods and willows marked the paths of the Wind River on the north and the Little Wind on the south. Where the rivers met, just east of the mission, was a cluster of greenery. He could see the church steeple rising among the cottonwoods.

And then the road headed into a canyon. The pavement

ended, replaced by a two-track with weeds and brush that scraped at the undercarriage. A thin forest of piñons and junipers sprouted on the slopes. He negotiated another turn. The high peaks, still covered in snow, came into view behind the ridge ahead. A barbed wire fence on the right ran to a small, log shack.

Father John eased on the brake and guided the pickup into the turnoff next to the shack. He stopped at the metal gate across a dirt road that wandered up-slope into the trees and turned off the tape player. The wind hissed in the trees.

A short, compact Indian with a rifle gripped in both hands stepped out of the shack and walked to the center of the gate. The round, flat face was turned toward him. Puebloan, Father John guessed, dressed in white buckskin with fringe running down the outside legs and across the chest. The partially laced V-shaped opening of the shirt exposed the thick tendons in the man's neck. An eagle feather rose over his head, held in place by a woven headband that wrapped around his forehead and kept the long, black hair close to his head. He wore beaded moccasins that made a shushing noise against the packed dirt.

"No outsiders allowed." The guard hunched over the top rail and lifted the rifle, squinting in the sun.

Father John leaned out the window and tried to ignore the rifle. "I'm here to see one of the dancers."

A look of incomprehension came into the stone black eyes. "Afternoon dancing's going on now. Dancers don't see nobody."

"Janis Beaver," Father John persisted.

"Nobody means you, white man. Back up and get on outta here." The Indian knocked the rifle against the top railing. A blue vein pulsed in his temple.

"What's going on?" Another Indian emerged from the trees and started toward the gate. He walked with a jerky motion, as if one leg was slightly shorter than the other. His buckskin suit looked like the guard's—an old woman somewhere, a traditional, might have made the clothing for both men, even beaded the moccasins. Black braids swung over the front of the man's shirt.

The guard threw a glance over one shoulder. "White man's lookin' for somebody. Told him to get goin'."

The other Indian lurched to the gate and grabbed hold of the top rail, as if to steady himself. The buckskin shirt wrinkled around the bulky shoulders and biceps. His eyes were so deeply set they looked like charcoal smudges on the flat face. He was several inches taller than the guard—a Plains Indian, maybe Lakota.

"Who are you?" His voice was high-pitched, tentative.

Father John got out of the pickup and slammed the door. The sun burned through his shirt. He gave his name and said he wanted to talk to Janis Beaver.

"Nobody here by that name."

Father John locked eyes with the man. "She's here, all right. I'm looking for a friend of hers, Dean Little Horse. I think she can help me find him."

Both Indians were quiet, faces unreadable. Finally the Lakota turned to the guard. "I guess Orlando's gonna want to see him," he said, his high voice trailing into a whine.

The faintest look of incredulity came into the other man's expression. He hesitated, then gestured with the rifle toward a clearing next to the shack.

"Park over there," he said. "No vehicles allowed in the village. Nothing here made by white people."

Father John parked where the guard had indicated, then

swung himself over the gate and hurried to catch up with the Lakota, who had started up the road, dragging his left leg, his shoulders and head bobbing as he went. The wind blew through the trees, as dry and hot as the wind off a fire. Father John pulled the brim of his hat low against the sun. His throat felt dry and scratchy. His shirt was clinging to his back. No telling how far they had to go. He wished he'd brought a bottle of water.

The Lakota started around a bend, past the clump of trees, and Father John sprinted ahead to catch up.

"Where we going?"

"To the village."

"Village? There's a village on Sherwood's ranch?"

"Name's Orlando." The man stopped and pivoted toward him. "You oughtta show respect for the prophet." He threw his shoulders around in an awkward motion and started out again, as if he didn't want to waste any more time.

Father John followed. The road narrowed into a steep path that switched back and forth up the slope. Strange, he thought. There was no sound of drums or rattles, and yet the guard had said the dancing was in progress.

"How long have you been with Orlando?"

Silence. Except for the breeze in the piñons, the Indian's moccasins scraping the hard ground, and the sound of his own breathing loud in his ears. Below, Father John could see the canyon he'd driven up, a winding chasm in the earth tossed with boulders and brush. The top of the ridge was about thirty feet above, he guessed. The switchbacks were shorter, the angles sharper. With each turn upward, he had the sense that he was climbing farther away from the ordinary, familiar world below.

The Indian came around a switchback, and Father John

saw the man's jaw muscles twitch, as if he were silently testing the answer. Finally he said, "Hospital in Denver, after I got my leg broke. I seen him die, and I seen him come back to life. He was different when he come back 'cause he'd gone to the shadow world. He started preaching right there, up and down the corridors, telling the rest of us Indian patients what we gotta do. Soon's he got out, the people started asking him to come to their homes and tell 'em how to get saved. He said we gotta start living like the new world was already come, even if it ain't come yet. Some of us come with him to the ranch." He stopped talking a moment, then hurried on: "Lot more comin'. People here gonna be saved from the event."

He took another switchback and bent forward up the incline. Father John could see the calf muscles of the man's right leg bulging through the buckskin. The left leg was stiff and thin, like a stick dragging beside him.

"What are you talking about? What event?"

The Indian glanced around, eyes slit in confusion and anger, as if he'd been goaded into saying more than he wished. "Don't concern white people." He braced himself against a boulder, then hurled himself upward with his shoulders before taking a final jump onto the top of the ridge. He set both hands on his hips and stood motionless, gazing out into the distances, black hair and white buckskin clothes gleaming in the sun.

Father John dug his boots into the ground to keep from sliding backward and, bending forward, his breath a hard knot in his chest, pulled himself over the boulders until he was standing next to the Indian. He took in a couple gulps of air. "Who are you," he said finally.

The Indian was still staring across the space that opened

below. "I am the prophet's disciple," he said, the high voice almost lost in the wind sweeping over the ridge. "My ancestors followed the messiah, Wovoka. Now I have heard the messiah's words from the prophet."

He turned and started across the bare strip of ground that curved away like the rim of a volcano, then disappeared down the other side.

Father John ran a hand over his face, wiping away the perspiration, still breathing hard in the thin, hot air. The wind smashed his shirt against his chest.

He walked to the opposite side. A cluster of ranch buildings stood in the meadow below: small, frame house, barn, two smaller structures, weathered-looking and run-down. A couple of horses paced in the corral next to the barn, and beyond the corral, a small herd of buffalo grazed in a pasture.

On the other side of the meadow was a village of about thirty tipis, arranged in a circle, white canvas lit by the sun. Inside the circle were the dancers, dressed in white, holding hands and moving clockwise in a slow, silent motion around a lodgepole set upright in the earth. Next to the pole, someone was seated in a chair that faced the east. A large man stood behind the chair, arms folded across his chest, watchfulness in his manner. From somewhere in the distance came the caw-caw sound of a crow.

Father John gazed at the scene below for a moment. His assistant was right. They couldn't ignore Orlando and his followers. This was a cult with its own messiah, its own prophet, isolated from the rest of the world. He should have spoken with the elders about the shadow dance and warned his parishioners. He wondered how many of his parishioners had already followed Orlando here.

He started after the Indian, who was working his way

down the narrow footpath in a hop-hop motion. Dropping closer to the village, Father John could see the bark on the clusters of poles that poked through the tops of the tipis. The sloped canvas walls shimmered in the breeze. The faint smells of manure and garbage floated toward him. The dancers were still circling about. He could still hear the crow—a frantic note in the sound now—but he couldn't see the bird.

"How many people are here?" he said to the Indian's back.

"You ask a lot of questions." The Indian glanced around, then slowed his pace, as if he were waiting until Father John caught up. "The saved are here. That's all you need to know. We're gettin' ready for the new world. Won't be nothing of white people then. Nothing made by whites. Everything we need is gonna be Indian. There's gonna be plenty of buffalo meat, roots, vegetables, berries. Everybody's gonna wear skins—all the women and children, just like the men. This way." He plunged ahead across the grassy area at the base of the slope, then they worked their way past the tipis. The crow had stopped cawing.

"We wait," the Indian said when they had reached the edge of the dance arena.

The dancers shuffled past, holding hands, silent except for the noise of their breathing—in and out like tiny bellows—as if they were in some kind of trance. Father John counted: twenty, twenty-five men and women, with the round, flat faces of the Navajo and Puebloans, the broad faces of the Sioux and Cheyenne, the narrow, defined faces of the Arapaho, none older than thirty, all dressed in white. Men in buckskins, women in loose, flimsy dresses that swayed about their legs. Across the shirts and dresses, painted in bright colors, were symbols of the Plains Indians: blue bands for the sky, yellow circles and crosses for the sun and the morning star, and red thunderbirds for the eagle that flies to the Creator.

As the dancers came around, they faced the rail-thin Indian who slumped in the webbed folding chair in the center, fingers spread over the knees of his buckskin trousers. Painted on the front of his shirt was a large, red crescent moon. He looked about thirty years old, with black hair cut just below his ears and intense, deep-set eyes that made his face appear skull-like. He was surprisingly pale, like a man who had been ill for a long time. As the dancers circled around, he held the gaze of each one for a long moment, and Father John could almost feel the electric charge that passed between them.

James Sherwood, he thought. A prophet who called himself Orlando.

The large Indian with shoulders like a bull, stationed beside the chair, was probably not much older than Orlando. He was also in white buckskin, arms folded across his chest, black hair pulled back into a ponytail, gaze fixed on the dancers passing by. He had a nose that curved like a beak, cheeks that jumped out from beneath the brown skin, and fleshy lips. A vivid red scar ran from the edge of his mouth to the tip of his ear.

The crow screamed again. Now Father John saw the bird, perched like an outsized black beetle on top of the lodgepole behind Orlando. Strips of brightly colored fabric wound around the pole, the ends flapping in the breeze. The bird turned its beaked head side to side, shiny eyes on the dancers below, then tilted its head upward and screamed into the sky.

Father John shifted his gaze to the dancers. He had no idea what Janis Beaver looked like. Arapaho from Oklahoma, Sam Harrison had said. "A fox, you know what I mean?" She could be any one of a half-dozen women swaying past, but his eyes kept coming back to the girl dancing between two muscled young men. She was very pretty, with brown, almond-shaped eyes, finely shaped nose and cheeks, rounded lips that she brought together in a small circle. Her black hair was parted in the middle and combed back. It hung like a veil to her waist. A white rope cinched her dress, emphasizing the full breasts and curved hips.

Out of the corner of his eye, Father John saw Orlando shift in his chair, then lift both arms in a kind of benediction. The dancers stopped immediately. The crow pivoted on its perch and cawed.

And then it was very still. Even the breeze died back. After several seconds, a deep, baritone voice broke the quiet. "My relations, hear my words. I have returned to you from the shadow world in the west. I have seen crow leading the armies of ancestors. The regeneration will come before the spring passes away. We will dance for two more days. Wovoka does not forget his promise."

The prophet got to his feet and started across the arena. The crow let out a scream and swooped down, perching on the man's thin shoulders. Walking close behind him like a bodyguard was the large Indian with the red scar that pulsed in his cheek. The dancers formed a long corridor through which they passed, Orlando lifting his hand, blessing those on the right, then on the left. He stopped in front of the tipi that faced the east, set apart from the others, then ducked inside, the crow still clinging to his shoulder. The bodyguard followed.

"Wait here." The Lakota beside Father John started loping toward the tipi.

Father John headed across the arena, through the dancers milling about. Several men came toward him, then parted, like water flowing around a rock, as if they hadn't seen him, and continued toward the northern curve of tipis. The women huddled together in small groups, moving toward the southern curve. They looked alike; he couldn't find the pretty girl with almond eyes.

Then he saw the Lakota coming along a diagonal path toward him, one shoulder thrust forward, left leg slightly behind. His eyes blazed with anger. "You got no right walking around," he said. Then he drew in a long breath. "Orlando'll see you now."

❖ 12 ❖

Father John ducked into the tipi. It was cool inside. The sun streamed down from the opening overhead and cast a mixture of light and shadow over the straw mats on the floor and the buffalo robes draped over the hay bales around the periphery. Daylight glowed through the canvas walls. He was aware of the Lakota and several other men crowding behind him, the rapid gasps of their breathing.

Orlando sat on a bale on the far side of the tipi, facing the east, the crow still on his shoulder. He looked straight ahead, but the dark, intense eyes seemed to take in the entire tipi. There was a half-smile about his mouth, an unhurried sense in the way he shifted forward on the hay bale. And something else: the shadow of fatigue in his pale face and the kind of transparency that Father John had seen in hospitals when patients were close to death.

The Indian with the scar on his cheek sat a few feet from Orlando, far enough away, Father John thought, to show respect, yet close enough to throw himself between the prophet and any danger.

"Down on your knees." Father John felt the jab of the

Lakota's fist in his back. "You are in the presence of the prophet."

Father John shrugged away and moved into the column of light, locking eyes with Orlando. "I want to talk to Janis Beaver," he said.

Orlando didn't say anything for a moment. His mouth moved silently, then the baritone voice burst across the tipi: "Why do you suppose someone called Janis Beaver is with us?"

"She's one of your followers."

"I have many followers." The man lifted both arms toward the village in a kind of benediction. "They've come here to be free of the white world. Soon the world will be cleansed and purified. We will have all that we need. Plenty of buffalo, wild vegetables and fruits. We will bend our own bows, straighten our arrows, and carve the tips from the finest flint. The women will tan the skins and sew beautiful garments. We need nothing from white people. Go away. You have no right to disturb us."

"I believe Janis can help me find her friend, Dean Little Horse," Father John persisted. "It's important that I talk to her."

Orlando lifted his hand and waved at the Lakota, who was now standing at attention beside Father John. "Leave this unbeliever with us," he said.

The Indian bobbed backward. There was the sound of the flap being pushed aside, moccasin feet slapping the ground. The crow lifted its head and gave three short cries.

"You know this man, Little Horse?" Orlando said.

"I know his grandmother. She can't sleep nights worrying about him. She raised him from the time he was an infant. He's like her own son."

"He has defiled our village." The baritone voice deepened. "He is an unbeliever. We do not want him here. We told him to go away. You must also go. Leave us."

"As soon as I talk to Janis," Father John said, "I'll be on my way."

"Why do you ask for these people?" Orlando started to his feet, then lurched backward. The Indian with the scar jumped up, took hold of his arm, and steadied him. "Janis!" Orlando flapped his free arm in the air. "I know no one by this name. Why do you white men come here and disturb our dance, looking for people we don't know? This morning, an FBI agent"—he enunciated each syllable, horror in his tone—"came to our village looking for Lakotas, interrupted our dancing, demanding to check the followers' IDs. And now you! You interrupt our afternoon dance. Shall we have no peace?"

He started forward, the guard holding one arm, the other still flapping in the air. The crow lifted off his shoulder and flitted up toward the poles tied at the top of the tipi. "What is it you want? To stop our dancing? Is that it?" Orlando was shouting now, spraying tiny flecks of spittle into the column of light between them. "I know you white people. You don't wish the new world to come. You want to stop it, just like before."

An absent look came into the dark eyes, as if some other scene had started playing out before him, demanding his attention. He flinched away from the other Indian's grip and lifted both hands overhead. The crow had started circling the tipi, screaming, flapping its black wings. "Here are the soldiers," Orlando shouted to the bird. "I see them on the horizon. I see the breaths of their horses in the morning frost. It is so cold. The snow is deep. I hear the hooves pounding in the snow. They are coming, coming."

Father John stared at the man. My God. It was as if Orlando were reliving the massacre of the last Ghost Dancers at Wounded Knee more than a hundred years ago.

"Run, run," Orlando shouted again, his voice raw with fear. "We must run through the snow. Everyone run!"

The other Indian placed an arm around the man and started to lead him backward toward the bale. "Medicine man!" he shouted. "Get the medicine man."

Orlando bent forward, coughing and crying out—a long wail of grief—gasping for breath. The crow perched on the bale of hay close by, head wobbling on its humped shoulders.

As Father John started toward the man, he felt a fist slam into his ribs. He stumbled sideways.

"Don't touch the prophet!" The Lakota lurched past and threw himself toward Orlando. He took the prophet's other arm, and the two Indians pulled him back onto the hay bale.

Father John heard the footsteps pounding outside, then dancers began plunging through the opening, two, three at a time. They gathered around Orlando, a deliberateness in their movements, as if they'd practiced the routine many times before, and each dancer knew exactly where to go.

Someone passed a bucket of water through the flap. The bodyguard with the scar on his face scooped a glass of water and held it to Orlando's lips.

He pushed it away and started coughing again, still bent in half, head dropping between his knees. Water dripped from the long fingers.

"Medicine man!" the bodyguard shouted again.

Another Indian stooped low into the tipi and the others

began peeling backward, clearing the way. Father John slipped outside.

He ran to the first tipi on the south and knocked against the canvas flap. "Janis!" he called.

There was no response. He pulled the flap aside. The inside was bare, except for the straw mats on the floor. Daylight pooled in the center. Beyond the light, three women lay curled on the mats, white dresses bunched around their bare feet. They looked half asleep, drugged, Father John thought, and whatever drug they'd taken hadn't yet worn off. The pretty girl wasn't there. An odor of exhaustion mixed with the smells of canvas and dried straw.

"Where's Janis Beaver?" he said.

One woman flopped over, turning her back to him. The others looked away, expressions as blank as sheets of paper.

He dropped the flap and ran to the next tipi, conscious of the commotion behind him, the footsteps pounding through the village, voices shouting. The crow was screaming from the top of the lodgepole.

He went through the same routine again: calling out, waiting, pulling the flap aside. There were four women lying in the shadows inside, shoulders touching. They might have been marooned in a blizzard, he thought, dependent on one another for warmth. "Janis Beaver?"

Heads shaking, eyes studying the straw mats. He'd started to back away when one woman gave him an almost imperceptible nod to the east. She lifted a hand and ran three fingers over her cheek.

He closed the flap and ran east past one tipi, then another. He stopped at the third and glanced back at the crowd of men pressing around Orlando's tipi. The cawing of the crow ripped through the air.

He leaned into the flap. "Janis," he said. "I have to talk to you about Dean." He waited a moment, then pushed back the flap and stepped inside.

The interior resembled Orlando's, with straw mats, hay bales, a buffalo robe draped over one bale. A woman was curled up on the floor, hands thrown over her head in exhaustion. On the right, propped against a bale, the pretty girl with knowing, almond eyes, face drained of color, long strands of black hair that fanned over the shoulders of her white dress. A red crescent, like that on Orlando's shirt, was splashed on the front of her dress.

She stared up at him a moment, then began scooting sideways, pushing herself with her bare feet, a frantic kind of fear and confusion in her expression.

"I won't hurt you." His voice was calm. He told her his name and said he was from the mission. "What can you tell me about Dean? He's been gone for five days. His grandmother's crazy with worry."

"You shouldn't've come here." Her voice had the flat, dead quality of an automatic machine. The almond eyes darted about the tipi.

He squatted in front of her and tried to hold her attention. "You must tell me what you know about Dean. You went to his apartment on Sunday looking for him, didn't you? Where is he?"

"It's forbidden for men to come to the women's tipis." She looked up, then to the side. Finally she began studying the edge of the hay bale.

"Please tell me, Janis." He could hear the voices outside coming closer.

"Only the prophet comes here." She was trying to dig a finger into the hay.

"What? Janis, try to concentrate. Where's Dean?"

"The prophet will choose the new people for the new world."

"What are you talking about?"

And then he knew. He felt his stomach turn over. "You mean children."

"Holy children," the woman said, her voice still on automatic. "We will bear the holy children for the new world."

He let out a long breath. God. He wondered if the women were already pregnant. Orlando! A man gasping for breath, and yet, he had seemed assured and confident gazing at the dancers, buoyed, Father John suspected, by their adoration.

"Listen to me, Janis," he said. "Is this what you want? You don't have to stay here." He glanced around at the other woman and wondered if she was really asleep. "You can both come with me. We'll get out of here." He could still see the guard at the gate with the rifle gleaming in the sun. He had no idea how they were going to get out.

She didn't answer for a moment, as if she were trying to remember something important. Finally she said, "The prophet was sent by Wovoka. He speaks only truth. I want to go into the new world."

"Do you have any family?" Father John tried another tack. "Do they know you're here? I can call them for you."

She was quiet; the almond eyes still darting about.

"What about Dean? He's in love with you, Janis."

For the first time, her eyes met his. "I tried to tell him, but he wouldn't listen. The prophet . . ." She hesitated, then crossed her arms over the red painted symbol on her chest. "The prophet is my life now. I could never love Dean the way . . . the way . . ." She struggled over the words, leaning back against the bale, as if searching for shelter. "He wouldn't listen. He went away."

"Where? Where did he go? His grandmother has the right to know."

Janis leaned back into the hay and began rolling her head, her eyes following the motion. "Lost. Lost. Lost. Tell the old woman to forget about him."

"What are you talking about?" Something moved at the corner of his eye—a disturbance in the atmosphere. The column of light through the opened flap widened.

"On your feet, white man." The Lakota's voice behind him, the man's grip, like a vise, on his shoulder.

Father John stood up. "Come with me now, Janis. I'll take you to the mission. You can call your family," he said, but she was staring beyond him, unseeing, as if she'd gone into another place that his voice couldn't reach.

"Out, white man!" A second hand took hold of his other shoulder. Father John swung around, wrenching himself free. The man with the scar stood next to the Lakota. Father John walked past them and stooped through the opening. The crowd was still gathered in front of Orlando's tipi. He started across the arena.

"You white men"—the Lakota was hopping beside him; the crow flapped and screeched overhead—"think you can do anything you want, stop our dancing, stop the new world . . ."

"You lied to me." Father John wheeled toward the Indian. "You said Janis wasn't here. What about Dean Little Horse? Are you hiding him someplace? Out on the ranch? In a shack? A cave? Where is he?"

"You heard what the prophet said. He's gone from here."

Father John held the man's gaze a moment. Then he

turned around and walked past the tipis and across the grassy area. He started climbing up the slope, the Lakota breathing hard behind him, like a pony snorting and scratching at the ground.

They crossed the top of the ridge and followed the foot-path down. The roof of the guard's shack poked through the piñons below; the bumper on the pickup flashed in the sun.

Father John cut through the trees and took a diagonal route down the slope, the Indian still behind him. He could see the guard inside the shed as he climbed over the gate. "I'm going to find Dean," he said, facing the Lakota again. "You might as well tell me where he is."

The Lakota met his eyes. "You're a foolish white man, priest. Go back to wherever you came from. You and your mission are not wanted here."

"Is that a threat?"

"You have heard the words." The Indian kept his gaze steady.

Father John felt the skin on his arms prickle. Had Dean threatened Orlando when he learned about the prophet's plans for Janis?

He got into the pickup, slammed the door, started the engine, and backed past the Indian standing on the other side of the gate. Then he slipped the gear into forward and jammed down the accelerator. The pickup skidded out onto the road, dust spattering the rear window. In the side mirror, he caught a glimpse of the guard framed in the doorway of the shack.

Father John reached Fort Washakie, pulled over, and punched in Gianelli's number on the cell phone. An answering machine clicked on at the other end; the agent's voice, disembodied and matter-of-fact, floated down the line. "I have to talk to you," Father John told the machine. Then he left his numbers: the cell phone, the office. "Call me," he said.

He drove back onto the street, turned left, and parked in front of the redbrick building with the sign in front: WIND RIVER LAW ENFORCEMENT. He waited in the small area inside the entry while the woman behind the glass pane disappeared into a hallway. After a few moments, she returned.

"Chief Banner says to come on back." She spoke into the round metal grate in the glass. A buzzer sounded, and he walked through the door on the left and down the corridor. The whiff of stale smoke and floor wax hung in the air. The chief was coming from the opposite direction, waving a sheaf of papers. He motioned him into an office with stacks of folders and papers toppling over the desk and file cabinets, an array of family photographs tucked among the stacks.

"You come about Ben's murder, we're doin' all we can." The chief dropped into the chair behind the desk and tossed the papers on some folders. Father John pulled over a metal-framed chair and sat down.

"This is fed business," the chief went on. "We're cooperating. My boys lifted prints and tire tracks. We been all over the res looking for a couple of Lakotas Vicky says that Ben met with Monday afternoon." He shrugged. "No luck. My guess is, those skins are out of here, laying low up at Pine Ridge 'til this gets settled."

"I just came from the shadow ranch," Father John said. "There are thirty Indians there from a lot of other tribes."

The chief nodded. "Number one on our list of places to look. Gianelli went up there himself this morning." The chief opened a file folder and consulted a typed sheet. "Roy He-Dog and Martin Crow Elk. Nobody by those names at the shadow ranch." He shifted forward, the navy blue uniform shirt wrinkling over the broad shoulders. "You ask me, it's not looking good for Vicky."

"You can't be serious."

"I'm not saying she shot Ben. I'm just saying, it's not looking good. She's got motive." He paused. "We both know how Ben treated her. She had opportunity and . . ." Another pause. He cleared his throat. "Vicky shot a guy last year."

True. All true. Father John set an elbow on the armrest, and blew into his fist. A perfect example of logic that added up to nonsense. "She didn't shoot Ben," he said.

The chief threw out both hands. "Let's hope the evidence proves her innocent. Gianelli's tracing the gun now. Should have the results tomorrow."

"You've got to find the two ranch hands Ben had trouble with," Father John said. "They could be calling themselves something else. Sherwood calls himself Orlando."

The smallest shade of doubt came over the chief's face. "The fed checked IDs on all the dancers. You got evidence those Lakotas are hiding at the ranch? We'd need evidence to get a search warrant." He raised an eyebrow and gave him a look of caution. "Something more than just a gut feeling, John."

Father John shook his head and glanced toward the window. The afternoon sunlight looked gray in the dust-smeared pane. He didn't have any evidence. Just a gut feeling that things were wrong at the shadow ranch.

"We been watching the place for two months." Banner crossed his arms over his chest. "Ever since Sherwood came back. He's probably harmless. Brilliant kid, once upon a time. You ever know him?"

Father John shook his head. He'd never seen him at Mass. And eight years ago, when he'd organized the Eagles, Sherwood would have been too old for the team.

"Walked away with a lot of honors at Indian High. Went to college in Denver. Became some kind of computer whiz, I heard." The chief raised one hand and snapped his thick fingers. "Hiking up around Boulder and gets hit by lightning. Spends a month in a coma and becomes a new man. Calls himself Orlando now. God knows why. Never heard of any Arapaho Orlandos."

"He has an armed guard at the gate and at least two other guards around the village. The followers all look drugged."

This brought the chief forward. He picked up a pencil and began stabbing at a folder. "You talk to people up there?"

Father John nodded. "A couple guards. Orlando himself, and an Arapaho girl from Oklahoma, Janis Beaver."

"Anybody tell you they're being held against their will?"

"No." The girl had wanted to stay, he was thinking. She could have left with him—he would have found a way—but she was in love with Orlando.

"Well, that's a problem. We've got consenting adults up there. Point is, John. There's no proof otherwise, and folks have the right to live as they please, long as they don't break the law. The American way, right?" A mirthless smile came into the man's face. "They want to live in a mountain valley with some nutcase, well, that's their right."

Father John was quiet a moment. The click, click sound of computer keys came from down the corridor. "How do they live?"

"We asked the same question when Indians from other tribes started showing up on the res asking for directions to the shadow dancers. Said they heard about Orlando on the Internet. So I drove up and paid a visit to Orlando. Turns out, he got severance pay from his company and disability insurance. He sends the dancers into Ethete and Fort Washakie every week. They preach and pass the collection baskets. Get a little money that way. Adds up to enough to feed people. They say they're gonna be self-sufficient, soon's the new world gets here. Got some buffalo. Planted a garden."

Banner shrugged, then went on: "Man didn't seem like the kid I remember, but I gotta admit, there's an intensity about him, and he's got that deep voice that sort of mesmerizes people. He claims he visited the shadow world. That gets people's attention. How come you went up there?"

Father John sat back and closed his eyes a moment. He'd assured Minnie Little Horse that he wouldn't talk to the police about Dean, and yet . . . Dean was missing; he'd been at the shadow ranch; and someone there—Janis? Orlando?—knew where the young man had gone.

"I'm trying to find Dean Little Horse," he said. He'd explain to Minnie later.

The chief tilted his head back and stared at him. "Dean's missing? We don't have a report."

Father John told the chief what he knew. Dean had been missing since last Thursday. He'd never had any trouble with the police. Minnie didn't want his name in the police files.

"Shit, John." Banner slammed a fist down, scattering a stack of papers. "Indian's missing, and nobody's looking for him except you? Minnie's got to get in here and file a report.

I'm gonna need everything she knows. Hell." He pulled a blank sheet of paper toward him. "I'm gonna start things rolling right now. What have you learned?"

Father John gave him the address of Dean's apartment and the Blue Crow Software Company, and the names of everybody he'd talked to, including Janis Beaver.

The chief's black scrawl covered half the page.

"Dean was at the shadow ranch recently," Father John went on. "I'm pretty sure Janis knows more than she was willing to tell me. She was looking for Dean on Sunday." He was quiet a moment. "Dean could be in danger."

The chief was still writing. "Ben Holden gets killed; Dean Little Horse goes missing. Two good men, John." He shook his head and laid the pen across the notepad. "Let's hope Dean's still alive. Maybe we'll get something out of Orlando, we lean on him enough. The shadow dancers are gonna get more attention than they want."

Father John got to his feet. He felt uneasy. Too much attention, and Orlando and his followers could feel threatened. There was no telling what a man who believed himself a prophet might do, if he felt threatened.

◆ 13 ◆

The late afternoon sun beat down on the baseball field. The air was bright. In the distance, the white-peaked mountains rose against the sky like furious waves in the ocean, but the sky itself was as still as blue glass. The end of a perfect summer day, Father John thought, except that summer was officially a couple of weeks away. He stood behind third base, dripping with sweat. The Eagles looked good. The batters connecting, Howard Night knowing when to throw a fastball, when to throw a curve ball, the infielders chasing down grounders, and the outfielders shagging fly balls. Charlie Moss had hit a line drive up the middle and sprinted to first, and Father John motioned up the next batter, his eye on Charlie. The kid was quick and smart. He had a good feel for the pitcher's delivery; he knew exactly when to run.

He was running now, head down, short legs pumping. Howard threw to the second baseman, but Charlie had already dived for the base.

"Safe." Eldon Antelope was on the side line, waving both hands overhead.

The batter struck out, and Father John motioned up the next kid. The breeze felt like a hot blow dryer on his arms and face. The sky was a brilliant blue, falling to the earth around them. Sometimes he had the illusion here, on the plains, that he was moving through the sky.

Out of the corner of his eye, Father John saw Vicky hunched on the bench behind home plate beside two of the mothers. Staring across the field, something different about her, something new mingling with the aura of bereavement, so that, even though she was only inches from the other women, she seemed completely alone. *Hisei ci nihi.* Woman Alone, the grandmothers called her.

How long had she been there? He'd been so intent on the game, he hadn't seen her arrive. He felt the same mild sense of surprise and gladness he'd felt the first time she'd appeared. Out of nowhere, standing in the doorway to his office: a slim figure; dark complexion and black hair smoothed away from her face; dark blue suit and white blouse; black bag hung over one shoulder.

The Arapaho lawyer, he remembered thinking, the subject of the gossip among the grandmothers at the senior women's meetings in Eagle Hall. Divorced a fine man like Ben Holden! Went off to Denver to become a *ho':xu'wu:ne'n.* Now she's back.

They hadn't said she was beautiful.

The batter sent the ball to center field and sprinted down the baseline. Charlie was heading home, head down, and then he was safe.

"All right!" Father John called. "That's it for today."

The kids hopped up and down, then started off the field in a run. They were good, and they knew it. "Listen up," he called, and began gathering a circle of brown faces with teeth too big for the mouths. "Practice on Thursday. What're we going to do Saturday morning?"

"Whip the Riverton Rangers."

"You got it."

"Clean up!" Eldon called. The man had already started stuffing the bats into green canvas bags, and the kids scattered about, gathering helmets, gloves, balls. Then the two mothers began herding several kids across the field to Circle Drive, where a line of pickups and old sedans were parked.

Father John walked over to Antelope. "Mind putting away the gear?"

The Indian glanced at the woman waiting on the bench, then motioned over two boys running across the field. "Nah. We'll take care of it, Father."

"Good practice," Vicky said when he sat down beside her. He wondered if she had taken in any of it.

"Any news?"

"Looks like Gianelli has a suspect." She kept her eyes ahead, and he followed her gaze across the deserted field, the path between second and third base worn into a gray line through the brown earth. The Indian man and boys dragging bags of equipment across Circle Drive headed toward the storage shed behind Eagle Hall. He wondered if she was registering the fact they were there. "Hugh Holden thinks I'm guilty," she said.

Now he understood. Hugh Holden had probably had a long meeting with Gianelli. Father John didn't say anything.

"Battered ex-wife, couldn't make a complete break from her ex without killing him," she went on, the words clipped and sharp.

"Gianelli doesn't have any evidence." He heard the counselor's note in his own voice, but it sounded slightly off-key, his own concern leaking through.

"You don't understand, John. Ben was shot with a twenty-two pistol. Anybody on the res could own the gun. It could be traced to someone who knows me."

"Look," he said after a moment. "Gianelli will work out what really happened. You have to be patient."

She tipped her head back and gave a tight laugh that sounded like a cry. "You and Adam Lone Eagle," she said. "White man and Lakota on the same side."

"Who are you talking about?"

"The criminal lawyer in Casper I just hired." She tossed off the information absentmindedly, then rose from the bench and walked to the end. Her heels scraped at the dried ground.

"What does Lone Eagle say?"

Vicky wheeled around and stared at him, as if she were trying to recall whom they were talking about. Then she said, "Be patient. Sit tight, as if nothing has changed. Everything has changed, John. Whoever killed Ben could have intended to make it look like I'm guilty. I can't sit tight."

"Listen to me, Vicky," he began, but she interrupted.

"I have to find the two Lakota ranch hands. They're involved, John. I don't know how, but they're involved, I'm sure of it." She was pacing, back and forth, back and forth. "Ben was mad enough to kill them. I'm sure he threatened them in some way. Gianelli thinks they took off for Pine Ridge last week, but he's wrong. They're hiding somewhere." She gestured toward the plains rolling into the far distance.

"Arapahos aren't going to hide two guys involved in Ben Holden's murder."

"Whoever's hiding them doesn't believe they had anything to do with the murder. They'll be protected. Nobody's going to turn two Indians over to the FBI. Gianelli will never find them."

He stood up and set a hand on her arm, stopping her in place. Then he told her about the shadow ranch and about the possibility—he was acutely aware of the fact that he had no proof—that the Lakotas could be hiding there under assumed identities. He explained that he'd gone there looking for a young man who was missing, Dean Little Horse, and told her about the guards and the village and the dancers. He said he'd talked to Orlando himself and to one of the followers, Dean's girlfriend, an Arapaho from Oklahoma named Janis Beaver.

"Shadow ranch. I saw some of the followers in front of the tribal offices." Vicky was staring at some image in her mind. Finally she locked eyes with him again. "The Lakotas are cowboys, John. Why would they get mixed up with a crazy Indian like Orlando?"

"Gianelli went to the ranch this morning. He didn't find them . . ." Father John paused. He was already regretting telling her about the shadow ranch. The guard at the gate had a rifle.

"Listen, Vicky," he went on, still holding her shoulder. "I've talked to Banner. He's starting a search for Dean, and he's going to check on the shadow ranch again. If the Lakotas are there, Banner'll find them."

"I have to find them," she said. Then she started down the base line toward Circle Drive.

He caught up with her. "No, Vicky. Let Banner and Gianelli handle this. You don't know what the Lakotas had against Ben. You get close to them, they could come after you."

"You don't understand, John." She kept walking. "They killed Ben, and they're going to get away with it unless I find them. They're hiding on the res somewhere. Ben found them. I can find them, too."

"It's not your investigation." He took hold of her arm and turned her toward him. It was then that he saw the moisture in her eyes.

"Ben was my husband once," she said. "And this is my life."

"Vicky." He held her name on his tongue a moment. "Then let me help you."

She pulled away from his grip and stepped backward, shaking her head. "You can't, John. You can't help me. Promise me you won't get involved."

"What are you saying?"

"Hugh Holden, all the Holdens think the same as Ben did. The only reason I didn't go back to Ben was . . ."

In her hesitation, he understood. He looked away a moment. Dear God, how obvious had his feelings for her been on the reservation? Had everyone seen his shadow self?

"Lucas and Susan will be with the Holdens," Vicky was saying. "They'll listen to all the lies Hugh tells them. If you help me, if we're seen together, my children will believe the lies."

Father John brought his eyes back to her. What she said was true, and he could see the force of it in the steady way she looked at him.

"You must promise me, John." Her voice was so soft that he had to bend toward her to hear.

He waited a moment, then he said, "I don't want anything to happen to you, Vicky. If you won't let me help you, then you have to promise me you won't put yourself in danger."

She smiled up at him. "Then we have a deal?" When he didn't say anything, she turned and started toward the Bronco. He walked alongside her, feeling a sense of help-lessness. She was so small and vulnerable, and he knew her so well. Nothing would stop her from finding the cowboys who had killed her ex-husband.

They reached the Bronco, and he opened the door. He waited until she'd slid behind the wheel and started the engine. Then he closed the door and watched the Bronco spin out into the drive, rear tires spitting back sprays of gravel. The vehicle plunged into the tunnel of cottonwoods and turned onto Seventeen-Mile Road.

Gracious God, he prayed. Keep her safe. He felt a pang of regret as sharp as a pain over the promise he'd given her. If she were in danger, he knew, he would have to break the promise.

Vicky drove back to Lander through the quiet heat settling over the asphalt. She avoided Rendezvous Road, taking Highway 789 south, the long way, reaching Lander with the sun blazing over the mountains and exploding in her windshield.

A red sedan sat in her parking space behind the apartment building. She parked beside it and hurried up the outside stairs to the second floor. Here and there, lights twinkled behind the windows of the apartment building across the street.

From thirty feet away, she could see the door slightly ajar

at the end of the corridor. Hushed, familiar voices drifted through the opening.

She found Susan and Lucas slumped on the living room sofa, leaning into the cushions for support, hands clasped in their laps. Vicki had asked the manager to let them in, should they arrive before she returned. She'd expected to be here first. Lucas must have held the pedal to the floor all the way from Denver.

He jumped to his feet and came around the coffee table toward her. It always took her breath away, the first time she saw her son, even if it were after an absence of only a few hours. He was so like Ben: tall and muscular and striking looking with chiseled features and black hair trimmed a little long. He wore faded blue jeans and a sporty gray shirt with the collar opened and sleeves rolled back, exposing thick brown forearms and capable hands.

And yet he was different from Ben, more at ease in the world that extended beyond the reservation. The corners of his mouth turned up in a smile, but he was looking at her out of deep-set brown eyes that still held the shock of his father's death.

"Hi, Mom," he said, encircling her in his arms.

When he let go, she turned to Susan, who was starting to get up, reluctance in the way she moved, her face rigid with grief and contempt.

Vicky reached out, took the girl's hand, and led her around the coffee table. Then she grasped her other hand and stood back, taking her in. She was looking in a mirror; the image that reflected back was her own, a lifetime ago. Her daughter had the same black, shoulder-length hair, parted in the middle, one side tucked behind her ear. Honey-colored skin, eyes like black agates shot through with light. Susan stood quite still, chest rising and falling beneath her pale blue T-shirt, hostility crackling about her. And yet, beneath the hostility, Vicky recognized the vulnerability, the *unformedness*. A chill ran through her at the thought of a man—a man like Ben—honing in on the unformedness and taking Susan over.

She pulled the girl closer—she was small and thin; the knobs of her spine poked through her shirt—not wanting to let her go, but Susan slipped free and dropped back onto the sofa. "It's the end of our family," she said, "now that Dad's dead. He was the only one trying to hold us together. He was the only one who cared. We don't have a family now."

"That isn't true," Vicky said. She was thinking, We have a sad, hurting family.

Lucas sat down beside his sister. "Do you know yet what happened?" Emotion surged beneath the calm surface of his voice.

She began explaining: The local FBI agent was handling the investigation. She was sure he'd make an arrest soon. (God, she could be the one arrested.) She pulled over a small side chair and sat across the coffee table from her children—hers and Ben's—twenty-two and twenty-four years old now. "Your father"—she chose the words carefully—"had a very important job running the ranch. He had a lot of responsibility. He was a strong man. He could have made enemies."

"You think somebody from the ranch killed him?" This from Susan, the anguish so palpable around her that Vicky had to check herself to keep from reaching out to shove it away.

"It's possible."

"The fed's checking on everybody Dad worked with?" Lucas, now.

Vicky nodded. She hoped that was the case.

Susan shifted forward until her knees knocked against the edge of the coffee table. "Uncle Hugh says you saw Dad just before he was killed."

Vicky was quiet a moment. "I don't know what Hugh might have told you, but . . ." God, the lies Hugh could have told her children.

"You got in a fight with Dad!" Anger and shock laced Susan's voice. "The last night of his life, and you were shouting at him in a restaurant."

"Hugh's very upset." Vicky held her daughter's eyes. "He's looking for someone to blame."

"You hated Dad! You wanted him dead!" Susan propelled herself to her feet, and Lucas rose beside her, an arm going around his sister's shoulders.

"Take it easy, Susan," he said, a soothing tone, rational.

Vicky stood up. She felt as if she were stumbling, being driven through an endless field. It was true. She had wanted Ben out of her life. Some part of her, a shadow that she didn't want to acknowledge, had willed him dead—and the truth of it lashed at her like a whip.

"Listen, Mom." Lucas waved his other hand toward her. "We'd better be going. We can talk later."

"Going?" she managed, the word clinging to her tongue. "I thought you'd stay here. There's an extra bedroom, and Susan can sleep in my bed." She'd thought Susan could sleep with her. "I'll take the sofa."

"I wouldn't stay in this place . . ."

"Enough, Susan," Lucas said, a new firmness in his tone. "I think you've said enough." He guided his sister around the coffee table and across the room. Glancing back, he said, "I'll call you tomorrow, Mom." Then they were through the door, the sounds of their footsteps receding down the carpeted corridor.

Vicky sank back into her chair. She felt that she would choke on the acid in her mouth. The kids would go to Hugh. Her children, absorbed into the Holden clan, Ben's people, blaming her, blaming her. And Gianelli. She'd always thought of the agent as a good investigator. She laughed out loud, startled at the sound; it was like a cry. A good investigator who would turn everything Hugh Holden said against her.

‹ 14 ›

Father John stood at the window in his office and listened to the buzzing sound of a phone ringing across the reservation. In the last five minutes two pickups had come around Circle Drive and stopped near the alley between the administration building and the church. Three members of the parish council had climbed out and headed down the alley toward Eagle Hall. Now a rusted orange pickup swung in alongside the others. The door opened and a knobbed stick, cut from a tree branch, stabbed the ground. Amos Walking Bear gripped the top of the stick and swung his massive weight out of the cab. Bent over, slowly picking his way with the stick like a blind man, he started down the alley.

The phone stopped buzzing.

"Hello?" It was Minnie Little Horse. She sounded out of breath, distracted.

He told her he'd talked to a few people about Dean. The exclamation of joy and relief that shot through the line made him wince. He didn't have good news.

"Listen, Minnie." He said that he'd already talked to Banner and that the chief had started a search for Dean.

Silence shaped by fear and grief filled the line. Finally the woman said, "We didn't wanna bring in the police."

"It's time, Minnie," he said. It was past time, he was thinking. He wanted to assure her that Dean had gone someplace, was hiding for some reason, but he didn't believe it. Instead, he told her that the chief was going to need her help.

He heard the sigh at the other end. Then the woman agreed to call Banner, and he set the receiver in place, a sense of inevitability pressing around him. Five days now. No one had seen Dean Little Horse in five days.

He dialed Gianelli's office again and left another message. Then he dialed the man's home. They'd been friends once. He thought of the agent as a friend. He'd had Sunday dinner not long ago at the agent's home. Spaghetti and meatballs and everybody talking at once—Ted and his wife and four little daughters who had somehow become teenagers—and he and Ted trying to stump each other on opera trivia. He hated to admit that Gianelli probably knew more about opera than he did.

"Agent Gianelli." The familiar voice was on the other end.

"I've been trying to reach you," Father John said. Then he told him about his visit to the shadow ranch. "The Lakota ranch hands could be hiding there," he said.

"We checked everybody's ID this morning. Nobody there named Roy He-Dog or Martin Crow Wolf."

"They could be using other names."

"We've got every law enforcement agency in Wyoming and South Dakota looking for those two Lakotas. We'll get them, John, and when we do, we're probably gonna find out that . . ." He paused.

"What?"

"That they left the res before Ben Holden was killed. If they had trouble with Holden, it wouldn't have been smart for them to hang around."

"Vicky says they were still on the res—"

The agent cut in. "That's what she'd like us to believe. I got the Holden clan on my tail. Hugh Holden thinks he knows who killed his brother."

"For godssake, Ted. Vicky didn't kill Ben."

Gianelli cleared his throat, a low, rumbling noise. "I don't want to think so. I have to go wherever the evidence takes me."

"The shadow dancers are on some kind of drugs," Father John said, trying another tack. "Dean Little Horse was there a few days ago. Now he's missing. Look, Ted . . ."

"No, you look, John. You think we aren't keeping a close eye on Orlando and the rest of the nuts up there? We can't go swooping down and close up the place without hard evidence. We find evidence they're harboring two Lakotas we want to talk to about a homicide, we find evidence they've got illegal drugs, we'll be all over them. Stick to your pastoring, John, and let me do my job."

The line went dead. Father John set the receiver in the cradle. His muscles felt tense and cramped. He knew the pattern. Gianelli: proceeding in a rational, logical order. And all the time, Vicky, out there alone somewhere looking for two killers. Dear God, he thought. She could find the killers before Gianelli did.

It took a few minutes to get his thoughts back to the mission. He collected the stapled copies of the annual report, the notes he'd made this morning. Then he turned off the desk lamp and walked over to Eagle Hall.

Seated on straight-back chairs arranged in a semicircle were four members of the parish council: Elvira and Justice Burns, Dave Buck, Amos Walking Bear. Four out of ten, Father John thought. Not even a quorum.

"Just about to start the meeting without you." Father George sat a few feet apart, facing the others, gripping a stack of papers.

Father John hooked a chair and pulled it over next to Amos, who turned stiffly and extended a bear-paw hand. "How ya doin', Father?" he said. His other hand cupped the top of the walking stick. He was in his seventies, with wispy gray hair and a broad face with hooded black eyes and heavy jowls. Behind the man's flat expression, Father John caught a look of reassurance. His assistant was wrong; the meeting wouldn't have started without the pastor. Nothing started until the time was right and everyone was ready.

Father John handed the reports to Amos, who removed the top copy and passed the others. Father George had already started copies of the financial reports from the other end. Minutes passed. Eyes floated over the stapled pages. The hall was quiet, except for the occasional sound of rustling papers.

"I believe it's clear"—Father George snapped his copies against one thigh—"the mission's debts have risen steadily over the past year. Income is sporadic. Last quarter, donations fell by half."

"Donations usually increase in the summer with tourists

coming to Mass," Father John began, but the other priest was shaking his head.

"The point is, we never know when the money might come in. We can't rely on miracles."

Father John stopped himself from saying that St. Francis Mission had operated on miracles for more than a hundred years. It was not the argument he needed for the board of directors this weekend.

"Excuse me, Father." Amos placed both hands over the stick and hoisted his shoulders forward toward Father George. The others turned, watching the elder. "Could you tell us what you're getting at?"

Father George cleared his throat. "The board of directors must consider the complete financial picture. It would be irresponsible to overlook the numbers. We may have to reallocate our resources."

"You mean close the mission." The old man sat back and glanced at Father John. "What do you say, Father?"

"I don't want to close St. Francis." *Dear Lord, how could we close the mission?* He glanced at the other council members: two men thumbing through the pages, as if they might discover better numbers; Elvira looking straight ahead, lips drawn into a tight line. "I won't have the final say," he managed.

Amos kept his gaze on him a moment, then turned back to the other priest. "Where the kids gonna get Catholic instruction? Where's the AA gonna meet? Who's gonna visit when we get sick? Where we gonna have Mass?"

"There are fine Catholic parishes in Lander and Riverton," Father George said.

Silence. The Indians were staring at the other priest. Finally, Elvira said, "This is our mission, been here since the

Old Time 'cause that's the way the chiefs wanted it."

"Look," Father John began. He could almost smell the tension. "You're welcome to come to the board meeting. You can tell them about the programs."

"The directors know about the programs," Father George said.

"We're gonna be there." Justice nodded toward the others. "Trouble is, rest of the council's got a lot going on right now."

One by one, the Indians rose to their feet, Justice and David retrieving cowboy hats from vacant chairs, tucking folded reports in jeans pockets; Elvira gathering up the floppy bag she'd set on the floor. Only four council members to speak up for the mission, and this, a number's game.

Father John took Amos's arm to help steady the old man and walked him to the door. The stick thumped on the hard floor. Behind them, he could hear Father George folding and stacking the chairs.

Outside, Father John said, "Do you have a few minutes?"

The hooded eyes glanced sideways at him. The old man nodded, and they turned around the corner to the administration building.

Amos Walking Bear *inhabited* the side chair: thick legs spread apart, forearms covering the armrests, one hand curled over the top of the walking stick. "That white man"—he gestured with his large head toward the rear office—"ain't the first thinks he's gonna close this place down. Him and those directors coming here from other places don't understand. Good things come down to us from the past, we gotta hold on to 'em."

Father John hoped that would be the case. He moved the other chair around and sat down facing the old man. "Couple of things I'd like to talk to you about, grandfather." He heard the suppliant tone in his voice. Here, in the office, he counseled other people; now he needed counseling.

The old man nodded. "I seen the worry following you around like a shadow. You thinking about Ben Holden's murder."

"Vicky could be indicted."

"Holden clan turned against her long time ago." The old man hunched over and shook his head. "They don't like to admit Ben Holden might've made himself some enemies. Sure, he got respect 'cause he handed out a lot of jobs. But he got to strutting around like he owned the res. Ordering folks about. Not our way." He shook his head. "Somebody could've gotten fed up."

Somebody else, Father John thought. Not Vicky. He said, "Vicky says he had trouble with a couple of Lakotas who stole something from the ranch. She thinks they could be involved, but the fed says they left the res a week ago."

Amos threw his head back and guffawed. "Only time the fed probably got it right. They stole from Ben Holden, most likely they lit out of here like lightning before he could get a hold of 'em."

Father John glanced toward the doorway. A shaft of light from the desk lamp flowed into the corridor, pushing through the shadows. Vicky was so certain Ben had seen the Lakotas yesterday. And this afternoon, at the shadow ranch— so many Indians from other places. And yet, Gianelli had gone to the ranch. He hadn't found the Lakotas.

Father John drew in a long breath. He was chasing shadows. He told Amos about his visit to the ranch and said he'd been trying to find Dean Little Horse.

"I hear he went missing." The old man sat very still. "You think he's following Sherwood?"

He said he didn't think so. "Dean's girlfriend is at the ranch. She called him an unbeliever because he refuses to accept Orlando as a prophet."

Amos began tapping out a steady rhythm on the floor with his cane. He was quiet a moment, then he said, "Wovoka, now he was a prophet, and the Ghost Dance he brought to the people, that's a good part of our tradition. Helped the people back in the Old Time when we didn't have nothing. Gave people hope."

Tap. Tap. Tap. "Wovoka came along and said if people do the Ghost Dance every six weeks for four days, the old world will come back like it was. Now Sherwood comes along. Says he died, went into the shadow land, and become Wovoka's spiritual son. Says Wovoka give him a new name, Orlando, and told him to go back to this world and preach the old religion." He paused, and in the creases of the old man's face, Father John saw the geography of pain passed down through the generations. "Maybe Indians up at the shadow ranch don't have nothing else to hold on to. Maybe they need hope for a little while, just like the people in the Old Time."

"They have armed guards at the ranch," Father John said. "The woman are being used sexually."

The cane knocked harder on the floor. "Indians won't put up with it for long. Soon's they see the new world ain't gonna be in this world, they're gonna find a way to get out of there." The old man shifted toward Father John. "Ghost Dance religion ended soon's people lost heart. They seen nothing was gonna change in this world, and they stopped dancing. Same thing's gonna happen with the shadow dancers. Let 'em be, Father. Sometimes people need a little hope, even if they're gonna be disappointed."

Father John walked the old man out to his truck, the last vehicle still parked in front of Eagle Hall. He waited until Amos had climbed behind the steering wheel and turned on the engine. Puffs of black smoke belched from the tailpipe as the truck made a U-turn, then lurched along Circle Drive. He started up the front stoop, the taillights blinking like red fireflies through the cottonwoods.

The building had settled into evening, shadows splayed over the corridor and across the office. In the silence, a dripping pipe, the creak of old wood. Father John searched the bookcase behind his desk, pulled out a large red-bound volume, with *History of the Plains Indians* printed in black across the top.

He sat down and opened the book. The pages were worn and dog-eared, marked with stick-ons and torn pieces of paper. There were checkmarks penciled in the margins alongside paragraphs that he'd wanted to be able to locate quickly. He flipped to the index, found "Ghost Dance," and turned to the page indicated.

Across the page: the photograph of a middle-aged Indian, with a frowning, somber expression seated on a chair draped in a buffalo robe. The camera flash had laid down a strip of light, like an interrupted halo, across his black hair, which was parted to the side and cut straight below his ears, like Orlando's. He wore a black vest buttoned over a white long-sleeved shirt. An arm band above his right elbow held an eagle feather that rose toward his shoulder. A white scarf

was tied at his neck. Beneath the photo, in bold type: WO-
VOKA, 1889.

Father John skimmed through the text:

*Sitting or lying around the fire were half a dozen Paiute,
including the messiah and his family, consisting of his young
wife, a boy about four years of age, of whom he seemed very
fond, and an infant. It was plain that he was a kind husband and father.*

*He had given the dance to his people after he received his
great revelation. He fell asleep in the daytime and was taken
up to the other world. Here he saw God, with all the people
who had died long ago engaged in their oldtime sports and
occupations, all happy and forever young. It was a pleasant
land and full of game. After showing him all, God told
him he must go back and tell his people they must be good
and love one another, have no quarreling, and live in peace
with the whites; that they must work, and not lie or steal;
that if they faithfully obeyed his instructions they would at
last be reunited with their friends in this other world, where
there would be no more death.*

Father John skimmed the following pages. The Ghost
Dance religion had spread across the plains. Cheyenne, Lakota, Arapaho, all the tribes crowded onto reservations, a vast
expanse of the prairies gone, the buffalo slaughtered, the
warriors dying, the children hungry. For two years, the people danced in hope of the new world and then—as Amos
had said—they had given up hope and stopped dancing.

Except for Big Foot's band.

He thumbed through the pages until he came to the section on the massacre at Wounded Knee, South Dakota, in

the freezing December of 1890. The last of the Ghost Dancers, led by Chief Big Foot, trying to outrun the Seventh Cavalry—Custer's regiment, bent on revenge, shouting, "Remember the Little Big Horn!" When the Hotchkiss guns were finally silent, more than two hundred people lay dying in the snow.

There were photos. He studied the grainy, black and white pictures for several minutes: brown humps of human bodies scattered across the frozen prairie, the narrow trench where the bodies were buried, stacked like cordwood.

Father John closed the book and sat for a long time, staring into the shadows. The Ghost Dance religion had ended in catastrophe. And now, Orlando, calling himself the prophet, the son of Wovoka, was preaching his own version of the old religion.

He couldn't shake off the feeling that it would end the same way.

‹ 15 ›

The morning seemed unnaturally still, the sun burning yellow through the blue sky, the day's heat already settling in. There were few vehicles on the highway, and Vicky eased up on the accelerator and leaned into the curves alongside the Wind River. Past Boysen Reservoir, north into the Wind River Canyon. Rock-strewn hills with thin stands of pines and sagebrush rolled past. The river dwindled to a narrow creek, stained brown by the muddy sludge beneath the surface.

She'd left instructions with Esther to call Norm Weedly at the tribal offices and arrange for her to meet with the JBC later. Later. The idea stabbed at her like a needle. The Wind River could dry up in the hot weather. She should be in the office now, refining her arguments for the tribal council, carrying on as if nothing had changed, the way Adam had advised.

She slowed through Thermopolis, then turned west along the edge of the Owl Creek mountains. She could imagine the gossip buzzing over the moccasin telegraph, dredging up her past—hers and Ben's. How could she talk to the business council about cleaning up the river? The council members, seated behind the curved desk on a platform—nodding, nodding—wondering if she was a murderer. As long as Gianelli and everybody else suspected her, Ben's killer would be free. She swallowed back the knot of tears in her throat. Ben—the man she'd once loved, the father of her children—Ben deserved justice.

Through the filters of junipers, she glimpsed the log bunkhouse at the Arapaho Ranch, the peaked red roof burning in the sun. She let up on the accelerator, turned right, and thumped across the cattle guard, then followed a narrow road another half-mile. Dust rising from beneath the tires laid a thin gray film over the windshield.

She parked close to the bunkhouse. A cowboy—black cowboy hat pushed back—stood on the narrow porch that ran along the front, eyes squinting in the sunlight, one thumb hooked into the belt of his blue jeans. His other hand cupped a cigarette backward, so that the smoke curled along the sleeve of his blue shirt.

She got out and walked up the wood steps. "Where can I find Don Redman," she said.

"He don't wanna see you." The man's voice was raspy, smoke-filled. He hadn't taken his eyes off her.

Vicky gestured toward the barns and ranch offices beyond the bunkhouse. "He in the office?"

The cowboy lifted the cigarette to his lips and took a long drag. Then he blew the smoke in her direction.

"Look," Vicky said, "whoever you are . . ."

"Friend of Ben's. He's got a lotta friends here. You better not hang around."

The screened door banged opened. Redman, Ben's right-hand man, stepped onto the porch and gave her a nod of recognition. He was big, middle-aged, with the slumped shoulders of a man who'd spent years in a saddle and permanent squint lines around his eyes from staring into the wind. A year ago, Ben had brought Don Redman to her office. She couldn't remember the reason, only that Redman had sat in the waiting room while the Ben she'd hated at times had railed at her in the private office about something she'd done or hadn't done. And that—how ironic, she thought now—was when she had believed that she and Ben might get back together.

She asked if she could have a few words.

Redman hesitated, arms dangling at his sides, brown hands clenching and unclenching. Finally he opened the door. "Inside," he said, the thin lips barely moving.

She crossed the porch, walking past the cowboy, and followed Redman into the spacious room that ran along the front. On the left, sofas and chairs draped with Indian blankets and a big-screen TV. On the right, kitchen cabinets that wrapped around a long table with scrub marks across the top and chairs pushed against the sides.

The manager nodded toward a chair and waited until she'd sat down. "Men are pretty torn up about Ben's murder," he said, taking the chair across from her. "Best foreman we ever had. Knew how to run the ranch, all right. Bought quality bulls, crossbred the stock, and produced calves with heavier wean weights. Not to mention, he grew the herd to the highest number ever. Put the Arapaho Ranch on the map, you might say. Got a reputation for being one of the best in Wyoming. Men are gonna miss Ben."

He pulled his mouth into a disapproving line and shook his head. "Fed come around yesterday, asking a lot of questions. Lot of questions about you."

Vicky felt a knot tighten in her stomach. *She did not have to defend herself. She was not guilty.* "I'm trying to find the ranch hands Ben fired last week," she said.

"He-Dog, Crow Elk." The man tapped a stained finger on the table top. "Only mistake Ben might've made, hiring those bastards, but we needed the extra hands. Ben had a lot of work lined up, what with you and him getting back together. Started building a couple rooms onto his cabin." He tossed his head in the direction of the cabin tucked among the trees. "Blasted out a new road and was gonna blast out some more trees for a pond. Said you were gonna keep a pony up there. Said you were gonna have your choice of the best pony in the corral."

"Where are the Lakotas?" She ignored the invitation in the man's eyes to keep the conversation on Ben.

Redman let out a short breath. "Pine Ridge, my guess. Took off with the bank bag . . ."

"They stole money?" Ben hadn't mentioned money.

"Cash and checks. Ben had 'em ready to take to the bank in Thermopolis. Bag was on the desk, time he told the Lakotas to pack their gear and get off the ranch. Didn't turn his back more'n a minute, and the bag was gone. So were the Lakotas."

A sense of relief washed over her like a cool blast of air. Vicky leaned back against her chair. So this was why Ben had been so angry. The ranch hands had stolen the bank bag from under his nose. He would have tracked them down, threatened to report them to the fed. But he wouldn't have *wanted* to report other Indians. He would have handled the matter himself. Return the money, he would have told them. No questions asked. Case closed. If they didn't—they would have understood—he would smash in their faces, then report them.

It made sense. It explained why the ranch hands had waited for him on Rendezvous Road.

But there was another possibility. Vicky looked away. The knot in her stomach felt like lead. It could also explain why the Lakotas would have left for Pine Ridge before Ben was shot.

And yet . . . Ben had met them that afternoon, she was sure. He had known where to find them.

She felt a path opening ahead, if she could only reach it. She clasped her hands over the table. "What else can you tell me?"

"Forget it, Vicky. Those guys are gone. They got the money and took off." Something caught his attention—boots clumping across the porch—and he scooted his chair back and glanced out the front window.

Vicky followed his gaze. Men in cowboy hats, backlit by the sunlight, moved like shadows beyond the glass. She was aware now of the low murmur of voices. She said, "Did the Lakotas have relatives on the res?"

Redman shifted back toward her. "You and the fed ask the same questions. Possible, I guess. They came and went as they pleased around here. Couldn't depend on 'em. Maybe visiting relatives. How do I know?" He shrugged. "Ben didn't like their ways. Had a couple arguments, gave 'em warnings. Trouble is, we were shorthanded. Finally he decided to let 'em go. Not soon enough, you ask me. Nobody liked 'em. Kept to themselves. Acted high and mighty, like they had some special power nobody else had. Lakotas!"

"They shot Ben," Vicky said after a moment.

Redman looked skeptical. "That's what you want the fed

to think." He glanced over his shoulder at the window. The sounds of boots pounding and scraping the floor and the murmur of voices drifted through the log walls.

Vicky kept her eyes on the man across from her. "I want the fed to find Ben's murderers."

Redman stood up and leaned over the table. "I don't know what went down out on Rendezvous Road." He hesitated. "But I know you had reason . . ."

Vicky jumped to her feet and locked eyes with him, daring him to recount her life to her: Ben's drinking, the beatings, the day she'd finally mustered up enough courage to take the kids to her mother and drive to Denver in a rusted-out Chevy with the reverse gear shot.

The man glanced away. "Ben getting involved with that white woman and all."

"What!" She felt as if she'd taken a blow in the face. "What white woman?"

He laughed and shook his head. "Don't tell me you don't know."

She started laughing, too. She had to hold her hand over her mouth against the rising sense of hysteria. How like Ben! Pleading with her to come back to him. *We'll be a family again.* And all the time, there was another woman.

"What's the woman's name?" She didn't care, she told herself. "She might know about the Lakotas."

Something different came into the man's eyes, as if he'd caught an unexpected glimpse of her, and in that glimpse had seen the determination to find Ben's killer. "Came to the ranch once. Blond hair, real pale face, big blue eyes. She's a looker. Stayed with Ben up at his cabin."

Vicky crossed to the window, struggling to calm the mixture of irony and grief that churned inside her. The little cabin nestled in the pines. Quiet and remote. *We'll be a family again.*

She stepped back. Outside, cowboys were shouldering together on the porch, crowding the steps. A couple of cowboys ran across the open field toward the bunkhouse, carrying coils of thick rope. All the hands gathering, all convinced of her guilt.

She turned back to the man watching her from across the table. "Her name, Redman. I have to know her name."

"Nobody around here poked into Ben's business."

"Did you tell the fed about her?"

"Wasn't his business. I ain't saying nothing that hurts Ben's reputation. He was a good man."

He was a bastard, she thought. A handsome, charming, manipulative bastard, but . . . She closed her eyes and took in a long breath. He didn't deserve to be murdered.

She started for the door.

"Hold on." The man's footsteps scraped the floor. He stepped between her and the door. "Let me see what's going on out there."

He cracked the door open. The voices outside went quiet. And then, someone shouted: "Where is she? Bring her out here. What's she got to say for herself?"

Redman slammed the door. "Looks like we got ourselves a lynch mob."

The room started to close in around her, hot and bright and airless. The buzz of voices came from far away. Her mouth felt dry. "I can't hide here forever," she said. "They think I killed Ben. I have to convince them they're wrong."

"You don't get it." Redman kept one hand flattened against the door, as if he might prevent it from bursting open. "Ben was the chief. We respected him. We would've followed him into fire, and now he's dead. They're riled up enough to kill whoever did it."

He lowered his head, a bull gathering strength for the charge. "Wait here." He flung open the door, stepped outside, and slammed the door behind him. His voice sounded hollow and distant through the log walls. "We don't want no more trouble around here. Ben's killer is gonna be arrested and convicted. He's gonna pay in the regular way."

"*She's* gonna pay our way." It was the raspy voice of the cowboy on the porch when she'd arrived. What had he done? Run back to the barn and office? Shouting, *She's here! Ben's killer!*

Vicky yanked open the door and stepped onto the porch.

"There she is!" the raspy voice yelled.

◆ 16 ◆

Vicky stared at the wall of cowboy shirts and blue jeans blocking her path to the steps and the Bronco below. The air crackled with hostility. Masculine smells of leather, perspiration, and tobacco clogged her nostrils. Most of the cowboys looked Arapaho. Her own people! A few familiar faces among them. Dark eyes stared back at her from beneath the brims of cowboy hats. Expressions were fixed, unreadable. The men seemed to breathe in unison, with long exhalations that sounded like the air hissing out of tires.

"Let's make room." Redman shouldered his way into the crowd, but the cowboys closed around him.

"Let me pass." Vicky started across the porch, aware of the stifling heat, her blouse damp against her back. The cowboy with the raspy voice blocked her way.

"Why'd you kill Ben."

She looked up into a brown face ignited with hatred. The silver snaps down the front of his yellow shirt glinted in the light.

"How dare you," she said, fighting for the implacable

courtroom voice that masked the sense of being on a precipice, the abyss yawning around her.

"Tell us the truth." A bassoon voice emerged from the shadows by the railing. "You hire somebody to shoot him?"

"Get out of my way." Vicky tried to sidestep the yellow shirt.

"Let her through," Redman shouted from over by the steps, but his voice was lost in the roar of voices that pressed around her.

"Ben wouldn't be dead, weren't for you."

"What happened, Vicky?"

She tried again to dodge past the heavy male bodies, but they formed a phalanx in front of her. She stepped back, trying to clear a little space. "I know Ben was your boss," she began, choosing the words, adjusting the inflections by the faintest twitch in the brown faces, the way she delivered a summation to a jury when her client's future depended on the impact. "You respected Ben. You loved him." She paused, giving them time to absorb the idea, reconnect with some lighter part of themselves. "I loved him, too," she said.

"You're lying." The yellow shirt leaned toward her. She could feel little pricks of spittle on her cheeks.

"I loved him once," she said. "You're forgetting Ben was the father of my children. I did not kill the father of my children." There, she'd said it again. She'd vowed she would not defend herself from something she hadn't done, but she'd said it.

A half-second passed. No one spoke. The breathing seemed quieter, resigned. The cowboy in the yellow shirt stepped to the side. "Time we head out for Ben's wake," he said, his voice cracking with smoke.

One by one, the other cowboys rearranged themselves on

either side of the porch until she could see down a narrow corridor to the top of the steps where Redman was beckoning her forward.

She kept her eyes straight ahead, not wanting to unhinge the brief pardon she'd received, and followed the man down the steps to the Bronco. Her hand shook over the door handle, the ignition. Finally the engine burst into life, and she drove toward the ranch entrance, vaguely aware of the shadows moving in the rearview mirror.

Not until she'd crossed the cattle guard did she feel her heart begin to return to its regular rhythm. She sped east, her thoughts on the white woman. She would be beautiful. Young and beautiful, that was certain. There had been a beautiful twenty-something in Ben's life a couple years ago. Another thing was certain: The white woman lived somewhere in the area. Ben never liked too much inconvenience with his affairs.

The roofs of Thermopolis shone through the trees ahead. She slowed through town, then sped up again on the highway south. Ben's wake was at Blue Sky Hall this evening. You're not welcome, Hugh Holden had told her. But Lucas and Susan would be there and, she resolved, so would she. The kids might need her.

It struck her that the white woman might also be there.

Father John reached across the desk and picked up the phone on the first ring. He felt a stab of impatience at the sound of a man's voice—another parishioner wanting to know about Ben Holden's wake. Father John told him what he'd heard. Blue Sky Hall, eight o'clock. No, he wouldn't be holding the service. The family wanted a traditional ceremony. Amos Walking Bear was in charge.

A trace of bewilderment worked into the voice at the other end of the line. Ben Holden. Such a big man. He'd expected a man like Ben Holden would be buried from the mission.

So would the board of directors, Father John thought, setting the receiver in place. He was already steeling himself for the questions and the sly comments masked as criticism. Explain, Father O'Malley, how you expect to attract Arapahos to Catholicism when a leading man, like Holden, is buried in the traditional manner? Should we, perhaps, direct our resources to places where we may expect a higher degree of success?

Father John went back to work on the changes he'd made in the annual report. He'd added a new section on the programs he hoped to start: day care and senior care; tutoring center for elementary kids; lay ministry for the sick and shut-ins. Above the section, he'd written: *St. Francis Mission in the Future.* Now he drew a black line through the title. Too grand and hopeful. He didn't want to alienate the directors. He wrote: *Proposals.*

He stuffed the loose sheets of paper inside the file folder, then picked up the phone again and dialed Minnie Little Horse's number. He'd been trying to reach the old woman all morning and hoping each time the phone rang that she was calling with news about Dean.

The buzzing noise continued. Minnie and Louise were probably at Banner's office, still providing names, addresses—which meant, he realized, that there was no news. Day six now, and Dean was still missing.

He grabbed the folder and strode down the corridor toward the source of computer keys clicking in the quiet. Father George was hunched over the monitor. The other priest glanced up, then sat back in his chair and began flexing his hands, like a pianist before a concert. "How's the report?"

Father John set the folder on the desk. "I think it's finished." He hoped he'd included everything, every possible reason to continue St. Francis Mission.

"Not a moment too soon."

His assistant had that right. The bishop would be pulling into Circle Drive at any moment; the directors would arrive tomorrow. The opening meeting was set for tomorrow night, and the tone for the weekend would be established.

Father George went on: "I'll make the changes and print out copies." His eyebrows came together in a concentrated line, and Father John realized that the man loved playing the keys, bringing the words to life on the screen, like a conductor calling forth the notes of the symphony in his mind.

"I must say, John"—now the other priest was rotating his shoulders and rolling his head—"you've advanced some strong arguments on behalf of the mission. However . . ."

Father John raised both hands. He didn't want to hear again about allocating resources and quantifying data. He pulled a metal chair next to the desk, straddled it backward, and rested his arms over the top.

"You were right about the shadow dancers," he said. "I went to the ranch yesterday."

The other priest's eyebrows shot up. "You went up there?"

He was looking for somebody, Father John said, tossing off the explanation. He didn't want to elaborate. Looking for a missing Arapaho probably wasn't the kind of thing the directors thought the pastor of St. Francis Mission should be doing.

He nodded toward the monitor. "Can you find the website?"

"If it's there, I can find it." Father George shifted forward and moved the mouse around the gray pad next to the keyboard. The screen began to change; columns of figures gave way to a maze of graphics and text with icons across the top and down the sides. Click. Click.

"Here we go," he said. The screen started to scroll and a photo of Orlando came into focus: long, white robe; straight black hair cut below the ears; eyes uplifted; hands outstretched.

Father John leaned closer and read the text.

Prepare yourself for the new world. The great event will sweep away all evil and destroy the oppressors of Indian people. The ancestors will walk among us once again. I, Orlando, the son of Wovoka, have gone into the shadow land and heard the words of my father. What Hesana'nin has promised will come to pass.

"How many followers so far?" Father George clicked on the mouse.

"About thirty, I'd guess." Another photo flashed onto the screen. Father John recognized the Charles Russell painting of a village in the Old Time. White tipis rising against the clear blue sky. A mountain meadow with streams carving through the wild grasses. Buffalo grazing in the distance. Children playing a stick game; women tending to iron kettles hung on tripods over the campfires; men lounging by the tipis, carving arrowheads, bending branches into bows.

A lodgepole stood in the middle of the village, a black crow perched on the top.

"So this is paradise." Father George clicked the mouse again. A map of the Wind River Reservation covered the screen. A black line traced the winding road into the mountains, a black circle outlined the ranch. Another click and the map was replaced by a photo of Orlando seated cross-legged inside a tipi, arms outstretched. The banner across the top read: JOIN THE SAVED AT THE SHADOW RANCH. COME TO ME.

"There's your strong, charismatic male leader." Father George tapped the screen. "Preaching an apocalyptic religion organized around core beliefs. Believers are cut off from families and friends in a secluded area." He swiveled toward Father John. "The classic attributes of a cult, just as I've been telling you. I say we denounce Orlando from the pulpit on Sunday."

Father John stared at the photo on the monitor. Orlando looked younger, more robust, a larger version of the frail, sick man he'd seen doubled over in a fit of coughing.

He said, "I spoke with Amos Walking Bear. The elder thinks the followers will drift away when they realize the new world isn't coming, just as the Ghost Dancers finally lost heart."

Except for Chief Big Foot's band, he was thinking, trudging through the snow, still clinging to Wovoka's message, with the horror moving toward them, like a storm darkening over the mountains.

"We have an obligation to guide our parishioners . . ." Father George hesitated. "As long as we're here."

The other priest was right. The armed guards, the women huddled in the tipis, and Dean Little Horse, the unbeliever, missing. Father John couldn't shake the unsettled feeling that had clung to him since he'd driven out of the ranch, as if some nameless force were approaching that couldn't be turned back.

"I'll talk to Amos about calling a parish meeting."

"Meeting?"

"Amos and the other elders can explain the old Ghost Dance religion and the fact that Wovoka preached peace and forgiveness. They can help the people understand the difference between a man like Wovoka and . . ." He swallowed hard. "A prophet like Orlando."

Father George sat back in his chair, rested his elbows on the armrest and steepled his hands together under his chin. "Maybe I'm missing something," he began, "but it seems to me that Wovoka proclaimed the end of the world, just like Orlando. Sounds like the same apocalyptic message."

"Not the same, George. Wovoka urged Indians to live good lives and work hard for their people while they waited for the new world. Orlando . . ." Father John glanced away a moment, the images of the shadow ranch imprinted in his mind. "Orlando has armed guards on the ranch. The dancers looked drugged, and he's taking advantage of the women. Wovoka believed a new and better world would come eventually. Who knows what Orlando might do to hasten the coming."

Father John stood up and swung the chair back into place against the wall. "You're right, George. The man could be dangerous."

The other priest was nodding. "We have to take a strong stand in the pulpit."

"We have to work with the Arapaho elders," Father John said.

• • •

It was midafternoon when Father John heard the tires skittering over the gravel on Circle Drive. He got up from his desk and went to the window. A blue sedan slowed past the administration building, then turned into the alley. Before the sedan disappeared past the corner, he caught a glimpse of the dark-haired, young-looking man with the round face and the fleshy chins folding over the white clerical collar.

He hurried out of the office, around the building, and down the alley. The sedan was parked in front of the guest house. Bishop Lawrence McCall was hauling his stocky frame out of the front seat. He shut the door and headed to the trunk, the top of which was rising in the air.

"Bishop, good to see you," Father John called.

The man swung around, set his left hand over his forehead, like the brim of a hat, and peered through the brightness. The breeze pulled at the front of his black suit coat and smashed his trousers against his thick legs.

"Father O'Malley," he said, extending his right hand. "Didn't see any reason to bother you. I know my way to the guest house."

Father John shook the man's hand. He had a firm grip, at odds, somehow, with the smooth, clean-shaven face, the round, reddish cheeks. A couple of times a year, the bishop managed to escape, as he put it, from the telephones and endless meetings in Cheyenne and spend a few days fishing on the reservation. He always stayed at the guest house.

"Let me get your bag." Father John lifted the small black bag from the trunk. Then he ushered the bishop toward the door and followed him inside. The one-room house was cool and drenched in shadows.

"Just what I need." The bishop spread his arms, as if the sofa bed, table, lamp, and closet-sized kitchen were his congregation. "Peace and quiet for twenty-four hours." He gestured toward the black suitcase. "Peaceful morning on the river, just me and the fish. Good mystery novel. And don't plan on me for dinner tonight. I'll be meeting friends in Riverton. In fact, don't plan on seeing me until the meeting tomorrow night. When do you expect the other directors?"

"Sometime tomorrow," Father John said.

"Good." The bishop gave him a conspiratorial look. "Don't tell them I'm here."

Father John smiled. "Enjoy fishing," he said. He let himself out, closing the door behind him, and headed back to the office.

The moment he sat down at his desk, he checked his phone messages. No word from Gianelli. Nothing from Vicky. He'd tried to call her all day, leaving messages with her secretary—*Ask her to call me.* And what is this about, Father? the secretary had wanted to know. Just ask her to call me, he'd said again. He wanted to hear her voice and know that she was safe.

❮ 17 ❯

Vicky could hear the rhythmic sound of the drums as she threaded her way among the parked pickups and sedans in front of Blue Sky Hall. She slipped past the solid wood door and stood next to a group of men leaning against the back wall. The hall was jammed: families crowded into the rows of folding chairs on both sides of the center aisle, other people standing along the walls. Most were Arapaho, although a few white people were scattered about.

The opened casket stood at the far end of the aisle. She could make out the crown of Ben's head, the black hair against the shiny white fabric inside the casket. Her heart lurched. An immense sadness and regret mixed with the flood of memories that washed over her. She'd seen Ben for the first time at a rodeo at Fort Washakie. She was seventeen, and she couldn't take her eyes off him. The way he'd hung on with one hand to the bronco bucking out of the chute, the other hand waving his cowboy hat overhead. Whooping with the sheer madness of it, shouting into the sky, and she'd fallen in love with him then. Then—she'd been so certain—he was everything she wanted.

He'd seen her, too, because after he'd slid off and the Bronco was bucking its way around the arena, Ben had walked straight over to her and said, "You and me, girl, we're gonna get together." Later, after the first time they'd made love, he'd told her he was whooping and shouting out of that chute because he'd spotted her over in the stands.

She pressed her fist against her mouth. From the front of the hall came the slow, deliberate beating of the drum that matched the rhythm of her heart. The singers' voices rose in the same song of grief that the ancestors would have sung for the fallen warriors.

She could see the Holden clan in the front rows: Susan and Lucas seated in the front row, next to Hugh, Ben's brother, which meant he was also their father, in the Arapaho Way. The realization made her flinch.

The air was stuffy. Fluorescent lights shone through a kind of fog that hung below the ceiling. The faint odor of coffee mingled with the smells of roasted meat and sugary cakes.

She'd missed the food. A couple of men beside her were still sipping from Styrofoam cups. Plates and boxes of leftovers were stacked on the tables in the back corner for people to take home to family members who hadn't been able to come. "We always eat first," she remembered her grandmother explaining. Years later she had understood. In the Old Time, the people never knew when they might eat again. They ate when they had the opportunity, then did whatever else they had gathered to do.

The song ended. Amos Walking Bear rose from the front row and, leaning on his cane, made his way to the casket.

The hall was quiet. The old man stood with head bowed, light glinting in his gray hair, black bolo tie pulled tightly against the collar of his white shirt. And then his voice boomed into the hall. *"Ani'qu ne'chawu'nani, Ani'qu ne'chawu'nani."*

Vicky set her head back against the wall, closed her eyes, and let the comforting sounds flow over her. She'd never learned to speak Arapaho—her parents were progressives—but she recognized the style. Formal and correct, the style in which the chiefs had addressed the villages. She caught snatches of words and phrases. The elder was calling the people to peace and forgiveness.

The voice stopped, and she opened her eyes, conscious of people turning in the chairs toward her, then looking away. The whispers sounded like the rush of the wind. Several men leaned out from the wall and craned their heads in her direction.

Amos was coming down the aisle, tapping his cane. Smoke curled over the top of the iron pan he held in one hand. Inside the pan, she knew, were smoldering chips of cottonwood and dried sage. He lifted the pan, allowing the smoke to drift over the people, to comfort and cleanse. Heads began to bow, and for a moment, Vicky felt free of the unwelcome glances.

The elder reached the end of the aisle. He stopped and held out the pan toward her. The sweet odor of sage floated over her. She felt a surge of panic. She wasn't sure if he was condemning her or forgiving her. Either way, her people believed she was guilty.

As he started back up the aisle, Vicky saw the thick-set man, muscles bulging beneath his denim shirt, striding down the side aisle toward her. One of Ben's cousins—she recognized the sway of his shoulders, the set of his jaw. He planted himself in front of her. His breath had a sour smell. "Hugh wants you out of here," he said, making no effort to lower his voice.

She moved sideways along the wall, aware of the rough concrete catching at her blouse. Heads turned again in her direction.

She gasped. Lucas had come up behind the man, and for a moment, she'd thought he was Ben. Ben, twenty years ago. He took her arm. "You stay if you want, Mom," he said, looking hard at his father's cousin, who shrugged his shoulders and started back toward the front.

"You can sit with me."

Vicky shook her head. "Not with the family."

Lucas stepped back and nodded toward someone farther down the wall. A moment passed before two folding chairs were pushed toward them. He guided her to one and took the other. Gradually she felt the gazes move away, like a breeze shifting in another direction.

The singers' voices rose over the beat of the drum. The elder was leaning over the casket now, applying the circles of sacred red paint to Ben's forehead and cheeks, marking him as one of the people so that the ancestors would recognize him in the shadow world.

Vicky closed her eyes and searched for the words to pray for Ben Holden. *Have mercy on him,* she managed. Then she said the prayer silently over and over again like a mantra. After a moment she opened her eyes and glanced about.

She saw the woman at once—when had she come in?— standing along the wall on the right, in a black, long-sleeved dress with a black scarf framing the pale, beautiful face and nearly obscuring the strip of blond hair along her forehead.

She looked vaguely familiar—a white woman from the area, no doubt. Vicky had the feeling that she should know the woman, and yet she couldn't remember any occasion in which they might have met. She'd never known a lot of white people in the years she'd spent married to Ben. Their life had revolved around family, powwows, rodeos, celebrations—all on the reservation. Occasionally white faces had appeared in the crowds, but no one she knew.

Now she was with white people every day: her office was in a white town, her apartment a few blocks away. She'd opened her office in Lander almost six years ago. Still she couldn't place the woman. Client? Opponent? The woman was nowhere in her life.

But Ben knew her, Vicky was certain. The truth of it sat like a weight against her heart. This was Ben's woman.

She was aware that the painting ceremony had ended; the drumming and singing had stopped. Quiet settled over the hall for a moment. Then, chairs scraped the floor and people started to their feet, grabbing purses and jackets, lifting sleeping toddlers. Groups of people surged into the center aisle.

Lucas stood up and leaned toward her. "Susan and I"—he hesitated—"and Uncle Hugh are going to stay with Dad."

Vicky nodded. Someone always stayed with the body through the night, until the burial in the morning. She kept her eyes on the woman in the crush of people at the side door.

"Do you want to see him?"

"What?" Vicky turned to her son.

"You know, to say goodbye."

Vicky glanced back toward the woman. She was about to

slip outside and into the oblivion from which she'd come, taking with her anything she might know about the Lakotas.

"Yes," she said, getting to her feet and pulling her eyes toward the casket almost hidden behind the groups of people making their way out of the rows and down the aisles. "I'd like to say goodbye."

Lucas took her hand and led her against the crowd flowing toward the entrance. A reverent quiet lay over the hall, broken by the shuffle of footsteps, the occasional hushed voice. Vicky saw the eyes turn away as she passed.

The Holden clan—two rows deep—remained seated, barely concealed anger rippling in the muscles of their clenched jaws. Hugh Holden sat ramrod straight, eyes locked on the far wall.

Vicky went to the casket, Lucas still beside her. Her breath jammed in her lungs. Ben was dressed in a blue, Western-cut jacket, and white shirt with a bolo tie—the tie she'd given him on their tenth anniversary. A white satin pillow had been arranged around his right temple where, she knew, he'd been shot. His hair was parted on the left, neatly combed and fanned over the edge of his shoulders. There were red circles painted on his forehead and cheeks. He looked like Ben and yet, not-Ben. Smaller, sunken, diminished by death.

She ran her fingers along the cool edge of the metal casket, then along the rough fabric of his sleeve. "Go in peace, Ben," she whispered. "Go in peace."

She felt Lucas's arm slip around her shoulders, and she leaned against him a moment. Then she stepped over to Susan in the front row. Her daughter lifted her chin and stared at her out of eyes clouded with incomprehension.

Moisture glistened on her thin cheeks. Vicky took her face in both hands, leaned over, and kissed her forehead. The dampness clung to her lips as she made her way past the rows of empty chairs and trailed the last of the crowd outside.

The white woman was nowhere in sight. Vicky waited in front a few moments, watching the parade of vehicles turning into the road. Finally she crossed through the beams of headlights to the Bronco.

She knew how to find Ben's white woman.

Thirty minutes later, Vicky parked in front of the Peppermill Restaurant and let herself through the double-glass doors. Faint odors of onions and spices floated into the quiet in the entry. A few couples were lingering over cups of coffee and half-eaten plates of dessert in the dining room. The waitress from Monday evening was carrying a tray loaded with dirty dishes toward the swinging doors in the rear.

"One?" The brown-haired hostess with her hair pulled into a bun beckoned her toward the dining room.

Vicky followed the woman past several other tables littered with dirty plates and coffee-rimmed cups. She felt a sense of relief when they passed the table where she and Ben had sat.

"Coffee?" The hostess laid the menu on a small table near the swinging doors that concealed the kitchen.

"That would be fine," Vicky said, taking the chair that faced the dining room. There was a low hum of conversation from the nearby tables, the sound of clanking dishes and gushing water behind the swinging doors.

The hostess returned and set a cup and saucer on the table,

then poured a stream of coffee from an aluminum pot. "The waitress will take your order in a moment," she announced before heading toward the front.

The doors pushed open. The waitress stood between them a moment, balancing a tray of dinner plates, black hair curled around the wary expression on her face. She pulled her gaze away, crossed the restaurant, and began distributing the plates in front of three men. Another moment passed before she came over, her gaze fixed on the small pad in her hand.

"What can I get you," she said, a peremptoriness in her tone. "Kitchen's about to close."

"You recognize me, don't you," Vicky said. "You saw me here Monday night with Ben Holden."

The woman didn't say anything. Vicky could see her throat muscles working as she swallowed. "Why'd you come back?"

"I want you to give me the name of the white woman Ben brought here."

"Don't know what you're talking about . . ."

"Yes, you do," Vicky said. She'd seen the quickly covered-up surprise in the waitress's face when she'd found someone else with Ben. She'd seen the conspiratorial look he'd given the woman.

"It's important," Vicky hurried on. "I have to talk to her."

The waitress glanced over her shoulder toward the hostess. Someone let out a long laugh that lingered over the muffled clanking of dishes. "I don't wanna get involved in murder," she said finally. "I don't need the cops in here asking me questions." She leaned over the table. "What I need is this job," she whispered. "I got a kid to take care of."

"I have two kids," Vicky said. "A lot of people think I killed their father. The white woman may know something that will help me."

The woman stood up straight and began flipping through the notepad. "You better give me your order." She held a pencil over the pad, as if she were already writing.

"Bring me a bowl of soup."

"We got creamy potato, vegetable—"

"It doesn't matter. Who is the woman?"

"Only time I ever seen her is when she come in here with"—she hesitated—"your husband."

"Ex-husband."

At this, the waitress gave her a smile of recognition. "I got me two of 'em," she said. "Roving eyes, both of 'em. I sure know how to pick 'em."

"Do you know her name?"

"I'll get your soup." The waitress stepped back, then disappeared behind the swinging doors.

Vicky took a sip of the coffee. Bitter, barely warm. This was a mistake, she thought, a long shot. How many white women lived in the area around the reservation? Ten thousand, at least. The waitress couldn't know them all.

The woman was back. She set down a bowl of butter yellow soup and an oblong dish stuffed with cellophane-wrapped crackers. "I heard him call her Marcia once," she said, positioning the dish in the center of the table.

"Anything else?" Vicky prodded. Marcia, she was thinking. There was something familiar about the name.

"I don't make a practice of listening in on my customers' conversations." She moved the dish closer to the bowl, and Vicky took a package of crackers.

"Of course not."

"She might've been a rancher. I'll get you some more coffee." The waitress hurried to the serving table, lifted the coffee server, and headed back, stopping to refill cups at another table, throwing quick glances over one shoulder toward the hostess in front.

"What makes you think the woman's a rancher?" Vicky asked, watching the brown liquid rise in her own cup.

"I heard them talking about ranch stuff, you know, cattle prices, best kind of hay, that kind of thing. One night . . ." She hesitated.

"What? Tell me, please."

The waitress drew in a breath. The rim of her nostrils inflated. "I heard her going on about her daddy dying and leaving her the ranch, like it was this big burden, and I'm thinking, I wish my daddy'd left me something other than a shit pile of bad memories, and Ben, he was giving her all kinds of sympathy, saying he sure knew how hard it was for a lady like herself to run a big ranch like the—" She stopped, eyes widening into circles of memory. "The Bishop Ranch, is what he said."

Vicky sank back against her chair. Marcia Bishop. Of course. The woman ran one of the biggest ranches in Fremont County. Vicky had never met the woman, but she'd seen photos of her in the newspaper, awarding trophies at the county rodeo, donating antique ranching gear to the historical society. She was blond and beautiful.

She started to thank the waitress, but the woman had turned away. A pink flush worked its way along the back of her neck, like a visible wave of regret at having said too much, having gotten involved.

Vicky fumbled with the cellophane wrapper, nibbled at the cracker, and took a few bites of the thick, lukewarm soup that tasted like congealed buttermilk. She threw a couple of bills on the table, enough for a large tip, and made her way back across the restaurant.

"How was everything?" The hostess's head snapped around.

"Just fine," Vicky said almost to herself. She was thinking that, first thing tomorrow, she was going to visit one of the most prominent white woman in Fremont County.

◆ 18 ◆

My relations, Wovoka has spoken to me a great truth. It is Wovoka's spirit that dwells within me. I am he, my relations. I am Wovoka come back to you. He has given me his great powers. I can control the elements. I will make the thunder and lightning. I will call forth the great cleansing waters. Oh, listen to me, my relations. The time approaches. You must dance and dance. There is nothing that will stand in our way. Together, we must prepare for the ancestors.

The AA meeting was about to get under way. Lights glowed through the oblong windows of Eagle Hall, and several pick-ups stood at various angles in front. From the alley, Father John could see a few people scattered about the rows of straight-back chairs. He'd considered canceling tonight's meeting—the AA members would probably go to Ben Holden's wake. Then he'd thought better of it. There might be someone who needed the meeting.

He needed the meeting; that was the truth of it. He'd wanted a drink all day. Each time the phone had rung, he'd thought it was Vicky, and he'd grabbed the receiver, reaching for her voice, a sense of premature relief flooding over him that she was safe. But it was never her voice on the line, and he'd felt the old tension grip his muscles. A sip of whiskey, that was all he needed. The tension would dissolve. He could remain calm and rational.

He stuck his head in the doorway and told the Indian woman in the back row that he'd be there in a moment. *He had to be there.* Then he walked through the darkness to the guest house and rapped on the door. The blue sedan stood a few feet away.

A moment passed, and he rapped again. The door swung open. Bishop McCall peered out over the half-moon glasses perched partway down his nose. He held a paperback book opened against his light-colored shirt.

"Everything all right?" Father John said.

"Ah, more than all right." The bishop stepped outside. "Would you look at that." He tilted his head toward the stars sparkling in the darkness overhead. "Peace, quiet, a good steak dinner with old friends, God's own beauty, a twelve-inch trout waiting for me in the morning." He pounded the book against his chest. "And a crackling good mystery novel tonight."

He lowered his head. Shadows sliced across his round face. "I understand there's a wake this evening. Well-known man murdered, is that true?"

"Ben Holden," Father John said.

"You have no part in the services?"

"The family wanted a traditional burial." The moccasin telegraph had reached the bishop's friends, Father John was thinking.

"Still a fair amount of tradition here." The man pushed the glasses up over his nose. "I understand there's a revival of the Ghost Dance religion on the reservation."

Father John said that was right.

The bishop was quiet a moment. Unspoken between them, the thought that somehow Father John had failed. The Arapahos still clung to the old ways. "Well"—the bishop glanced up at the stars again—"it'll be a shame to close this place. We both love it here, John, but . . ." Dropping his head now, staring into the darkness. "We mustn't think only of ourselves."

"The mission belongs to the people, Bishop."

The man gave him a sideways smile, and Father John could see a flash of white teeth. "Don't lobby me, O'Malley. I'm on to all the tricks. Every pastor thinks the world will end if his bailiwick's closed."

Father John was aware of the sound of his own breathing in the evening quiet. He could almost taste the whiskey on his tongue—Dear God, would he never forget the taste? He'd been right. The board was planning to recommend the closure of St. Francis. Even the bishop knew about the plan. Everyone seemed to know except the pastor.

Out on Circle Drive, an engine screamed and accelerated, tires skidded in a burst of gravel. Father John wheeled about, expecting a truck to careen down the alley and slam to a stop at Eagle Hall. Someone was shouting: "Get outta here! Whites outta here!"

A dark-colored pickup sped past the end of the alley, kicking out a cloud of gravel, then was lost behind the church, the engine roaring into the night. The pickup came around the far side of Circle Drive. A man raised himself through the passenger window and pointed the barrel of a rifle into the sky. "Sonsobitch!" he shouted.

"Get down!" Father John grabbed the bishop around the

shoulders and pushed him to the ground, then dropped down beside him. The gunshots were coming faster, recoiling around them, punctuating the noise of the truck, the sound of glass shattering, and the shouting and laughing. He could feel the bishop shaking under his arm. People were spilling out of Eagle Hall, running about, screaming and shaking fists into the air.

Father John lifted his head and shouted, "Go back," but his voice was lost in the crackle of gunfire. The pickup careened past the alley on two tires, and he threw himself across the bishop's head and shoulders.

He counted the seconds. At twenty, he realized the roar of the pickup was farther away, and an eery kind of quiet was moving across the mission, like the quiet following a whirlwind. He waited another ten seconds. The pickup was gone.

He scrambled to his feet, then helped the bishop upright. "You okay?" he said.

The man was still trembling, and Father John kept an arm around his shoulder and walked him back to the guest house. His face looked white in the lamplight. He tried to adjust his glasses, both hands shaking against the frame, a perplexed look in his eyes. One of the lenses was shattered.

"Stay inside," Father John said. Then he left the man standing next to the sofa bed and ran outside, past the paperback book tossed under the sedan's bumper, down the alley. Two vacant parking spots yawned in front of Eagle Hall. Three women stood outside the door, one towering over the others. "You all right, Father?" she called.

"Get back inside!" He pushed his hand against the air. "They might be back."

"Bastards won't be back," she yelled, her voice edged with

hysteria. "Joe and Lou chased 'em outta here."

Father John could taste the acid in his mouth. Dear God, they might have been killed. "Are you all right?" he shouted.

"We know rifle fire when we hear it." The tall woman raised a fist. "We hit the floor."

He gestured toward the hall. "Call the police," he shouted, then he ran past the church, through the grassy area in the middle of Circle Drive to the Toyota pickup in front of the residence. He gunned the engine and, pulling the door shut, wheeled out onto the drive, then onto the straightaway, glancing both ways on Seventeen-Mile Road before running the stop sign and heading west. He drove into the darkness, his thoughts collapsed into a single intention: He had to catch the pickups chasing the gunmen before somebody was killed.

‹ 19 ›

They were nowhere. Father John kept the accelerator to the floor and peered into the darkness beyond the headlights. Shadows rushed past the windows. And then, around a wide bend, taillights blinked in the distance. He stomped harder on the accelerator, aware of the chassis and doors shaking around him, the pickup bed bouncing behind.

He drew up behind the taillights: an old sedan doing about forty, tiny head barely visible above the front seat. But there were headlights in the oncoming lane ahead. A light-colored pickup drove past, then another. He hit the brake and made a U-turn. The pickups had already pulled over, and he stopped alongside the first.

"We lost 'em, Father. Sorry." Lou LeBois was leaning out the window, one of the breeds on the reservation, descended from an Arapaho woman and a French trader.

"You guys okay?"

"No problem."

"They could have shot you." He hadn't meant to chastise them.

"We was prepared." The breed lifted a rifle off the front seat.

Father John squeezed his eyes closed a moment against the feeling washing over him that some horrible event had been averted. "Mind coming back to the mission," he said. "The police will want to talk to you."

"You got any idea who them bastards are?" The Indian in the other pickup leaned out his window and crooked his head back.

"Yeah," Father John said. "I know who they are."

"Who'd want to do this?" Ted Gianelli said.

Father John stood at the window in his office. Three BIA police cars were parked in Circle Drive, blue and white lights blinking on the roofs. Several officers were walking about, stopping from time to time to scoop up something. The office window had been blown out, and a warm breeze blew past the jagged pieces of glass hanging from the frame.

He turned around. Shards of glass littered the carpet and winked on the papers strewn over his desk. The FBI agent sat on one of the side chairs, a matter-of-fact look about the man, dressed in the usual blue sport coat and tan slacks, balancing a small notepad on one thigh. His thick fingers wrapped around a gold pen.

Father George slumped in the other chair, elbows locked at his sides, chin dropped onto a fist. Father John had found his assistant standing in the middle of Circle Drive, talking to the officers. The other priest had broken away and walked over to the pickup. "God, what's going on around here?" he'd said. Then he'd explained that he'd been in the kitchen, he and Walks-On. He'd dove under the table and pulled the dog—howling and shaking—with him.

Father John walked over and leaned back against the edge of the desk across from the fed. "I told you. I had a run-in with one of the guards at the shadow ranch. He warned me to leave the reservation."

The fed dipped his head and scribbled across the notepad. Then he looked up. "Good time to shoot up the mission. Everybody else is at Blue Sky Hall tonight for Holden's wake. Can you ID the shooters?"

Father John shook his head. He'd already told the agent that he hadn't even gotten the make of the truck. Lou LeBois thought it was a Ford, but he wasn't certain. Nobody had gotten the license.

Father George jumped to his feet and announced he was going to check on the bishop. The man had quite a fright, he said, shaking his head. He crossed the office and started down the corridor, his heels clicking on the wood floor. The front door slammed shut.

Father John swept up another pile of glass specks. George and the bishop. That was great. Tomorrow they would be recommending that St. Francis Mission be closed before somebody was killed.

He realized the fed had asked again about the shadow ranch. "Start at the beginning," he said. "Give me all the details."

Father John walked back to the window. The scene below was the same: blinking lights, shadowy figures moving about. He told the fed about the armed guard and the two other guards. About Orlando and Janis and Dean Little Horse. "They know where Dean is."

"What makes you so sure?"

"I think Dean went to the ranch Thursday night after he left work. Maybe he stayed for a while, trying to talk Janis into leaving with him. He was gone by Sunday evening, because Janis Beaver went looking for him then."

"That's it?" Gianelli got to his feet and stuffed the notepad back into the inside pocket of his sport coat. "Jesus, John. You're jumping to a hellava lot of conclusions. All you got from your snooping was a visit from a couple of trigger-happy hotheads who don't happen to like whites. Lucky nobody was killed." He started toward the corridor, head down, a linebacker coming off the bench and into the action.

Father John followed the man outside. "Wait a minute," he said.

Gianelli was partway down the steps. He turned and glanced up. The lights threw blue and yellow stripes over his face. "Make it quick. I want to get to the shadow ranch while the tires on any truck in the vicinity are still hot."

"What do you have on Holden's murder?"

The fed looked away, his gaze following an officer coming down the drive, picking up something, slipping it into a Ziploc bag. "I have to go where the evidence takes me," he said.

"Vicky didn't have anything to do with it."

"I hope that's true." He met Father John's eyes again. "I expect to have a report on the murder weapon tomorrow."

"Then you'll have the killer."

Gianelli started down the steps. "We'll have an indictment," he called over one shoulder. Then he walked over to the officer, who held up the plastic bag.

"We've found six shells," the officer said.

"Get a hold of Chief Banner," Gianelli said. "I need a

couple of BIA cars at the shadow ranch." He brushed past the officer and walked over to the white Blazer in the middle of the drive.

"Might want more than a couple," the officer hollered. Then he went over to the squad car behind the Blazer, leaned inside, and lifted out a black radio. "That's a tight community," he called over the static and whining noise. "Don't like outsiders, especially cops."

The Blazer was already pulling around the squad car. It sped out of the mission toward Seventeen-Mile Road.

Father John crossed the alley and walked along the front of the church, searching the shadows that washed over the white stucco for signs of damage. There was one small chip near the door. He walked down the far side, then circled back and made his way down the alley, checking the walls and windows. The stained glass windows were intact, for which he gave silent thanks. Two windows shot out at the administration building, another two at the residence. A warning, this time.

He spotted Lou LeBois sitting on the stoop outside Eagle Hall, holding a cigarette off one knee. The end glowed orange. Father John walked over and sat down next to the Indian.

"You okay?"

The Indian nodded. "Why do you stay here?"

The question caught him by surprise. "This is home," he said.

"Them Indians want to run you off."

"We don't run off easily." He hoped that was true.

The man laughed, then took a long draw on the cigarette and blew a gray plume of smoke into the shadows. "Indians like that don't make rules for the rest of us."

"I'm glad to hear it."

"Can't live backward. Past is dead. Every day's new." He threw his head back toward the hall. "So they say in AA."

"Hey, Father." Leonard Bizzel, the caretaker at the mission as long as Father John had been there, emerged from the alley and walked over. A group of men in blue jeans and cowboy hats crowded behind him. "We been lookin' for you. We got a lot of warriors on the way over. We're gonna hang around tonight."

"It isn't necessary." Father John pushed himself to his feet. The last thing he wanted was an armed guard. "The police will keep an eye on the place."

"We got a pickup out at the entrance," Leonard went on, as if he hadn't heard. "Another pickup's gonna be parked by the church. That oughtta discourage the bastards. They're gonna figure we got guns."

"Look," Father John began. *God, somebody could get shot!* "I appreciate it, but the cops—"

The man interrupted. "This is our mission, Father. We're not leaving."

"Okay," he said after a moment. "It's your mission."

◀ 20 ▶

Vicky drove down the long driveway, through the pi-ñons and junipers, and parked in front of the two-story, log ranch house. A tall, slender woman with large blue eyes and an oval face framed with curly blond hair that looked white in the sunlight stepped onto the porch, almost as if she'd been watching from behind the curtain at a front window.

"You must be Vicky," she called, moving to the railing with the litheness of an expert horsewoman whose muscles flowed in rhythm with those of the horse.

Vicky came up the wood steps. "And you must be Marcia Bishop," she said. The woman was even more beautiful up close.

"We might as well get this over with." Marcia Bishop wheeled around and stepped back into the house. Vicky followed her through the door and down a hallway into a spacious room. Blocks of sunlight lay on the overstuffed sofa and chairs and winked in the large, glass-topped coffee table. A wall of windows overlooked a meadow with a barn and a corral where a couple of ponies nuzzled the fence, and be-

yond, the rock-bound slopes of the mountains west of
Lander.

The woman planted herself in the center of the room.
"Something to drink?" she said, as if politeness required her
to ask. She was dressed in a tan, silky blouse, unbuttoned
in a long V that exposed her slim neck and pale skin, and
brown jeans that hugged the smooth curve of her hips and
made her look comfortable and at ease.

Vicky shook her head, acutely aware of the stiffness of her
lawyer clothes: the linen dress and high-heeled sandals that
cut into the tops of her feet.

"Sit down, please." Marcia Bishop gestured toward the
sofa behind the glass-topped table. She waited until Vicky
settled herself, then sat in the flower-printed chair across
from the table. "I've been expecting you, I must say." She
spoke in a precise manner that seemed natural and easy, like
a long-accustomed habit.

"Ben was . . ." She drew in a long breath; her nostrils
flared. "A lovely man. Ben was a lovely man."

Vicky had to glance away from the cold certainty in the
blue eyes. She could imagine what had attracted Ben to this
woman: her beauty and position. It would be like coming
home from the rodeo with the championship trophy, and
Ben was always the champion.

But what had attracted this white woman to Ben?

She knew. Oh, she knew. She and Marcia Bishop had
fallen in love with the same man—the handsome, charming,
confident Indian chief. The difference between them was
that Vicky had fallen out of love with him.

"Did you know him long?" she said after a moment.

"Eight months. We met at the county rodeo last fall. Sure
I can't get you something to drink?"

"A glass of water would be nice." Vicky tried for a smile. Her tongue clung to the roof of her mouth. The air felt close and warm.

The woman rose from the chair and let herself through the door at the far end of the room. A few seconds later she crossed the room and handed Vicky a crystal glass filled almost to the brim with water and ice and a slice of lemon. She sat back down. "It's only fair you should know that Ben and I were going to be married," she said.

Vicky took a long drink. She could still see Ben across from her, hear his voice begging her to come back to him. And after all the years, she finally understood. Ben was a chief, and a chief needed his wife and family and respectability. All of that had nothing to do with the parade of women through his life.

She was barely aware of the white woman prattling on about how the Holden clan hadn't approved, she being a white woman. Didn't want her at the wake last night. Well, Vicky must know all about that because they didn't want her there either, but they'd both gone, hadn't they? And Ben was being interred at this moment, on the Holden ranch, and think of it, neither of them were welcome on the ranch.

She drew in a long breath. "We would have been married by now, if you hadn't returned to Lander."

Vicky tried to focus on what the woman was saying. "What possible difference could my return have made?"

Marcia laughed and shook her head. "You're very clever, Vicky. You think I don't know? Ben told me everything: how you could never accept the fact that it was over between you; how you insisted on getting back with him. He wanted to, shall we say, let you down easy. You were the mother of his children, he kept reminding me, and he hoped to remain on good terms for the kids' sake. So naturally I agreed to postpone our plans. He was very fond of you, Vicky, I'm sure. I don't mean to be cruel, but you must accept the fact that it was over between you."

Vicky made herself take a sip of water. "I didn't come here to discuss my relationship with Ben," she managed. "I'm trying to find the Lakota ranch hands he fired last week. I'm hoping you can help me."

"Are you certain that's what brought you here?"

"I don't understand," Vicky said.

A dilemma seemed to be playing out behind the blue eyes, as if the woman couldn't decide whether to press on. Finally, she said, "You should know that the FBI agent has already called. He's bound to come around soon. I was hoping you'd show up first."

Vicky set the glass on the table and waited.

Finally, the woman said, "Ben and I were in Cheyenne at a horse show when he got an e-mail. Some emergency, he said, so we drove back Monday morning. I've been waiting to hear your explanation." Mockery seeped into the woman's tone. "Naturally you'll want to convince me that you know nothing about the e-mail and that the so-called emergency had nothing to do with Ben's murder before I speak with the fed and tell him everything. I'm surprised you didn't show up sooner."

"You're mistaken if you think I had anything to do with Ben's murder," Vicky said. "You must tell Gianelli the truth."

"The truth?" Marcia lifted her chin and stared at her out of half-closed eyes. "That you were insanely jealous? That you couldn't stand the idea of Ben with a white woman?

That if you couldn't have him back, no one would have him? I intend to tell the truth. You can count on it."

For a moment, Marcia Bishop seemed to blur into the bright light at the windows, and Vicky realized that Ben had convinced everyone—this blurred woman, Hugh Holden, even Lucas and Susan—that *she* was the one who had tormented him. He had given her the perfect motive.

Beyond the blurred woman, Vicky could see the cottonwood branches moving in the breeze, a colt trotting after a mare in the corral. She felt like a wild animal caught in a trap on a normal, peaceful day, the iron jaws tightening around her. The harder she tried to escape, the more she howled into the wind, the tighter the jaws became.

She blinked and tried to bring the woman back into focus. "What about the ranch hands?" she said. "Where are they?"

"They had nothing to do with his murder."

"How can you be certain?"

Vicky instantly regretted the question. How could the Lakotas have killed Ben when *she* was the murderer? She hurried on: "Ben saw them before he was killed."

"That's what you'd like the FBI to believe, I'm sure."

"Please, Marcia," Vicky said. "They stole money from the ranch and Ben went after them. He might have said something—please try to remember—about where they were hiding."

"Ben was right. You really never understood him."

"What?"

"You think he cared about the money?" She leaned forward. "It was the dynamite, Vicky. A hell of a lot of dynamite. Enough to blow up the reservation."

"Dynamite! No one at the ranch mentioned dynamite."

Marcia Bishop propelled herself upright, walked to the

window, and stared outside. "No one else knows. Ben kept control of the dynamite. He's the only one who knew the amount in the magazine."

Vicky got to her feet. A picture was emerging in her mind, like blocks of color scrolling onto a monitor. It was Ben who had the permit to buy dynamite to blast out tree stumps, build new roads and ponds. Ben who kept the dynamite in the magazine, locked and secure. He wouldn't have wanted anyone to know it had been stolen.

"You have to tell Gianelli." Vicky heard the stunned note in her voice.

"I have no intention of telling anyone." The other woman turned toward her. Light shone through the white-blond hair and flashed in the blue eyes. "I'll deny everything I've said. I'll say you made it up out of desperation to save yourself. Let the Lakotas blow the reservation into the dinosaur age. What do I care? You killed Ben. You destroyed everything. You deserve whatever happens."

◀ 21 ▶

The road wound down the mountain slope through sparse stands of evergreens. An occasional branch scraped at the side of the Bronco. Lander lay in the sunshine below, gray ribbon streets and roofs floating through trees. To the north, tiny, blocklike houses and clumps of buildings dotted the open spaces of the reservation. And somewhere, two Lakotas with dynamite. *God. God. God.*

She felt the rear tires skid in the gravel. Dust floated in the rush of air over the half-opened windows. It was so like Ben to take charge. He wouldn't have wanted the moccasin telegraph spreading the news that Lakotas had stolen dynamite from the Arapaho Ranch. He would have gone after them. He would have gotten the dynamite back. He was a chief. He protected the people. He gave his life . . .

It made sense, except . . .

Except for something else in the woman's eyes—the dark shadow of hatred, pure and unrelenting. Vicky couldn't get it out of her mind. She had a sense—odd, she thought—that Marcia Bishop loved and hated Ben at the same time.

Promising to marry her, yet calling his ex-wife and taking *her* to dinner. The woman could have followed Ben to the Peppermill. All her suspicions—surely, she'd had suspicions—would have been confirmed. The woman could have seen her with Ben.

Possible, Vicky thought. Marcia had known what she looked like. "We were both at the wake," the woman had said, and she'd called Vicky by name this morning.

Vicky slowed through the residential neighborhood on the west side of Lander, allowing this new picture to develop in her mind. How else could Marcia have known her? Unless . . . The picture still emerging, taking on a new and unexpected shape. Unless Ben had carried her photo.

It could be true, and the realization brought new waves of sadness and regret at the way things had turned out. My God, Ben might have been carrying her photo after all the years.

She gripped the steering wheel, steadying herself. Her nails dug into her palms. She would call Gianelli the minute she reached the office. The agent had to convince Marcia Bishop to tell everything she knew. And Gianelli could check the dynamite records at the ranch. He'd see that there were other people with motives to kill Ben Holden.

She pulled into the curb in front of her office and watched the green Chevrolet truck in the rearview mirror draw in behind her. Adam Lone Eagle loomed in the windshield a moment, then ducked out the door. He walked toward her as she was getting out of the Bronco.

"Vicky, we have to talk," he said. His tie was loosened below the opened neck of his light blue shirt. The cuffs were rolled back, exposing the hard line of muscles in his forearm. His eyes were as black and opaque as pebbles in a river.

Vicky shoved her door closed and told herself to stay calm. The lawyer had made the two-hour drive from Casper when he might have called. Her heart was pounding. She felt as if a flash flood had roared over her.

"We can talk inside." She started around the front of the Bronco, but the pressure of his hand—hard and definite—stopped her, and she turned toward him.

"There's a place I always like to visit when I'm in the area," he said. "It's beautiful, calm, and peaceful. Do you mind if we go there?" He turned without waiting for an answer and walked back to the truck.

She followed and let herself into the passenger seat. The minute he turned the ignition, the sounds of Count Basie surrounded her, the rhythms low and insistent. "You like jazz," he said.

"Is that what you came here to talk about?"

"No."

"Then, what?"

He threw her a sideways glance, a little smile. "Be patient," he said. "Wait for the right time."

Vicky left her eyes on the man a moment. She liked that in him, the patience. It called her to the old ways and to herself.

She turned and looked out the window. The rhythm of drums and blare of saxophones occupied the space between them, like another passenger. Outside the downtown storefronts blurred past, the sun winking in the plate glass windows. She understood that he would tell her what he'd come to tell her when the time was ready.

They were out of town now, heading east. Count Basie gave way to Ella Fitzgerald. The sign alongside the road read: ENTERING THE WIND RIVER RESERVATION. A couple of miles passed, then another sign: SCENIC VIEW. Adam turned into the wide pullout.

The minute the truck stopped, Vicky got out and walked across the gravel to the horizontal metal bar that marked the drop-off. The plains stretched below—vast, quiet, and secluded. Buttes and arroyos melded together in shadows that created a sense of flatness and sameness that, she knew, was not the reality, only the shadow of reality.

"Makes you think of the ancestors." Adam gripped the metal bar next to her and leaned into the view. "You can almost see warriors riding out on the hunt. Problem is"— he turned toward her—"the warriors are gone, and so is the buffalo. The people aren't in charge anymore. We have to live by their rules." He gestured with his head toward the dark blue shadow of Lander in the distance.

"You'd better tell me what happened," Vicky said. The sun burned through her blouse, but her skin felt cold and clammy.

"I talked to Gianelli this morning. He has the report on the twenty-two pistol that killed your ex-husband. He's linked the murder to you."

"What!"

"The gun was registered to the deceased Lester White Plume."

Vicky felt frozen in place, her mind trying to absorb what she'd heard. Uncle Lester's gun. She could see the black gun cradled among the white socks and underwear in Aunt Rose's dresser drawer. When was that? A month ago, after she'd gotten back from Denver? "You don't have to worry about me none," Aunt Rose had assured her. "I'll be just fine. I still got Lester's gun."

"There's more, Vicky," Adam said. "The gun was obviously wiped clean, but the lab picked up a partial fingerprint on the barrel. It's yours."

Vicky looked around for someplace to sit down, but there was no place except the graveled earth rising toward her. She was only half aware of Adam's grip on her arm.

"Well, Gianelli has everything now," she managed. "Motive, opportunity, gun, fingerprint. I'll be indicted." This was why Adam had brought her out here. To give her the news in a place of the ancestors, where she could draw the strength she was going to need from their spirits. A sense of gratitude toward the man mixed with the fear and anger that clasped her like a vise.

She turned toward the shadows moving over the plains. "Someone wanted me to look guilty. Whoever killed Ben stole the gun from my aunt, then left it on Rendezvous Road knowing it would be traced to me."

"Who, Vicky? Who could have taken the gun?"

"Dozens of people." Vicky pushed back from the metal bar and walked over to the truck, then back to the bar. Back and forth, back and forth, kicking at the gravel. "Aunt Rose took in all kinds of people. Teenagers in trouble, people just out of jail. Her heart's as big as that." She waved toward the space below. "Gianelli has to check out her recent houseguests."

"He thinks he has the murderer." Adam's voice was low.

She stopped pacing and faced him. "And you, Adam? What do you think? Oh, forgive me." She threw up one hand. "I forgot that you don't care whether your client is guilty or innocent as long as you win the case."

Adam reached out and took her arm. "I think the fed is full of shit, and I told him so. I told him there has to be another explanation." His fingers dug into her flesh. "Listen to me, Vicky. It's likely the grand jury in Casper will indict you. Maybe tomorrow, maybe the next day. If it happens, I've asked Gianelli to let you surrender. I don't want him bursting into your office, handcuffing you, and dragging you to the county jail. He agreed. If you have any unfinished business, you should take care of it. I'm sure I can get you released on bond, but—"

"Stop it, Adam." Vicky ducked free of his hand and turned away. She crossed her arms, struggling to contain the terror and confusion coming at her like a storm blowing over the plains. She'd stumbled into another reality, incomprehensible. Beyond the metal bar was the real world—the world of the ancestors in another time, another life. A part of her—the part untouched by the white world—would have been at home there.

A crow flapped over a butte and cawed into the wind.

She had to think! The Lakota ranch hands had a motive; they'd stolen the dynamite. But other people could have wanted Ben dead. Marcia Bishop? The white woman could have stalked Ben and shot him in a fit of jealousy.

She locked eyes with Adam and told him about Marcia Bishop and the dynamite.

"Dynamite!" The lawyer's eyebrows cocked upward in an arch of surprise.

"Ben was determined to get it back. He would have made trouble for the Lakotas."

Adam was shaking his head. "They've taken off, Vicky, disappeared into thin air. I talked to some folks at Pine Ridge. Nobody's seen them. He-Dog's aunt thinks he could sill be on the Wind River Reservation, but there's no sign of him here."

Vicky stared out at the plains. She prayed silently to the spirits of the ancestors. "Help me."

Then she turned back to the lawyer waiting a few feet behind her. "There are Indians from other tribes at the shadow ranch. The Lakotas could be hiding there."

"Thirty Indians . . ." Still shaking his head. "Gianelli has IDs on every one. They aren't there, Vicky." Adam leaned closer. She could smell the trace of aftershave, the faint whiff of perspiration. "Let's say you're right. How did the Lakotas get your aunt's gun? She's an old woman, right? Is it likely that she took in a couple of male Lakotas?"

Vicky didn't think so. And yet, if they had stayed at the house, they would have heard about her and Ben. Aunt Rose: passing the time of day over a cup of coffee, making small talk. Her niece had been married to the foreman at the Arapaho Ranch, did they know? A very important man. Would have been a chief in the Old Time. Had a bad breakup, those two.

"What about Marcia Bishop." Vicky heard the desperation in her voice. Nothing was making sense. "She could have gotten a hold of the gun somehow."

Adam didn't say anything, and she knew he'd heard the desperation.

"Take me back to the office," she said, starting for the truck. She flung open the door and got inside.

Adam came around the other side and crawled in behind the wheel. "Listen, Vicky, I want you to take care of your own affairs."

"This is my affair."

"I'm your lawyer. Let me handle this." He hesitated, some new idea taking shape behind the black eyes. "I'm going to lay it on the line, Vicky. You've got a reputation for getting involved in matters you have no business getting involved in. You've put yourself in dangerous situations. You had to shoot a man."

Vicky flinched. She felt the warm flush in her cheeks, the stab of pain that always came with the memory. She tried to concentrate on what the man was saying: If the Lakotas got wind that she was looking for them, they'd come after her. She should concentrate on putting her affairs in order. Didn't she have a report on Bull Lake Dam to finish for the JBC? She should do normal things. He would take care of the rest.

He started the engine and wheeled back onto the road. Gravel peppered the undercarriage for several moments.

"I'm dead serious, Vicky." He glanced at her out of the corner of his eye. "You do things my way, or you find another attorney."

‹ 22 ›

"**B**astards had it in for us." Leonard Bizzel kicked at the glass shards that winked in the morning light, then positioned the metal ladder below the window space in Father John's office. The Arapaho knew the grounds and buildings—the location of every hammer, box of nails, and cleaning fluid. He took the attack personally.

"Don't you worry, Father. I'll have the windows fixed in no time, and we'll be back to normal." He started toward the shed around the corner where he kept his tools. "Oh, almost forgot." He looked back, eyes shadowed with concern. "Warriors are gonna hang around the mission, case those bastards decide to show their ugly faces again." He threw a brown fist toward the cottonwoods.

Father John followed the man's gesture. Parked in the trees along the drive was a green pickup. Two men inside the cab, as still as mannequins, cowboy hats pulled forward. He took in a deep breath. The warriors would have a rifle stashed between them, and he didn't want anybody killed. On the other hand, he doubted that last night's shooters would drive past the pickup. A part of him, he had to admit, was glad for the guard.

"Tell them thanks," he called to Leonard, who was out of sight. He could hear the man jiggling the door of the shed.

"They don't need thanks, Father," the Indian shouted. "Just doin' their job."

Father John started up the front steps, his eyes on the truck. He wondered if the men were parishioners. It didn't matter. They were warriors protecting what belonged to the people.

He shoved open the heavy wood door and stepped inside. The building felt cool, the night air still clinging to the stucco walls. The quiet amplified the thud of his boots on the floorboards. He could see the door at the far end of the corridor. Father George had left an hour ago for the Riverton Airport. At any minute, Father John expected the other priest's sedan to roll around Circle Drive and disgorge the three new members of the board of directors, all former colleagues of his assistant, who would help decide the future of St. Francis Mission.

The hot breeze blew through the open space in the window and rustled the papers on his desk. He sat down, pulled the phone onto a stack of paper, and dialed Gianelli's office. He listened to the mechanical voice that barely resembled the agent's, then left his name. Gianelli would know he was calling to see if last night's shooters were in custody. And the agent would know if the BIA police had anything new on Dean.

There was something else: By now Gianelli would also have the report on the twenty-two used to kill Ben Holden.

Both Vicky and Dean had been on his mind all night, threading their way through crazy dreams that made no sense: the dark pickup chasing them across the mission grounds, fire bursting through the windows, and he, trying to run after them, wanting to protect them, his legs paralyzed, two stumps frozen into the ground.

He woke in a tangle of sheets and perspiration, and he'd offered Mass this morning for them both. *Let them be safe.*

He held down the disconnect button half a second, then dialed Vicky's office. The clank-clank sound of a chisel burst through the window opening.

"Vicky Holden's office." The woman's voice was still unfamiliar, still tentative. The new secretary in Vicky's new office. Everything seemed new and unfamiliar since she'd returned from Denver, as if she'd stepped into a life in which he had no part. No, Ms. Holden wasn't in today. What was this about?

To reassure her, he supposed, and reassure himself that she was okay. He said, "Ask her to call Father O'Malley."

She repeated his name, emphasizing each syllable, as if she were still trying to comprehend the purpose of his call.

"When do you expect her?"

"I really can't say."

He hung up and walked over to the window opening. Leonard was bent over a folding wood table he'd dragged from the shed, fitting a pane of glass into the frame. The ladder was still against the wall, the pickup still parked in the trees.

A blue sedan turned into Circle Drive.

Father John came down the front steps as his assistant sprang out of the sedan and opened the rear door. A tall angular man with a full head of white hair that framed a composed, aristocratic face unfolded himself from the backseat. Father Niles Johnston, president emeritus of two Jesuit colleges, dressed in black clericals and starched white collar. The man looked like an older version of the photos Father John had seen in the Jesuit magazines. It was Niles Johnston who had written him a letter insisting the board scrutinize the "long-term goals"—he'd ended with a question mark— of St. Francis Mission.

Father John walked over and shook the man's hand. "Good to meet you," he said.

Two other priests, also in clericals, were climbing out of the other side: Father James Bourne, an old friend from the seminary who'd taken a straight path, with no detours for treatment at Grace House, and was now a college vice president. Father John didn't recognize the other man: Father Allen Beckner. Short, rotund, with a horseshoe of black hair laid around a pink scalp and alert, penetrating eyes behind the rimless glasses that rode partway down his bulbous nose. He looked like the artistic renditions of Thomas Aquinas. Fitting, Father John thought, for a philosopher and Thomistic scholar.

Father John walked around the sedan, shook hands, and welcomed the priests to the mission.

"What's going on?" Father Niles was staring at Leonard clambering up the ladder.

"An unfortunate incident—" Father John began.

Father George cut in: "Four windows shot out last night."

"Shot out, you say?" The philosopher stepped forward.

"Yes, well—" Father John began again, groping for the words that might allay the bewilderment in the philosopher's eyes. There was no room for such incidents in the cool, logical contemplation of the higher truths. "We had a little trouble last night . . ."

Father George took hold of the philosopher's arm. "A

pickup with two crazy men sped through the grounds. There was a lot of rifle fire. Fortunately, no one was hurt."

"Well, well." Father Niles threw his white head back and straightened his thin shoulders, as if the suggestion, implied in his letter that St. Francis had outlived its usefulness, had just been confirmed.

The phone had started ringing inside the office, a faraway sound, oddly insistent. Father John started toward the steps, but the ringing stopped. Either the answering machine had picked up, or Elena had answered in the residence.

"Windows'll be fixed by tomorrow," Leonard called from his perch on the ladder. He was adjusting the new frame into the space. "Won't be any more trouble with the warriors here." He nodded toward the cottonwoods.

Father John saw the other priests turn in a precise maneuver and stare fixedly at the green pickup, their expressions dissolving from curiosity to dismay. "You have warriors here?" Father Niles said.

"What happened, John?" Father James, his old friend from the seminary, came around the sedan toward him, sympathy in the man's eyes.

Father John started to explain that a cult had gotten started and the followers wanted whites off the res. He stopped. It was complicated, and the sun was beating down on the bare heads and black clericals of the other priests, who were blinking in the brightness in an obvious effort to understand what in heaven's name he was talking about.

He said, "Why don't we go to the residence. You look like you could use a cool drink."

The other priests threw each other a look of relief, then started trudging single-file down a path through the field of wild grasses in the center of the drive, Father George in the lead.

Father John started after the others. He caught snatches of the small talk: mission looked pretty much as they had imagined. Fewer windows, Father Niles observed. Everybody laughed.

They were crossing the far side of the drive when Elena burst from the residence and propelled herself down the steps, arms flapping ahead. "Father, Father," she yelled, fear and hysteria in her voice.

Father John darted around the others and ran to her. "What is it?"

"They found him." She was shouting, her chest heaving with the effort.

"Take it easy." He laid a hand on her shoulder. "Who are you talking about?"

The other priests were pressing around, heads bending toward the housekeeper.

"Amos called. Says they found Dean Little Horse in the foothills west of Fort Washakie. He's been shot, Father."

The other priests jumped backward, as if she'd cracked a whip in their direction.

She let out a long wail: "Somebody shot him to death."

‹ 23 ›

A phalanx of official vehicles stood at the side of the dirt road: five white Ford sedans with the blue and yellow insignia of the Wind River Police; Gianelli's white Blazer; a paneled truck with FREMONT COUNTY on the side. A dozen blue-uniformed police officers and several men in slacks and sports coats milled through the trees about fifty feet off the road.

Father John parked behind the paneled truck and started through the trees. Pine needles snapped under his boots. He'd left Father George and the others staring after him and driven out of the mission. They were probably seated at the kitchen table now, sipping iced tea, discussing homicide on the reservation and last night's shooting. He could hear the gravelly voice of Father Niles Johnston: *We really must consider . . . In view of everything . . . A dangerous place.*

Now he could see Ted Gianelli and two uniforms leaning over a dark object that looked like rags, a pile of bones. The agent broke away and came toward him. "Coroner's about to bag the body," he said. "You want to offer a prayer?"

Father John nodded and kept walking. The uniforms and

rts coats stepped back, and he saw the mud-caked blue jeans and yellow shirt and brown flesh in a heap on the ground. He went down on one knee and caught his breath. The body had been hollowed out. Where the stomach and abdomen had been was a jagged hole with torn masses of flesh and intestines. The plaid shirt was bunched and ripped, the chest matted with brown blood. He pulled his eyes to the face smeared with dirt, the hollow eye sockets, and the expression frozen in fear and shock.

He made the sign of the cross. "May the good and merciful Lord remember you, Dean, forgive you your sins, whatever they may have been, and grant you the peace and love you longed for here."

He tried to swallow back the knot of revulsion and anger in his throat at the senselessness, the absence of reason—there was no reason. The two men from the coroner's office began smoothing a gray plastic bag across the ground a few feet away. Father John got to his feet and turned back to the agent.

"What happened to him?"

Gunshot wound in the chest. Bullet probably hit his heart. We'll know after the autopsy. Coroner says he's been dead several days. Killer tried to bury him." He nodded toward clods of earth around a shallow trench several feet away. "Mountain lion probably dragged him out, started at him. Tom Hizer lives up the road. He spotted the body this morning."

Father John looked away a moment, trying to force his thoughts into a logical sequence. He turned back. "What kind of gun?"

The agent was rubbing his fingers into his temple, squint-

ing in discomfort. "Have to wait for the autopsy, but . . ."
He paused.

"It's a small wound."

"A twenty-two? Like the gun that killed Ben Holden?"

"Don't get your hopes up there's any connection, John. We have the murder weapon in the Holden case. We know the owner. Registered to Lester White Plume, deceased husband of Rose White Plume." He drew in a long breath that expanded the chest of his navy sport coat. "Look, John . . ." He paused. "We got a fingerprint off the barrel. It matches Vicky's."

The implications hit Father John like a fist in the chest. The physical evidence, the final piece that would tie everything together and convince a grand jury to indict Vicky.

"There has to be some explanation," he said. "Vicky's not capable of murder."

"She killed a man once."

"Give me a break. That was in defense of human life." *Defense of his life.* "Now we're talking about premeditated murder."

"I don't like the idea any more than you do." Gianelli was digging his fingers into his temple again, as if to rub out some invisible pain.

"What if it turns out the same twenty-two killed Holden and Dean?" Father John pushed on. "Vicky didn't even know Dean."

"So you're trying to tell me that two Lakotas shot Ben, then shot Little Horse? Put your famous logic to work, John. How the hell did they get the gun from Rose White Plume? And what beef would a couple of cowboys have with some guy like Dean, spent all day writing computer software. Where the hell's the connection?"

Father John glanced away. Two sports coats struggled toward the road with the bulky gray plastic bag between them. They dropped the bag onto a gurney, then shoved the gurney into the paneled truck. There had to be a connection. What was the connection?

A new idea flitted like a shadow at the edge of his mind. Two men, Dean and Ben, Arapahos, born and raised on the res. They belonged here. Two Lakotas, outsiders who might not care about the res or the people. The idea was coming into focus, assuming logical order. The outsiders posed some kind of threat, created some kind of danger. Dean and Ben had tried to stop them. They'd been killed.

He said, "Dean stayed at the shadow ranch. The Lakotas could have been there at the same time."

"Shadow ranch again." Gianelli shook his head and glanced away a moment. Then he said, "Look, John. Let me do my job, okay? I'm gonna push Orlando and his bunch real hard. If there's some connection, I'll find it."

"What about the guys that shot up the mission? Have you found them?"

"No vehicles at the ranch. Village was lit up with bonfires. The followers were doing their dance, dressed in white, circling around, holding on to one another. We interviewed Orlando himself and about a dozen others. They claimed they didn't know what we were talking about. Without evidence . . ." He shook his head. "You want to give Dean's grandmother the bad news?"

It was probably all over the moccasin telegraph, Father John was thinking. Minnie and Louise would have heard by now. He said, "I'll stop by the house."

❮ 24 ❯

"**Y**ou bless the boy?" Minnie said.

Father John scooted his chair close to the sofa where the old woman sat with her sister, their hands intertwined. The living room was crowded with Arapahos seated on the other chairs, huddled in the corners. The low buzz of conversation ran like an electric current through the air.

He told the old women that he had blessed Dean's body.

The information seemed to give them some degree of comfort, as if Dean could now start on the road to the shadow world.

Someone handed him a mug of coffee and Father John took a sip. Then he told them he'd found Dean's girlfriend. "She said Dean had been at the shadow ranch."

Both women were shaking their heads. "That's an untrue story," Minnie said. "Dean wouldn't stay with those Indians. They think the world is gonna end."

Louise said, "I knew he got himself a girlfriend. He might've gone up there to see her."

"I suppose." Minnie patted her sister's hand. "He

would've been worried about her, if she took up with that cult. But he wouldn't have *stayed* there. He had a future, that boy. He was going someplace." Her voice began to crack, and she paused. "He didn't think the world was ever gonna end."

Father John didn't say anything for a moment. Then he asked if Dean had known Ben Holden.

The two women stared at him out of eyes round with surprise. "Ben Holden? Everybody knew Ben Holden. He got murdered a few days ago. What's that got to do with Dean getting murdered?"

"Did he ever work at the Arapaho Ranch?"

"What're you saying, Father?" A rail-thin man sat down on the sofa armrest. "You think the same bastard shot 'em both?"

"I don't know," Father John said after a moment. "I'm trying to figure out if there's a connection."

Louise waved away the idea. "Dean never took to ranching. He was a thinker, that boy. Stayed in school. Used his head. Nothing in common with Ben Holden."

"Hell," said the man on the armrest. "Ben was a whiskey man. Dean didn't even drink."

He was chasing shadows, Father John thought. Connections that didn't exist. He tried to focus on the conversation: Minnie and Louise saying that Dean had to be buried within three days—buried at the mission, Father—so that his spirit could find the way to the ancestors, and he trying to explain the mysterious workings of the white bureaucracy. First, the coroner had to release the body. He promised to hold the funeral as soon as possible.

Then he got to his feet and made his way to the door, shaking hands, clasping shoulders as he went, trying to corral the sadness running inside him. He should've insisted that Minnie go to the police when he'd first talked to her—why hadn't he insisted? And yet, what good would it have done? Dean was already dead by then.

Outside, the sun glistened on the open spaces. He climbed into the pickup and headed south. It would take most of an hour to get back to the mission. The other members of the board of directors had probably arrived by now. The first meeting would get under way in a couple hours. He was going to be late.

The offices of Blue Water Software had the vacant end-of-the-day look, but a light glimmered through the front window and the door opened when Father John tried the knob. A wall of refrigerated air hit him. The hum of an air-conditioning unit mingled with the click of computer keys.

The receptionist looked up from the papers she was arranging into neat stacks on the desk. "We're about to close, Father," she said.

He asked if Sam Harrison was still there.

The woman picked up the phone and pressed a key. "The priest from the other day," she began, bringing the thin-penciled eyebrows together.

"Father O'Malley," he said.

"Yes, of course. Father O'Malley's here to see you."

A second passed before Sam Harrison emerged from the maze of cubicles. "Come on back, Father," he said, waving him into the aisle.

Father John followed the young man past vacant cubicles with monitors gleaming with iridescent images of mountains and lakes and dams. They turned into a cubicle with two desks set at right angles. A long, fluorescent lamp emitted a glow of light over the papers and the computer monitor on one desk. The lamp on the other desk was turned off; the monitor was dark.

"I heard the news," Harrison said, brushing his brown curly hair off his forehead and sinking into a chair in front of the monitor filled with tiny words and numbers that seemed to make no sense. Father John took the chair in front of the blank monitor.

"Dean! Man, I can't believe it," Harrison said. "Just yesterday, a police officer was here, asking questions, nosing into Dean's files." He nodded toward the blank monitor. "Why'd anybody want to kill him?"

"I need your help," Father John said.

"Anything, Father. You name it, and I'll do it." Harrison scooted his chair forward.

"Did he ever mention an Arapaho named Ben Holden?"

The young man tilted his head toward the ceiling. "Not that I can recall." He looked back. "Wait a minute. Isn't that the Indian got shot the other night? Big man on the res?"

Father John said that was the man. "What about the Arapaho Ranch? Dean ever talk about the ranch?"

Harrison was shaking his head. "Dean wasn't the cowboy type. He was a desk jockey." He gave another nod toward the monitor. "Liked putting computers through their paces. What're you saying, Father? Dean's murder has something to do with the murder of the big guy?"

"I'm not sure." Father John got to his feet. It was a long shot; he'd been grasping for some connection. Nothing tied Dean Little Horse to Ben Holden, except for the fact they'd been shot by a twenty-two. "Look, Harrison," he said, "if you think of anything . . ."

"Hold on, Father." The young man jumped up, pushed back the chair that Father John had just vacated, then sat down in front of the blank monitor. He flipped a switch; blue, red, and yellow icons began to form in the white light. Harrison leaned closer and clicked on the mouse by the keyboard. Black boxes of text replaced the icons. He tapped on the keys, and tiny x's appeared in one box.

"Dean and I, we worked pretty close," he said. "Troubleshooting glitches in our software. You know, gate doesn't open at the dam way it should, we find out what the computer's ordering and tell it to order something else. He had my password. I have his. Made life simpler."

A column of names began scrolling downward. "Police officer printed out Dean's contacts. Mostly clients, looks like. Dam operators. People we work with every day. Hold on." He hunched forward and clicked the mouse. The scrolling stopped. "Whatd'ya say the big man's name was, Ben Holden? Here we go." A blue line highlighted a name and e-mail address that began with BH.

"Let's see if Dean saved the messages he sent out." Harrison clicked again. "Here we go. Good old Dean. Saved everything."

Lines of text started to form. Father John leaned around the young man and peered at the monitor. "Urgent!" appeared in the subject box. The message read: "I'm a Rap like you. Must talk to you immediately. I know about the day box."

The e-mail had been sent on Sunday at 8 P.M.

"I'll get a printout." Harrison was on his feet, striding into the corridor.

So there was a connection, Father John thought. Dean had tried to get a hold of Ben Holden. But he didn't know

Holden—he'd had to explain that he was also Arapaho. He'd wanted to give Holden some information: he knew about a day box. It was urgent. Urgent enough to get them both killed.

Harrison stepped back into the cubicle and handed him a printed sheet of paper. "Hope this helps find whoever shot Dean."

Father John thanked the man and made his way back down the aisle and into the late afternoon heat. He walked back to the pickup, fished the cell phone out of the glove compartment, and left another message for Gianelli: "I've found the connection."

‹ 25 ›

Vicky kept her eyes on the belt of gray asphalt rolling under the hood of the Bronco and struggled against the feeling that the sky and the plains were closing in on her. She'd checked her messages when Adam dropped her off at the office. Four or five calls from Aunt Rose. Two calls from the mission priest, her secretary's term for John O'Malley. Oh, and a call from Norm Weedly. The JBC had decided to pursue other avenues concerning the Wind River and Bull Lake. Thank you very much for your efforts. Your fee will be mailed shortly, his exact words, the secretary said.

Vicky tightened her grip on the wheel and turned onto Blue Sky Highway. She understood. Gianelli thought he'd solved Ben's homicide, and the JBC had decided not to retain a lawyer about to be indicted for murder. No matter what Adam said, she intended to find out how the Lakotas or Marcia Bishop or whoever had shot Ben had gotten Aunt Rose's gun. Adam wouldn't approve. He was the type of lawyer—it was obvious—who expected clients to follow his advice. She was the same. She wouldn't keep a client who didn't follow her advice. It hit her that tomorrow she'd probably be arrested, and she wouldn't have a lawyer.

She eased on the brake and turned into the bare-dirt yard in front of Aunt Rose's house. The old woman was already at the door, as if she'd been waiting for the sound of the Bronco. She looked disheveled, sleepless. Her eyes were bruised red from crying.

"Oh, Vicky." She reached out, took Vicky's hand, and pulled her into the house. "I don't know what happened. I don't understand." She started sobbing and taking in great gulps of air.

Vicky hugged the old woman. She could feel her trembling beneath her cotton dress. "We'll figure it out, Auntie." She guided her to the worn upholstered chair, then perched on the ottoman and waited until Aunt Rose had dug a tissue out of the front of her dress and dabbed at her eyes.

"The fed was here first thing this morning." She waved the wad of tissue at the door. "What's the FBI want with an old lady, I said. He said, what do I know about Ben Holden getting himself shot? He wanted to know if I got a gun. I seen clear as day what he was up to. You got it all wrong, white man, I told him, but he kept wanting to know if I owned a gun. I said no. Well, that was the truth, 'cause Lester was the one that owned the gun. So the fed said, your husband had a license for a twenty-two pistol. So what if he did, I says, and then he told me that Lester's gun killed Ben Holden."

The old woman paused. Moisture glistened in the creases of her brown face. "I went back into the bedroom to get the gun and prove he was crazy; the fed was right behind me. I opened the dresser drawer and . . ." She dabbed at the tears, smearing the moisture across her cheeks. "Maybe I put the gun somewheres else, I said. I started looking everywhere, pulled out the drawers, looked in the closet. I'm telling the fed how I'm an old woman, and maybe I got forgetful and put the gun someplace I can't remember. But it's nowhere."

Aunt Rose dropped her face into her hands and emitted a soft, wailing noise. Her shoulders shook. Vicky patted her hand and said it was okay, everything would be okay. She wished she believed it.

"You're wrong, Vicky." Aunt Rose glanced over the wad of tissue. "The fed thinks you shot Ben. He wanted to know all the times you been here." Her features rearranged themselves into a look of defiance. "I told him, I'm not talking to you no more without a lawyer."

Vicky smiled at the image of Aunt Rose standing up to Ted Gianelli. "You may have to answer the question in court." She made her voice matter-of-fact. "You'll have to tell the truth."

The truth, she was thinking: She'd come to Aunt Rose after Ben was killed; she'd spent three days here after she'd returned from Denver. She always came to Aunt Rose when she was off-balance. But there was another truth. Somebody else had taken the twenty-two.

"Would you like some coffee?" she said after a moment.

The old woman nodded, and Vicky went into the kitchen. She found the coffee canister, measured out the grounds, filled the glass container—going through the motions, her thoughts on Gianelli. He would have talked to the neighbors down the road. Arapahos paid attention; they knew who was visiting who. It kept the moccasin telegraph humming. He would know the exact dates she'd been here.

She stared at the brown liquid dripping into the glass container and tried to breathe slowly. She could feel her ribs squeezing her heart.

After a moment, she poured a mug of coffee, then found a notepad and pencil by the phone and went back into the living room. Aunt Rose lay with her head tilted back against the chair.

Vicky set the mug on the table next to the chair and dropped back onto the ottoman. "Listen, Auntie," she said, "have any whites stayed here? Anyone connected to the Bishop Ranch?"

Aunt Rose locked eyes with her, surprise mingling with disbelief in the woman's expression. "What're you talking about?"

"Marcia Bishop, Ben's girlfriend. Has anyone stayed here who knew her?"

In the way that the old woman shrugged, closed her eyes, shook her head, Vicky knew she was clutching at shadows. It wasn't Marcia Bishop who had found her way into Aunt Rose's bedroom and taken the gun.

She said, "How about any Lakotas, Auntie? Two Lakota ranch hands stole dynamite from Ben. They might have been looking for a place to hide out."

"Lakotas? Lakotas took dynamite? What're they gonna do? Blow up our reservation?"

"Roy He-Dog. Martin Crow Elk. Do those names ring a bell?"

Aunt Rose sat very still, like a child searching for the right answer to please the teacher. Finally she shook her head.

"What about Indians from other tribes," Vicky pressed on.

"I know Lakotas when I see 'em. Even if they said they was some other tribe, I'd know 'em."

Vicky felt the vise clamping in her chest again. "Let's

start with the most recent visitors and work back."

Aunt Rose shifted her gaze to some point across the room. "Two girls social services sent last Saturday. Stayed the night."

Vicky wrote Saturday. Two days before Ben was killed. Then she made a note to check identities with social services.

"Week before," Aunt Rose went on, "Mark Shield stayed a couple days. Dad goes on a drunk once in a while, and Mark comes over. He's a good boy."

Vicky wrote down the name. She knew the Shield family. Mark was about fourteen. "Before Mark," she said.

"Well, that'd be, about a month ago. Let me see—couple girls stayed one night. They were from Montana."

Vicky held the pencil over the notepad and waited.

"Come here to join up with the shadow dancers. Seen all about 'em on the Internet. Cop stopped them late at night on 287 for driving too fast and they told him where they were going. So he tells them to come here first, get some sleep and food, before they headed into the mountains. Maybe he was thinking they might change their minds, but soon's they woke up in the morning, they took off."

"Did you get their names?"

"Sue and Mary. They was sisters. Last name was Buckle."

Vicky wrote down the names, then shadow ranch. She felt a little surge of excitement.

"Gun was here when they left," Aunt Rose said.

"Are you sure, Auntie?"

"Oh, I'm sure. I was doing some spring cleaning. Gun was right there in the drawer where Lester kept it. Let me see, there might've been somebody else . . ."

Vicky dropped her head into her hand. It was impossible. The truth was, anyone could have walked into Aunt Rose's house and taken the gun. No telling how many people knew about it. People worried about Rose White Plume taking in strangers, and Aunt Rose assured them, just as she'd assured her. No need to worry. I got Lester's gun.

"Janis . . ."

Vicky dropped her hand. She felt her heart turn over. John O'Malley said he'd talk to a girl named Janis—what was her last name?—at the shadow ranch.

"Stayed here couple weeks ago. Oklahoma girl."

Oklahoma girl! Vicky felt as if the gears had suddenly snapped into place. The girl was from Oklahoma.

"Come to the res last winter," Aunt Rose was going on. "Seen the shadow dancers at Ethete and decided to join 'em. Met Orlando himself. Oh, she wanted to live up at the ranch in the worst way, but her boyfriend, well, he didn't want her to go. So she showed up at the door." She paused, as if she were groping for the memory. "Wanted to know if she could stay a little while. Needed a place to think. I don't know how she heard of me."

Vicky didn't say anything. Everybody's heard what a soft touch you are, she was thinking.

"All she talked about was Orlando," Aunt Rose went on. "How he's the son of Wovoka. How the new world didn't come before, but now it was gonna come. No more trouble and suffering, no more kids getting kicked around. I figured she'd been kicked around plenty, poor girl, and sure enough, one morning she gets up and says she had a vision. Orlando was calling her, and she had to go. Last week, her boyfriend comes looking for her, and I had to tell him she went to the ranch. Dean Little Horse. Seemed real nice. Too bad what happened to him."

Vicky stared at her aunt. "What happened?"

"You don't get the moccasin telegraph in Lander?"

She heard the news on the radio this morning, Vicky was thinking. Nothing earthshaking. And this afternoon, Adam was playing a jazz CD, and she hadn't turned on the radio on the drive to Aunt Rose's. She could think better with the noise of the wind crashing through the Bronco.

"What, Auntie?" she pleaded.

"Found his body out in the foothills. Shot to death, like Ben."

Vicky sprang to her feet. "What else have you heard, Auntie?"

The old woman shook her head and looked up at her. "Last I heard—Josephine Cleary called just before you drove up—they don't know who shot him. He'd been dead three, four days."

Vicky started pacing. The door. The window. The ottoman. She sat back down. "Think, Auntie. Could Janis have taken the twenty-two?"

Aunt Rose's lips moved silently a moment. Then she said, "Can't say for sure. Maybe it's what happened."

It was what happened. Vicky could feel the truth of it. The girl named Janis had taken the gun to the shadow ranch, which meant the Lakotas had been at the ranch. They'd brought the dynamite to Orlando! Ben must have gone to the ranch and confronted the Lakotas Monday afternoon. They'd grabbed the gun—a perfect weapon, registered to someone else. They probably didn't even know it was registered to the uncle of Ben's ex-wife. They'd followed Ben to the restaurant, then to Rendezvous Road.

Vicky jumped up and began carving out another circle over the braided rug, conscious of Aunt Rose's dark eyes following her. There was more. Dean had probably gone to the ranch and tried to get Janis to leave. Probably caused trouble, and someone—the Lakotas?—had shot him. They could have used the same gun.

And yet . . . Gianelli had already checked the ranch. The Lakotas weren't there, but . . . *they had been there.* She was going to have to convince the fed to get a search warrant. She had to get some evidence.

It hit her like a clap of thunder. The dynamite could still be at the ranch. If she could get a photo . . .

"I'm sorry, Auntie," she said, starting for the door, grabbing her black bag from the table as she went. "I have to go."

Aunt Rose's voice behind her, as if she'd seen into her head: "You're not goin' to the shadow ranch! The dancing's going on. Outsiders aren't allowed."

Vicky opened the door and turned back. "What did Wovoka preach, Auntie? How was the new world supposed to come?"

Aunt Rose stood very still a moment, as if she were trying to grasp a memory. Then she staggered backward into the table. The mug turned over and a stream of coffee ran onto the floor. "He preached . . ." She hesitated, then swallowed and started again. "The new world's gonna come after the great event. The Ghost Dancers was supposed to dance for four days. Every six weeks they danced for four days. They was supposed to keep dancing until the great event happened. There was gonna be an explosion and a great flood that would wash the earth clean. They didn't know when the event was gonna happen, but it was gonna be on the last day of the dance."

Vicky stood very still, trying to pull from her memory what Norm Weedly had said: *They're starting the dance today.*

That was Monday and this was Thursday, the fourth day.

Today was the last day!

"I'll call you later, Auntie." Vicky wheeled about and ran outside to the Bronco. She jammed her key into the ignition and shot onto the road, past Aunt Rose standing on the stoop, gesturing with both hands, as if she could pull her back.

‹ 26 ›

I t was almost six when Vicky reached Lander. Offices and shops had closed an hour ago. She left the Bronco in the lot behind her apartment building and ran up two flights of stairs. In the living room, she leaned over the desk, struggled to catch her breath, and played back her phone messages. Adam Lone Eagle's voice: They had to talk. It surprised her that the man was still in town. She deleted the message.

Two calls from Lucas. He and Susan were leaving tomorrow. Could they get together tonight? Call as soon as you get in. He left the number. They were still at Hugh's house.

She picked up the receiver. The familiar longing clung to her like a worn dress. She'd hardly seen the kids since they'd arrived for Ben's funeral, and tomorrow Lucas would be starting for Denver, Susan for L.A. How would they hear that she'd been indicted? From the radio? Somewhere between Laramie and Cheyenne? She had to talk to them first, prepare them. God only knew what Hugh Holden had told them.

She tapped out the first three numbers, then stopped, her

fingers numb against the keys. The shadow dance would end tonight. Whatever great event Orlando had planned would happen tonight.

She dropped the receiver, went into the bedroom, and stripped off the lawyer clothes—the beige linen dress, the hose and sandals she'd worn all day. If everything went okay, she'd be home by ten. She'd call the kids and arrange to meet them for breakfast tomorrow before they left.

She pulled on a pair of blue jeans and a black T-shirt and jammed her feet into her sneakers. Then she tied her hair in a short ponytail. Rummaging through a closet shelf, she found a black waist pack and walked back through the apartment, gathering up the items she might need: screwdriver, tiny flashlight that fit in the palm of her hand, metal nail file. She pulled her cell phone and apartment key from her bag. Then she found her camera in the desk drawer and inserted a new roll of film. She jammed the items into the waist pack, except for the small key, which she stuck in the pocket of her jeans where she could find it without rummaging through the pack.

Ten minutes later she was driving north onto the reservation, trying to recall everything John O'Malley had said about the shadow ranch. Armed guard at the entrance. Dirt road over the ridge into the village, guards around the periphery. When she was a child, she'd gone to the ranch with her grandfather to buy a bull. There was no guardhouse then, no village. Just a log ranch house where she'd sat at the kitchen table and licked at the sucker Mrs. Sherwood had given her. Through the window, she'd watched her grandfather and Mr. Sherwood leaning onto the top rail of the fence, the black bull pawing at the ground on the other side.

She turned west at Fort Washakie and began winding up a graveled road. Dusk was moving down the slopes like a storm. She tried to fix the map of the ranch in her mind. Ranch house, barn and corral, a couple of shacks. The dynamite would be in one of the shacks, away from the house.

She turned right where the road branched into a Y and continued climbing. The gravel road stopped, and the Bronco bounced along the dirt two-track that cut through the boulders and scraggly pines spilling down the slope. Around a bend, in the gray light, a small wood structure with a peaked roof came into view.

She turned off the headlights, let up on the accelerator, and crept forward. The guardhouse was coming closer.

And then she saw the clearing outside the passenger window. She maneuvered out of the two-track, across a narrow ditch, and through the clearing. She set the Bronco under a canopy of branches, the bumper nosing against a boulder, and cut the engine. The guardhouse was about a hundred feet away.

She waited, not breathing, half-expecting the guard to appear in the rearview mirror. The wind hissed in the trees around her. She was alone. She tried to locate her position on the map in her mind. The road to the ranch cut over the ridge on the south. Guards could be patrolling the road. She had to stay north and work her way upward around the trees and boulders.

She got out and, keeping her eyes on the guardhouse, buckled on her waist pack. Then she ducked low and started through the trees, her sneakers crunching the pine needles. The air was clogged with odors of pine and dried earth. She moved from shadow to shadow, plotting the route as she went, staying close to the branches that scratched at her hands and pricked at her T-shirt and jeans.

The line of trees gave way to another clearing with patches of grass and scrub brush at the base of the slope. On the left, the two-track intersected with the dirt road that curved out of sight. The guardhouse was close; she could see a shadow moving inside.

She moved back into the trees. A large man filled the doorway, then stepped outside. The white buckskin shirt and trousers, the flat, round face and ponytail—she took all of it in, but her gaze fastened on the rifle in his hands. He walked down the two-track, glancing in the direction she'd come, then swung around and started into the clearing.

She held very still, watching him come closer. The rifle, a black cannon pointing toward her. He stopped, turned around, and went back into the guardhouse. A light flickered on, and the guard hunched over a shelf, as if he were writing something. He was making out a report!

She ran across the clearing and, still running, started up the slope. Darkness was coming on fast. It was getting harder to see. The ground rose steeply beneath her; she could feel the pull in her calf muscles.

She leaned onto the cold surface of a boulder and gasped for breath. A wall of rock loomed above, too high to climb. She edged along the base until she came to a place where the boulders looked manageable. Jamming one foot into a crevice, she propelled herself upward, the air burning in her lungs. She steadied herself and lunged for a higher boulder.

And then she saw the flash of white as another guard came along the top of the ridge, rifle slung over one shoulder. She held still, the edge of the boulder cold and jagged against her palms. She could feel the guard's eyes on her.

The seconds crawled past. It was a long time—a life-time—before she heard the shush of footsteps rocking away, as if the man were limping. She edged along the boulder until she could see the white suit silhouetted against the gray sky, the dark head bobbing. Then she pulled herself onto the top and, crouching low, darted across the flat, tree-less ridge.

Directly below, sheltering in a stand of cottonwoods, was the dark shadow of a log ranch house with dim lights twin-kling in the windows. Behind the house were the shadows of the barn and two small sheds. In the meadow to the left was the village: about twenty tipis arranged around a clear-ing filled with white figures circling silently around the bonfires. The orange flames licked at the white clothing.

A crowd was milling about the tipi that stood apart from the others, facing the east. Orlando's tipi, she realized. The tipis of the leading men were always set apart. People ducked in and out of the opening, a deliberate intensity in the motion. She was wondering if Orlando himself might appear, when, out of the corner of her eye, she saw the flash of white moving toward her on the ridge.

She slid down the slope and crouched behind a boulder, still watching the guard. Coming closer. Then he turned and started back the way he'd come. He was dragging his left leg.

Vicky began working her way downward, slicing off the slope in dog legs. She reached the bottom and sprinted through the cottonwoods toward the house. She stopped next to the porch that extended across the front, watching the windows for some movement inside. There was nothing.

After a moment, she walked up the steps and peered through one of the windows. Pushed against the living room wall were several tables covered with computers and monitors with white, ghostly lights shining into the shadows. Odd, after all these years, how she remembered the interior: living room, dining area, and kitchen on the left; bedroom on the right. But the wood-framed sofa and chairs, the crocheted doilies over the backs, the braided rug were gone.

She moved past the door to the other window. She could make out a cot and a small table. There were no sounds. The house was vacant.

She stepped back and tried the door. To her surprise, it opened and she went inside. There were no cabinets or chests in the living room, nothing in which to store dynamite. She pulled her flashlight out of her pack, went into the kitchen, and started flinging open the cabinet doors. The tiny beam played over paper plates, a can of coffee, and in one cabinet, stacks of brown prescription bottles. She focused the beam on one of the labels: James Sherwood. Valium. Take two pills daily for muscle spasms. The beam moved to another label: James Sherwood. Vicodin-ES. Take two pills daily for pain.

She ran the light over the other labels: the same prescriptions from different pharmacies. Some pharmacies were in Denver, others in Riverton and Lander. It struck her that Sherwood had been stockpiling the drugs. She shook several bottles. They were empty.

She retraced her steps through the living room to the bedroom. The closet was empty. She checked under the cot. Nothing.

She went back into the living room, leaned over a monitor, and tapped a key. The white light dissolved into a blue background with rows of brightly colored icons. She clicked on the e-mail program—there could be something, some hint of what Orlando was planning. Even that might prove the dynamite was here.

She waited until the white blocks outlined in black began to take shape. Thirty new messages flashed on the in-box, all with similar subjects: "We love you, Orlando." "Pray for us, Orlando." "My offering."

She opened the last message. "I'm sending two hundred dollars to you for your preaching. I want to join you in the new world." She opened another and another. They were like the first. She wanted to laugh. Orlando, preaching a return to the old Indian ways, using the Internet.

She clicked on bookmarks. A list of website URLs popped up. She was about to select the URL for the shadow ranch when her eyes fell on the line below—the address for the Bureau of Reclamation, Bull Lake Dam. She highlighted the box and brought up the site. A color photo of Bull Lake, like the photo in the tribal engineer's office, rolled onto the monitor. The lake wrapped into the mountain slopes, as quiet and blue as the sky.

Black lines of text started forming below. She slid into the chair in front of the monitor, not taking her eyes away. She was reading the specifications for the dam! Height, ninety feet. Materials, earth covered with concrete on the inside and boulders and rock on the outside. Capacity, 156,000 acre-feet of water. Enough—the realization made her cold—for a great flood. She scrolled back to the photo of the lake and the dam. With sickening clarity, she understood why the Lakotas had brought the stolen dynamite to the shadow ranch. Orlando intended to blow up Bull Lake Dam.

Voices, a snatch of conversation, broke into her thoughts. She glanced at the window. Shadows were moving across the porch toward the door.

❮ 27 ❯

Vicky slid off the chair and moved into the kitchen. The scuff of her sneakers was like drumbeats on the plank floor. Behind her, the front door creaked open. She lunged for the back door. The knob froze in her hand. The orange and yellow lights from the bonfires reflected in the window next to the door. It was then that she saw the man dressed in white standing out back.

She stepped away from the window, heart thumping, legs shaking, and glanced about the kitchen. Cabinets too small to hide in. Table. Three chairs. Stove. Refrigerator in the corner.

"I tell ya, somebody's here." A high-pitched, nervous voice bounced through the quiet. Light burst on in the living room and spilled into the kitchen.

"Check the bedroom." There was an edge of anger in the second voice. "I'll get the kitchen."

The sound of footsteps rose toward her. Vicky darted past the table and squeezed into the corner on the far side of the refrigerator. The footsteps stopped, and a fluorescent bulb staggered into life overhead. She blinked in the brightness

and pressed against the cool, smooth surface of the refrigerator. The man outside plastered his face against the window, his breath making a gray smudge on the glass. The
slightest turn to the left and he would be looking right at
her. She stopped breathing.

The man in the kitchen stood near the table. She could
see a slice of him: the thick shoulders and thigh beneath the
buckskin suit, the brown fist at his side. A maroon scar
seemed to pulse in his cheek. An odor of male perspiration
floated toward her. The sound of his breathing was quiet
and controlled, like that of a wolf stalking its prey, ready to
lunge at the smallest movement.

"Bedroom's clear." The high-pitched voice from the living room broke through the quiet.

The man with the scar relaxed his shoulders into a flabby
mound. He gave a wave toward the window, switched off the
light, then moved out of sight, and the footsteps, steadier,
more relaxed, receded into the living room. "Called me in
here for nothing," he said. The living room light went off.
"Get back on the ridge. This ain't the time to get nervous."

The guard outside was still peering through the window,
shining a flashlight beam over the kitchen. The slim beam
shimmered over the countertops and the table. Coming
closer. Vicky slid back along the refrigerator until her shoulder and arm jammed into the wall and the plug in an electric
socket scraped her leg.

"I seen somebody running across the ridge." An ag-
grieved, squealing sound came into the high voice. "I know
what I seen, and I ain't seein' shadows."

"Yeah? Nobody's here."

"Hold on." The high voice again. "Looks like somebody's
been messin' with this here computer."

Oh, God. She'd left the website on the monitor. She pressed her face into the smooth, cold refrigerator and tried to swallow the bile rising in her throat. She was going to be sick.

"What the hell?" The light switched on again in the living room, and now the kitchen window reflected the image of the broad-shouldered man with the scar standing next to a shorter man with one shoulder lower than the other. They bent over the monitor.

"Tol' ya somebody's—"

"Jesus, Martin," the big man interrupted. "Orlando must've sent somebody over to check the dam, that's all. We don't want no mistakes. All the same, I don't want nobody in here I don't know about." He drew himself upright and moved out of view. Vicky heard the sound of a key rattling in the front door. Then, his reflection in the window again, moving toward the kitchen. The shorter man fell in beside him, walking in a jerky motion.

Their reflections were gone from the window, and they were in the kitchen now. Vicky had a clear view of them in the shadows at the door. The man with the scar uncurled his fist, inserted a key in the lock, and yanked the door open.

"You giving orders for the prophet now, Roy?" the other Indian said.

Roy. The man with thick shoulders and the maroon scar was Roy He-Dog. The short, limping man was probably Martin Crow Elk. She was close enough to reach out and touch Ben's killers.

"Nobody's gonna bother the prophet," He-Dog said, stepping outside. "Medicine man's taking care of him. All we gotta do is follow our instructions. Can't have any mess-ups."

The door closed with a force that rattled the windowpane and ran through Vicky like an electric shock. There was another jingling noise, and she realized that He-Dog had reinserted the key and was locking her inside.

They were gone. She could hear the voices receding toward the village. She crept to the door and grabbed the knob. Rigid. Struggling against the waves of panic that flooded over her, she moved to the window. There was no one outside; the guard must have left with the others. The tipis glowed through the trees, and light from the bonfires striped the ground and sides of the barn. The perfect ad for a dude ranch, she thought: Come experience the Old West. She gave a burst of laughter that sounded like a cry.

The window was the old-fashioned type with two vertically sliding panes. She turned the lock in the center, then gripped the metal handle at the bottom and pulled. The window held fast. She examined the thick globs of paint around the edges and realized the window was painted shut. She made her way around the periphery of the house. All the windows, painted shut.

She pulled the cell phone out of her waist pack and punched in 911. The Lakotas were here now; she'd seen them. The police, Gianelli, somebody had to get here. The phone felt inert in her hand, and she stared at the tiny green letters in the readout: NO SERVICE. A sense of unreality floated over her. She was in an unreal world, far from the normal, everyday things.

She went back to the kitchen, took the screwdriver out of her waist pack, and started chipping at the frame. Little specks of paint pricked her hands. She cringed at the noise, then tried the window again. Still stuck. She stepped back.

She could keep chipping—maybe it would work—but the noise could attract the guards.

Think! she told herself.

The big man had locked the doors with a key, which meant the other guards could also have keys, and that meant an extra key might be stashed somewhere. She raised herself on her toes and groped along the top of the door frame until her fingers ran over a small piece of metal, cool and jagged, wedged in the crack. She managed to coax the metal over the lip of the frame. The key dropped at her feet.

She picked it up, unlocked the door, and ran outside, down a path to the barn, still gripping the key, trying to stay in the shadows. About thirty yards away, the tipis wrapped around an arena filled with the orange and red light of bonfires. A large crow perched on top of the pole in the center. The dancers were wheeling in slow motion through the flickering light, their long shadows moving over the tipis. At the entrance to the tipi that faced the east, a guard stood motionless, one hand gripping the black barrel of a rifle.

Vicky climbed through a log fence behind the barn, ran to a small shed, and tried the door. Locked. She moved sideways until enough light fell over the door that she could see the keyhole. She jabbed in the key, hoping the same key would fit all the locks on the ranch buildings. The lock remained rigid. Glancing back at the tipis, she inched around the corner to the window. It was black inside. She dug out her flashlight. The light beam fractured in the black glass, then spread over the shelves inside crowded with stacks of folded blankets, bolts of white cloth, industrial-sized cans of food. The labels weaved in the light: BEANS. STEWED TOMATOES. CHICKEN SOUP. In one corner was a pile of logs and branches, the kind Grandfather always kept to start campfires.

She let the light rest on each shelf for a moment. No sign of dynamite. The dynamite would be in the other shed, as far away as possible from the food and computers.

Switching off the flashlight, she picked her way past the pine branches toward the flat-roofed shed outlined against the gray sky. Through the trees, she saw the guard coming along the periphery of the village. She stood still until he was out of sight, then hurried to the door.

It was also locked, and she tried the key, but it stuck in the keyhole. She had to yank hard to disengage it. She walked around the outside. There were no windows. She could imagine the oily, pungent odor of dynamite in the darkness.

She found her nail file in the waist pack, then knelt in front of the door, shone the flashlight in the keyhole, and probed the gears with the file. It was an old lock, cast in bronze, the kind Grandfather had used on the barn. She could hear the gears clicking over.

She shoved the door open and slid inside, closing it softly behind her. Then she ran the light beam over the walls: metal shelves crowded with spurs and bit chains and folded saddle blankets. An old saddle thrown over a wooden saddle horse, and a small white box in the far corner. She moved closer and focused the beam on the black letters stamped on the side: ARAPAHO RANCH.

She set the flashlight on the dirt floor and took out her camera. The light flickered over the ceiling. Her hands shook, her fingers fumbled for the correct buttons, then she raised the camera, located the dynamite crate in the lens, and pressed the top button. Another picture, then another, moving in closer now, going down on one knee, the flash sizzling in her eyes.

The door snapped open behind her, and smoky air rushed into the small space. She felt something hard—fist? boot?—crash into her back, and she sprawled forward over the hard dirt floor. She was breathing dirt. Dirt in her nose. The gritty, bitter taste of dirt in her mouth. Another blow sent a white hot flash of pain through her ribs, and she drew in her legs and curled into herself. Before the blackness, she was aware of the low, confident voice of He-Dog floating above her: "Goddamn. A woman!"

‹ 28 ›

Father John turned off Seventeen-Mile Road into the mission grounds, the sun lost behind the mountains, the sky layered in reds and violets. He checked his watch. Almost eight-thirty. The board of directors had been meeting for thirty minutes. Father George was a stickler for starting on time.

He followed the blinking red taillights through the tunnel of cottonwoods, past the green pickup with the two Arapahos, cowboy hats pushed back, seated in front. He waved to the guards and turned onto Circle Drive. Several pickups and old cars were parked in front of the church and administration building. He stopped alongside an orange truck just as the driver's door swung open. Amos Walking Bear gripped the top of the door and lifted himself out. Another elder, Clarence Wilbur, was climbing out of the passenger seat.

"Good to see you, grandfathers," Father John said. He walked over and clapped Amos's shoulder.

The elder reached inside the cab, grabbed his cane, then waved the cane toward the alley leading to Eagle Hall.

"Okay if we come to this here big meeting?"

"Absolutely." Father John smiled at the two old men in plaid shirts and blue jeans and cowboy hats outlined against the fiery sky, faces creased in shadow. He'd been hoping Amos and some of the parish council members would attend the board of directors meeting.

He ushered the elders down the alley, Clarence hunched forward, Amos tapping the cane ahead. Old warriors more accustomed to riding than walking over the dried, hard earth. He left them at the entrance to Eagle Hall.

Then he walked back to the concrete steps in front of the administration building and took them two at a time. Cool shadows stretched across the corridor into his office. The new windowpane glowed red in the sunset. He flipped on the desk lamp and checked his messages. No message from Gianelli.

He lifted the phone. He had to warn Vicky. There was some connection between Ben and Dean, something that had gotten them both killed. And they had both gone to the shadow ranch. Vicky might stumble on the connection— he knew her; she wouldn't stop until she'd found Ben's killer. She could be sucked into the vortex of a madman.

He tried her office first: "You've reached the law office . . ."

He hit the disconnect button, tapped out her home number, and listened to the ringing. Pick up. Pick up. An electronic voice told him to leave a message.

"Call me as soon as you get in," he said to the machine. "This is John," he added.

He pressed the disconnect again, wondering how he was going to convince her to be careful, not take risks. Not take risks? That was a laugh. There was no telling what risks she

might take. He stared at the phone in his hand a moment
before dialing Gianelli's office. Another answering service.
"I have to speak to you right away, Ted," he said. "It's urgent."

Urgent. That was how Dean Little Horse had termed the
message he'd sent to Ben Holden. He replaced the receiver
and headed for the meeting.

Two long tables where the parishioners usually sat for feasts
or for donuts and coffee after Sunday Mass had been pushed
together at the end of Eagle Hall. Seated on the far side were
the directors: Father George and the bishop in the center.
The three Jesuits who had arrived this morning sat on the
left, and on the right, five other Jesuits who had trickled in
during the afternoon, heads bent over copies of the annual
report. Amos, Clarence, Leonard Bizzel, the caretaker, and
half a dozen other Arapahos were scattered around the folding chairs in front of the tables, holding up copies of the
report, squinting in the bright, fluorescent light.

"Sorry to be late." Father John took the vacant chair at
the far end, next to Father Niles Johnston, who nodded his
white head and continued running a finger down the column
of figures on the page in front of him. Amos was in the front
row, and in the elder's eyes, Father John recognized the fear
that had been gnawing at his own insides the last couple of
weeks. There was no denying the truth in the financial report.

A stapled packet of papers was handed down the table to
him. "We've been going over the finances," Father George
said.

Father John left the packet unopened. He'd written the

report, totaled up the columns again and again in the quiet of the night, hoping that each addition would yield a different sum, but it was always the same. Expenses exceeded income.

"We don't understand . . ." Father Niles hesitated, then cleared his throat and, like the university professor he'd been for thirty years, launched into a discourse on the impossibility of operating a business with accounts in the red. Indeed, no business—he was warming to the subject now—could consider being in the red *normal*.

"St. Francis is not a business." Father John set his elbows on the table and clasped his hands. He was the superior here, he reminded himself. The officer-in-charge, in the military hierarchy of the Jesuits—officer-in-charge of a backwater post—but in charge nonetheless. Not his assistant, not the directors, not even the bishop, who was leaning forward, looking at him along the line of black coats. They were advisers. They would probably advise the Provincial that the mission should be closed, but they would do so without the acquiescence of the Superior.

"What this report doesn't take into account"—Father John had waited until the other priest stopped for a breath—"are the random acts of generosity."

"Random acts?" One of the priests at the far end spoke up, making no attempt to hide the contempt in his voice. Rumbling noises of distain erupted down the line and the other priests shifted over the table, like soldiers ready to charge.

Father John went on: "Donations always arrive when we least expect them." The little miracles, he almost added. He'd depended on the little miracles for the past eight years.

He was aware of the other priests' eyes on him, the expressions of disbelief in their pale, flushed faces. But the Arapahos sat straight-shouldered, nodding, smiling. From outside came the sounds of tires on gravel, and Father John felt his muscles tense. Dear God, don't let the shooter return.

"Surely, John, you can't expect the mission to operate . . ." The dead ringer for Thomas Aquinas presenting a logical, reasoned argument. "It's foolish to presume . . . Random donations cannot be counted upon . . . Bankruptcy . . ."

The door opened and six Arapaho men filed inside. They moved silently into the last row, sat down, and dipped their heads in respect to the elders seated ahead.

"Welcome," Father John said. "We're discussing finances."

The Indians nodded.

Father Niles lifted his white head and said, "Without either an endowment or a reliable source of income—and may I inject that St. Francis has neither—how do you intend to meet the current bills?"

"That would appear to be one of the great mysteries of the universe," said the Thomistic scholar.

Father George cleared his throat. "As it happens, Father, two checks arrived in today's mail." There was a note almost of apology in his tone. "They should cover the month's expenses."

The Arapahos exchanged sideways glances. Warriors, Father John thought, watching for the next skirmish.

It came at once. "We must not ignore the other issues." Father James, his old friend from the seminary, always wanting to take the broad perspective. "The Society is stretched thin, as we know. Universities, colleges, high schools, missions, and not enough priests to fill the positions. We have to reevaluate each situation."

"You've seen our schedule of programs," Father John began.

"Yes, yes, yes." Father Niles gave an impatient wave. "Despite the programs, it appears that not everyone on the reservation would like the mission to continue."

There was a slight change in the atmosphere, a stillness falling over the hall. Finally, Father John said, "The shooting last night was an isolated incident."

"Isolated!" The bishop gave a bark of laughter. "You say it's isolated, and yet two guards are posted at the entrance to keep out other riflemen. Please, Father."

The door squealed open again, and more people crowded inside: two, three, four families, several grandmothers and elders. They filled up the remaining chairs. Leonard jumped up and began unfolding other chairs stacked along the back wall.

Amos Walking Bear got to his feet and leaned forward on the cane. "Can I speak, Father?" he said, locking eyes with him.

"Of course, grandfather." Father John could feel the impatience bristling along the table. Father Niles let out a long exhalation of breath.

"Long time ago," Amos began, the dark eyes moving along the row of priests, "hundred and twenty years ago, the chiefs made a pact with the Jesuits. You come here and teach our children and we'll give you land. We'll put up buildings and take care of the place. So the Jesuits—they was all white men—said they'd come and help the people. They kept their word, and that surprised us." There was a little undercurrent of laughter in the audience; heads started nodding. Several other Arapahos were filing through the door, finding places along the back wall.

The elder went on. "Now you come here from some other places and you say you're gonna do like the rest of the whites and go back on your word. You say—"

"I believe," the bishop interrupted, "that you're talking about the past. We have to consider the state of the mission now."

"Excuse me, but I'm talkin' about now, Bishop." Amos kept his tone polite, steady. "Mission's still here. People still need help. You gonna go back on your word?"

People were still crowding into the hall, a sea of dark faces pressing toward them. Leonard was backing through the door, dragging four chairs.

"If you insist upon looking at the matter in those terms," another Jesuit at the far end spoke up—an historian. "It would seem that, after all this time, the Society has certainly . . ."

Leonard hurried past the crowd standing along the side wall and leaned over the table. "Important message, Father," he whispered. "Phone was ringing when I went to the office for more chairs. Rose White Plume says it's an emergency." He pushed a slip of paper scribbled with a telephone number across the table.

Father John got to his feet. "Excuse me," he said, interrupting the historian in the middle of explaining the relationship between the Jesuits and the Plains Indians in 1874. "There's an emergency. Please continue." This last he directed to Father George.

Then he hurried through the crowd in the side aisle and nearly collided with another group coming through the door. He waved them inside, then broke into a run down the alley, around the corner of the administration building, up the concrete steps. He turned on the light in his office and dialed the number.

Aunt Rose picked up on the first ring. He could feel the fear vibrating through the wires.

"Father John, grandmother. What's happened?"

"Oh, Father. I didn't know who else to call."

"Tell me what it is," he said, trying to soften the bite of impatience in his tone.

"It's Vicky."

"Is she all right?"

"I don't know. I don't think so. That's why I called you. Somebody's gotta find her."

"Find her? What are you talking about?"

"She's not home. She's not at her office. I been callin' and callin' and nobody answers. I tried callin' her boy, Lucas. He's over there with the Holden clan, but nobody answered there, either. She says she had to find a couple of Lakotas that killed Ben. She could be in trouble, and nobody around to help her!"

"Where did she go, grandmother?"

"Up in the mountains to see the shadow dancers."

"The shadow ranch?" God, she went alone to the shadow ranch. "When did she leave?"

"Four hours ago. Should've called me by now. She says the Lakotas have the dynamite. They're gonna blow up something."

Father John heard his own gasp of air, sudden and disembodied. The box Dean had wanted to tell Holden about contained dynamite! It was probably a day box that Holden—or the Lakotas—would have used to carry sticks of dynamite to someplace on the Arapaho Ranch where they intended to blow out tree stumps or build a road or pond. Vicky must have found out that the dynamite was at the shadow ranch.

And so were the killers.

He tried to remember what he'd read about Wovoka: The event would occur on the final night of a dance session. Tonight was the final night of the current session.

"Listen to me, grandmother. I want you to call the fed."

"I already did. He's got his answering machine on."

"Call him again. Leave a message. Tell him everything you've told me. Tell him he has to get up to the shadow ranch, that Vicky's in danger."

There was a sharp gasp at the other end.

"I'm going up there right away," he said. Then he said, "Try not to worry." He was talking to himself, as well as to the old woman.

He hung up, rummaged in a bottom desk drawer for a flashlight, then grabbed a jacket from the coat tree and ran for the Toyota.

It was only when he drove past the guards still parked under the trees and sped toward Seventeen-Mile Road that he remembered the board meeting. The fate of St. Francis Mission could be settled tonight, and he wouldn't be there.

◆ 29 ◆

From far away away came the sound of drumbeats calling her back to life. Vicky struggled to fight her way up through layers of blackness, dimly aware of the vibrations pulsing through the ground beneath her. Her arms and legs felt stiff, dead. She couldn't dislodge whatever was jammed in her mouth. It was foul and tasted of gasoline. It made her retch.

The drum beat faster, the sound crashing through the blackness. Footsteps thudded nearby. Men were shouting and, over the shouts, the sound of women wailing.

Vicky snapped into consciousness and blinked in the dim light. Something was going on outside. The village had been enveloped in silence, and now—drums, shouting. She tried to raise her head. Pain shot down her neck and into her shoulders. She realized she was tied up—trussed up like an animal carcass—arms pulled back, wrists looped together, ankles and legs squeezed tight. She twisted her fingers about until they grasped the rough surface of a rope—the same rope crossing over her arms and chest and squeezing her ribs against her lungs. Her head was throbbing.

She maneuvered around in a half-circle, trying to get her bearings. She was still in the shed. In the thin thread of light that traced the edges of the door, she could see the metal shelving on the right and the crate of dynamite. The dynamite was still here! That gave her an odd sense of hope. Whatever Orlando intended to destroy, he hadn't destroyed it yet. There was still time.

She had to get out of here. By pulling sideways, she could see her waist. The waist pack was gone—the screwdriver, nail file, flashlight, every piece of metal she might have used. She searched the shadows on the floor. The pack wasn't here.

The drums beat harder, cutting through a cacophony of panic—shouting and wailing—that matched her own. Her eyes raced around the walls looking for a nail, a hook, a piece of metal, something sharp, that she could reach. There was nothing, except the metal shelving that held the containers of insecticide and rodenticide.

She scooted toward the shelves, rolling her hips and shouldering herself sideways, panting through her nose, fighting back the gorge in her throat. Finally she managed to back up against the vertical metal frame.

She tried to lift herself on one hip, fingers running up the frame, searching for a sharp edge. Her fingertips brushed a crack in the metal. A loose piece jutted out, but it was too high. She couldn't get a grip on it. The rope pulled her legs, keeping them straight, like two dead stumps attached to her body. Her knees wouldn't bend; she couldn't get any leverage.

She maneuvered around, flipped onto her stomach, and lifting her legs, thrust her feet at the frame, trying to push the broken strip downward. The rope cutting into her flesh made her retch with pain. She kicked again. The frame shivered, but the broken strip stayed in place.

She lay with the side of her face pressed into the dirt floor, exhausted, breathing in dust mixed with the smell of chemicals and her own perspiration and fear. Outside people were shouting and running about. She could feel the frenzy vibrating through the shed. God, what was going on? The dance must have ended. *They*—the Lakotas, Ben's killers—would come for the dynamite. They'd come for her.

She flipped to her side and slid upward along the frame. The hard, rounded edge bit into her spine. Her fingers curled around the metal, and she pulled herself higher, wincing with the pain that ripped through the sockets of her arms. Her eyes blurred; the tears burned on her cheeks. She strained upward, forcing her fingers to climb higher— an inch, a half-inch. Something warm and wet—blood— ran along her hand.

She'd found the broken metal. She pulled as hard as she could until she felt the strip give way and bend downward, the edge cutting into her fingers. It was as sharp as a knife.

Suddenly she was aware of the silence. The drumming and shouting—when had they stopped? She was enveloped in silence, as if the shed had been deposited in the middle of the plains surrounded by the endless stillness of the sky and something else: the stillness of a tornado before it touches down.

She thrust the rope around her wrists into the sharp edge and started sawing. Up and down, pain ripping across her shoulders, numbness flowing down her arms. The tears were coming fast, blurring the shed in the dim light, until she felt as if she were moving under water. Up and down. Up and down.

There was a barely perceptible loosening, a slackening so slight she feared she'd imagined it out of her own desperation. She kept sawing, buoyed with new hope and strength. She wondered if the drums and shouting had been as frightening as the silence outside.

The rope gave way. She could raise one wrist above the other and managed to slip one hand free. She yanked at the rope until it dangled loosely around her chest and she was able to reach one arm around and rip the rag out of her mouth—the stinking rag! She took in hugh gulps of air, then tore away the rope, spasms racing down her arms.

She was scrambling upright when she heard the thud of footsteps outside.

"Get a grip on yourself." It was He-Dog, the confident voice, sharp with anger. "We got work to finish."

Vicky tugged at the rope still around her legs, then started rolling—propelling herself—across the shed to where they'd left her. Then she remembered she'd left the gag by the shelving.

"But Orlando . . ." The high, whiny voice of the man with the limp.

"Shut up!" Something blocked the light around the door, and the shed plunged into blackness.

She scooted back to the frame and threw herself facedown, hands scrambling over the dirt trying to find the gag.

"He said he was the messiah," the whiny voice went on. "He said nobody was gonna die in the new world . . ."

"I said, shut up, you fool!"

Her hand clamped over the soggy cloth. She jammed it into her mouth and started scooting sideways, pushing herself with her hands.

"We gotta keep going. Do just like we promised, so the

new world can come." The door burst open, orange-tinged light flooding into the shed. Vicky slid downward and tried to make herself small, part of the shadows.

"He's waiting for us." The boots stomped past her, as if the men had forgotten about her. "He's bringing the ancestors."

"I don't know . . ."

"Get the box. The trucks are coming up." Then, in a softer tone, "You heard what the messiah said. We gotta go on."

The men crossed back to the door as He-Dog kicked it wide open, then stepped aside and waited for the other man to haul the box outside. There was the low rumble of a truck engine cutting back.

Vicky shut her eyes; she could feel He-Dog's gaze burning into her. Then, the boots clumped out the door, and her eyes snapped open. She could see the men pushing the box into the bed of a truck, then slamming the tailgate. Someone stood by the door, the end of a cigarette glowing red in the orange light.

"Take care of the woman," He-Dog said.

"You hit her pretty hard." The high-pitched whine again. "She's dead."

He-Dog walked alongside the truck and lifted a gun out of the rack at the rear window. He handed the gun to the other Indian. "Make sure. We gotta get to the dam before somebody comes looking for her. We can't take any chances." He nodded toward the shed. "Do like I say."

And then the man with the limp stood in the doorway, blocking the light. Vicky could hear the engines revving up behind him, the tires spinning against the earth as the black barrels of the rifle turned toward her.

• • •

In the half-light of the moon breaking through the clouds, the trees on the uphill slope looked like a wilderness of spirits. Another mile, Father John guessed, before he reached the guardhouse. He'd turned off the headlights a mile or so back, and the two-track disappeared ahead in the grayness.

As he came around a curve, he saw the glow of light through the trees. He slowed down and inched forward until he spotted the narrow clearing. He jerked the wheel right, drove into the trees, and stopped a few inches behind a bumper that glinted in the dim light. Vicky's Bronco. She'd done exactly what he planned to do: avoid the guardhouse and hike over the ridge.

He found the flashlight under the seat, got out, and shone the light into the Bronco. It was stamped with her absence. The pines around the vehicle glowed in the light beam. He switched off the flashlight and gave himself a moment for his eyes to adjust in the moonlight that filtered through the branches. Gradually the darkness seemed to lift, and he walked back to the pickup.

A gunshot reverberated overhead. The retort rolled through the trees and echoed off the mountainside.

Father John dropped down alongside the pickup and waited for the next shot. A guard on top must have spotted him. Except for the wind in the trees and the sound of his own heart, an immense silence closed around him.

He waited. Only one shot. He tried to think logically. The sound had been close, yet muffled, which meant it hadn't come from on top. It must have come from the valley on the other side. From the village. Where Vicky was.

Dear God, he prayed, the only prayer he could manage. Dear God, Dear God.

He plunged into the trees, dismissing the idea of checking the toolbox in the back of the pickup for a wrench or screwdriver. There were no weapons to match a rifle.

He'd gone about thirty feet when he spotted the clearing, moonlight running like a river between the trees and the upward thrust of the ridge.

He stopped at the edge. To the left was the guardhouse, a black shadow straddling the earth a dim light inside. Something was different, he could sense it. No sign of movement. The guardhouse was deserted.

Father John stayed in the trees, trying to decide what to do. He could work his way to the guardhouse, then take the main road into the village—the shorter route. But the guard might have just stepped away for a moment, gone to check on the rifle shot. And he ran the risk of meeting other guards on the road.

He was about to cross the clearing when headlights flashed across the guardhouse. A truck roared past and turned onto the two-track. Another truck squealed out behind. Through the trees, Father John could see the headlights streaming in the direction of the reservation.

He stared after the trucks for a couple seconds, trying to grasp the logic. There was no one in the guardhouse, and the other guards could have just driven off. Something had happened, and whatever it was, it was not good. And Vicky was still at the ranch.

He plunged back into the trees, crashing through the branches that scratched at his face and hands. Then he backed the pickup onto the two-track, rammed the gear into forward, and drove for the guardhouse, headlights blazing ahead. He thumped past the opened gate and started climbing up the switchbacks that he'd taken with the Lakota two days ago.

At the summit, the road narrowed, then started downward. Father John hunched forward, gripping the wheel tight, trying to keep the tires from slipping sideways down the slope on the tight turns. An orange light glowed from the center of the village below. There were no other vehicles in sight, no sign of movement, and the absence of human activity created a void that struck him as more ominous than a phalanx of guards. It was the void at the end of the world.

He bounced across the meadow past the log house and hit the brake. The pickup was still rolling forward when he grabbed the flashlight, jumped out, and ran toward the village. Bonfires were scattered about the arena, casting orange and red shadows over the white tipis.

He was thirty feet away when he saw the large white mounds, like mounds of snow, among the bonfires. He stopped. He was breathing hard, his heart was thumping. The reality came to him in fragments, small enough to absorb one at a time, until he understood. The crumpled bodies in white, the naked arms and legs, the hands splayed in the dirt, the bare feet and stray moccasins flung about. Gray smoke that smelled like charred cottonwood hung over the arena. He had a sense that he'd stepped into the past, and the heaps of bodies lying around the bonfires, locked in the silence of death, were Chief Big Foot's followers. That the massacre at Wounded Knee was still taking place.

He made himself go to the nearest body—a young woman. He dropped down on both knees beside her, grabbing for her wrist and probing for a pulse. Where was the pulse? Her eyes were closed, as if she'd dropped into a peaceful sleep. It was a couple seconds before he could feel it: the almost imperceptible rhythm of her blood coursing through her veins. He saw the slight movement of her chest. She was breathing! He knew instantly that she was drugged—drugged, but alive—and he felt almost sick with relief.

He got to his feet and went to the next body. A round-faced, pudgy man, his eyelids flickering, his breath slow and quiet. Dropping down again, Father John felt the steady pulse in the thick neck. Then he got to his feet and went to the next dancer and the next, working his way around the arena, some part of his mind keeping count: five, six, seven. A total of twenty-six dancers, drugged and unconscious. Alive, thank God, alive.

He looked around. Vicky had to be here somewhere. In the house, the sheds. He'd started across the arena when he saw the flap thrown back on Orlando's tipi and candles inside flickering over the canvas walls. He ran over and stooped inside. Across from the opening, Orlando lay on a buffalo robe spread over three hay bales. He was dressed in white buckskin, arms crossed over his chest, bare feet emerging from the trousers, black hair spread out like a fan. Three small candles at his head gave off a yellowish light and the faint smell of wax and sulfur.

Father John walked over and lay one hand on the cool, soft wrist, trying to detect some sign of life. The flesh was inert, the man's chest was still. "May God forgive you," he said.

Then, with a sickening clarity, he realized the man had been *laid out*. He must have died earlier, and then what? Had the dancers wanted to follow him into the afterworld? It must have been part of a plan. The dancers were supposed to die, like Orlando. The guards had probably distributed whatever drugs they'd taken, but something had gone wrong and the drugs hadn't worked the way Orlando had intended. But the guards had already sped off.

And Vicky could be with them.

He wanted to believe, but a part of him knew that if they'd found her here, they would never have allowed her to live. The sound of the rifle shot screamed through his mind. They'd shot her. Left her somewhere in the village. In one of the tipis, in the ranch house or the barn or the sheds. He would search every inch of the shadow ranch until he found her.

He lurched through the opening and started toward the other tipis. The breeze was hot and smoky, reeking of death.

On the far side of the arena, beyond the prone figures of the dancers and the bonfires, almost imperceptible but present nonetheless: a moving shadow. He ran toward it, then stopped. Vicky emerged from between two tipis, face blanched, eyes wide in shock.

◆ 30 ◆

She walked into the arena as if she hadn't seen him, arms extended, gaze darting around the drugged dancers. The bonfires glowed orange and red on her face.

"Vicky!" Father John shouted, but she kept walking. He shouted her name again, then grabbed her by the shoulders, stopping her in place. He turned her toward him, aware of the warmth of her, the reality of her, in his hands. "Are you all right?"

She tilted her head back and blinked up at him, as if she were trying to bring into focus some specter that had materialized in front of her. He felt her trembling beneath his hands.

"Orlando killed them!" Vicky strained toward the white mounds.

"They're unconscious, Vicky," he said. "We have to get help. They've been drugged."

"Drugged!" She let out a little cry and cupped one hand over her mouth. Then she said, "My God, John. It's started. They've gone into the shadow world to welcome the ancestors. The new world is coming. The Lakotas are going to blow up Bull Lake Dam."

He could read the truth in her eyes, as if fragments had arranged themselves into a coherent whole that he could finally grasp. Before the new world could come, the old world had to be washed away. The Lakotas had stolen the dynamite for Orlando. Bull Lake Dam! The water would crash down over the reservation. Ethete, Arapaho, Riverton—St. Francis Mission.

"We have to get to a phone," he said, taking her arm and guiding her through the tipis toward the pickup.

Father John drove down the two-track and onto the graveled road, taking the bends on two tires, Vicky tapping at the buttons on his cell phone. "No service," she screamed.

They were careening toward Fort Washakie when the sound of sirens rose like a wall of granite down the road, then the red, blue, and yellow lights flashed into the night. Father John pulled onto the shoulder as three BIA police cars sped by.

"They're on the way to the ranch." He could hear the feeling of relief in his voice.

"How . . . ?" Vicky turned toward him. She was gripping the phone in one hand. A residue of yellow light washed over her.

"Aunt Rose called them," he said, pulling the pickup back onto the road.

She started tapping the buttons again. "It's working," she cried. Then, into the phone: "Vicky Holden." She was shouting. "Get medical help to the shadow ranch. The dancers are unconscious. They've been drugged." She hesitated, then plunged on. "They took Valium and Vicodin. I saw the empty prescription bottles. And now, two Lakotas are on the way to Bull Lake to blow up the dam. That's right. They have dynamite."

Vicky was quiet a moment, then she clicked off the phone. "There's an officer on patrol in the area. He's on his way."

Dear God, Father John thought, let the officer get there in time.

Father John slowed through Fort Washakie and turned north. Highway 287 lengthened into the darkness beyond the headlights. There were no other vehicles. He jammed down on the accelerator. Black shadows of trees raced by outside his window.

"Orlando has everything planned," Vicky said. "He wants to make sure his prophecy comes true. He's going to destroy the reservation."

"Orlando's dead, Vicky." Father John glanced over. She was staring at him, pinpricks of light flashing in her eyes.

"I don't understand. He was waiting for the new world. Why did he die and not the . . ." She halted, as if another thought had intercepted the one she'd been following. "The prescriptions were his," she said. "He must have built up a tolerance, so he took more pills than the dancers. He must have taken an overdose."

Possible, Father John thought. The man was sick. He'd probably been using the drugs for some time. He must have taken a lot to make sure they worked.

Father John eased up on the accelerator and guided the pickup around a bend. The road cut through a shadowy landscape of treeless bluffs, the flat surfaces soaking up the moonlight. He was acutely aware of Vicky beside him, her profile outlined in the moonlight.

He looked at her. She was alive; thank God, she was alive. "I was afraid they'd killed you," he said. "What happened?"

She began slowly, then hurried along, the story spilling out: the climb up the ridge, the house, the guards, the dynamite box, the shed. He could feel his muscles tense as she talked. They'd knocked her unconscious in the shed; she could have been killed.

"They came back for the dynamite." Her eyes were still on him. "After everything got quiet, they came back. They took the box outside, and I heard He-Dog say, 'Shoot the bitch.' Crow Elk came back into the shed." Hysteria had begun to seep into her voice.

He reached over and took her hand. "You're okay, Vicky. You're safe."

She gripped his hand in both of hers. "He was pointing the rifle at me, John. I could see down the barrel. It was a long, black tunnel. It was very still. And then I saw the fear in his eyes. He was looking at something he'd never seen before and it was horrible, and that's when I knew he couldn't do it. He jerked the rifle up and everything exploded around me, and he ran out. I heard the trucks drive off."

Father John was quiet for a long time, watching the road ahead, unable to imagine a world in which she did not exist. He tried to follow what she was saying: how Orlando must have sent the Lakotas to the Arapaho Ranch to steal the dynamite. There would be dynamite on the ranch to clear out stumps, build roads, create waterholes; Orlando would have known that.

"Ben could have called Gianelli," Father John said.

"Admit somebody had stolen dynamite from him? You didn't know Ben."

"I knew him." Recovering alcoholic. Determined to get *everything* back that belonged to him, including Vicky.

"He went after the Lakotas himself." Vicky paused. "I don't understand how he knew they'd gone to the shadow ranch."

"Dean Little Horse," Father John said. "He was there for three days, trying to get Janis to leave. He must have seen the dynamite, and . . ." A new idea shoved its way into his mind. "He wrote the operating software for the gate at Bull Lake Dam. He must have guessed what Orlando had in mind. If Orlando blew up the dam, he would cause the flood he'd been prophecizing. Dean left the ranch on Sunday, went to his office, and e-mailed Ben Holden."

Neither spoke for a few moments, then Vicky said, "They were alike, Dean and Ben. Dean had his own reason for not going to Gianelli. He was probably trying to protect the girl. He didn't want the fed to go to the ranch, not with Janis still one of Orlando's followers."

It made sense, Father John was thinking, except for one thing. Dean must have begged Janis to leave with him, but she hadn't gone with him. And yet, she went to Dean's apartment on Sunday evening, looking for him. Maybe she'd decided to leave the ranch after all. But it was too late by then. The Lakotas had already found Dean. And she'd gone back to the ranch, back to Orlando.

He tried to follow what Vicky was saying, something about Janis Beaver staying with Aunt Rose and stealing the gun. "The perfect weapon," she said. "It could be traced right back to me." The sound of her laughter was forced and tight. It drifted over the thrum of the tires on the asphalt.

They were climbing now, the pickup bouncing over the narrow road. The slopes on either side blocked out the moonlight, so that only the headlights shone through the darkness. He could still see Janis Beaver, huddled in the tipi, the pretty face hard with certitude. Dean had come for her. He'd loved her, but in the end, she'd chosen Orlando. And now she was lying unconscious—God, let the ambulances be there!

Father John wheeled through a sharp curve, trying to remember. Where was Janis lying? There were several young women close together by one of the bonfires. Had she been among them? In another group? A solitary mound in front of one of the tipis? Had all the faces simply blurred together in his own shock?

The road was climbing along Bull Creek; the trees were sparse now, crowded out by clumps of willows that looked black and grotesque in the moonlight. He eased on the brake and peered ahead for the turnoff into the area of Bull Lake.

He steered around another curve, then spotted the break in the willows. He turned left. The willows crept close to the sides of the pickup, the tires chattered on the gravel. He could see the dam ahead, a black wall rising out of the earth, backlit by the moonlight. The road veered to the right, climbing toward the top of the dam. Another quarter-mile, and he could see the lake, an enormous body of black water. A metallic sheen rippled over the surface.

A white Wind River police car, a kaleidoscope of lights whirling over the roof, blocked the road ahead. The driver's door hung open. Father John jammed down the brake pedal. In the headlights, he could see the bulky figure slumped next to the door.

‹ 31 ›

ather John got out and ran to the prone body. A hole
as big as a crater gaped in the officer's chest and a pool
of oil-black blood was soaking into the fragments of his
blue uniform shirt. The holster on the black belt was pushed
back, the flap still snapped over the gun handle. Father John
lay a hand against the man's neck. It was as inert as leather.

He looked up through the whirling red and blue lights
at the sky. It was immense, a vast and impersonal darkness
with moon-edged clouds moving eastward and breaking up
at intervals to reveal a scattering of stars that flickered in
the void. They were too late. The Lakotas were here, and
when the officer had tried to stop them, they'd shot him. It
was a moment before he could summon a prayer: "God, have
mercy on us."

He got to his feet. Stepping around the body, he reached
inside and grabbed the black radio. He fumbled with the
buttons a moment. A shrill noise mixed with static, then a
woman's voice. "Go ahead."

"This is Father O'Malley," he managed. "The officer at
Bull Lake . . ." The name, what was the man's name? He

leaned over the body, unable to read the blood-smeared badge. "He's been shot. Get some other officers up here. The dam's going to be dynamited."

"Cars are on the way, Father." The woman was shouting at the other end. "Father, you better get out of there."

He replaced the radio and turned to Vicky. The blue and red lights washed intermittently over her face and black T-shirt. "The Lakotas are at the spillway," she said.

She was right, he knew. There was no movement along the top of the dam, no sign of anyone, only the flat concrete surface that held back the lake from the darkness dropping away below. The Lakotas would plant the dynamite deep inside the spillway; the dynamite would blow a hole in the base; the water would surge through and bring down the dam. And the flood . . .

"Listen to me," he said. "This whole place is going to be obliterated. Get the flashlight out of the pickup. Start climbing. Climb as high as you can. Please, Vicky."

She stared at him in disbelief. "For goddsakes, John. We have to get to the spillway." She shouldered past and threw herself into the passenger seat.

He got in behind the wheel, and started maneuvering the pickup backward into a narrow clearing. There was no time to argue, and it wouldn't do any good. She would never run away. They hurtled down a narrow path that angled along the side of the dam.

In the gray light, he could see the boulder and rock face of the dam rising higher and higher outside Vicky's window as they dropped toward the creek below. The sound of running water grew louder, and then the creek came into view, a narrow funnel of silver pouring out of the concrete spillway that resembled the entrance to a tunnel. The cuts of other service roads converged through the brush and rock.

Vicky leaned forward, braced her hands on the dashboard, and stared down at the roads. "They've already left," she yelled. "The trucks are gone!"

Father John tightened his grip on the wheel. The roads below were vacant. He felt a stillness settling over him—the stillness of death. The Lakotas had already set the dynamite and gotten out of there. The dam would blow at any moment.

They were close to the creek now; he could feel the cool moisture in the air. He turned right, and the pickup lurched to a stop in a clump of willows. "Wait here," he said. "Let me take a look around."

"It's my world that's about to be destroyed, John." Vicky threw her door open and started to slide out.

He took hold of her arm. "Listen to me, Vicky. I need you to stay here. Watch for the trucks, do you understand? You can see the roads from here. The Lakotas might not have finished setting the dynamite. They could come back."

It was a moment before she nodded. He grabbed the flashlight from under the seat, got out, and started through the willows, moving at a diagonal toward the edge of the spillway, sweeping the flashlight beam ahead. The squish of his boots in the muck mixed with the sounds of the creek. He was breathing in the damp spray.

He reached the base of the dam and started edging along the sloped rock-faced wall. At the entrance, he grabbed the rough corner and swung himself around. It was pitch black inside. The flashlight beam was no more than a thin strand of light penetrating the darkness. He waved the beam along the wall, then across the opposite wall. Webs of green moss crawled over the concrete and glistened in the light. Deep inside, almost lost in the blackness, was the faint metallic sheen of the gate. Water ran beneath and spilled out into the creek, sending up little jets of spray.

He was about to start up the spillway when the light beam hit the dynamite. Twelve sticks taped together, dangling from some kind of hook embedded in the concrete. Extending from the middle tube were two thin leg wires—one blue, the other yellow. They ran above the surface of the water, then angled out the entrance.

He kept the light beam on the wires: along the creek, into the willows. Suddenly they disappeared. He stooped close to the ground and pushed aside the branches until the beam found the yellow wire, thin and stiff, running in a straight line into an area of trampled grasses. He traced the wire toward the small metal object glinting in the light.

He moved closer. A clock, he could see it clearly now: the black numerals circling the white face and the yellow wire attached to the hour hand. A black wire ran from the minute hand. He struggled to pull from his memory everything he'd ever heard about dynamite. The tiniest electric spark—that much he knew—and it would detonate.

He went down on one knee and shone the light over the wiring, conscious of the sound of his own breathing against the water lapping over the rocks. The hour hand was on 12; the minute hand was a little more than one minute before 12. One minute, and the hands would touch, and when they touched, an electrical charge would shoot through the wires to the dynamite.

Something had to deliver the charge—a battery. That was it! The blue wire he'd lost in the willows was attached to a battery; so was the black wire on the minute hand, making a complete circuit. He had to detach the wires.

He reached for the clock, then drew back his hand. The minute hand was a hair's breath from 12. The wires so close, he could accidentally jam them together and set off the dynamite. He had one minute now to find the battery.

He started following the black wire from the minute hand, crouching low, stumbling through the bramble, throwing back the willow stalks, counting off the seconds. The flashlight flickered off, then on again.

Twenty-five seconds, twenty. The wire twisted through the brush and disappeared in the undergrowth. He stepped backward, picked up the trail again, then lunged into the brush. He had it now, the tiny black wire snaking close to the ground. He kept the light on top of it all the way to the oblong black box set on a bed of willow branches.

Ten seconds. He threw himself toward the box and fell on his knees. The wire from the minute hand looped over the positive pole. The blue wire attached to the dynamite was twisted around the negative pole. He yanked at one wire, then the other. They strangled the poles, refusing to let go. He threw down the flashlight and fumbled for the end of the black wire and started unwinding it, his mind still ticking off the seconds.

Six. Five. Four.

"Come on," he shouted, yanking as hard as he could. The wire popped free, and the recoil sent him backward into the mud and trampled branches. He lay still for several minutes, gasping for air, his heart pounding against his ribs.

He didn't see the shadow until it flickered across the beam of light.

‹ 32 ›

"**W**hat the hell . . ." a voice shouted.

Father John felt something hard crash against his ribs and he flipped sideways. His face pushed into the wet, mushy earth and sharp roots. The crash came again and again, his shoulder this time, then his back. A jagged line of pain ran down his spine and into both legs. The pain seared his lungs. He couldn't breathe.

He clawed at the ground and managed to get enough leverage to raise himself up so that he could see the large, broad-shouldered Indian standing over him, the white buckskin trousers splashed with mud. Moonlight splayed across his dark face, and Father John could see the scar carved into the man's cheek. Orlando's body guard, a rifle gripped in one hand.

"It's that damn priest," the man hollered to a shadow on the other side of the creek, half-hidden in the willows.

"What'd he do? Pull one of the battery wires?" Another Indian started wading toward them, boots slapping at the water. He climbed onto the bank, slipped backward, then caught himself and stumbled forward, dragging his left leg.

Mud covered his buckskin pants almost to his knees.

"We gotta kill him, Martin," the man with the scar said.

Martin Crow Elk, Father John thought, the Indian who'd taken him over the ridge to the shadow ranch. The other man was Roy He-Dog, Orlando's bodyguard. He wondered what kind of fake IDs they'd used to convince Ted Gianelli they were not the Lakotas he was looking for.

"Don't see it makes any difference how he dies," Crow Elk said, his voice high-pitched with the whine of an adolescent. "He oughtta die like the rest of the evil ones." He leaned over and examined the battery. "All we gotta do is put the wires back and reset the clock, and they're all gonna die."

He-Dog seemed to consider this a moment, then he wheeled around and started back into the willows. "I'll take care of the clock. Ten minutes'll be enough for us to get out of here." His voice trailed behind him like a shadow, and Father John understood. The two men had set the clock and given themselves enough time to drive up one of the roads on the other side of the dam. When the dam didn't explode, they'd come back.

Crow Elk stooped over, his left leg outstretched, his moccasin slipping in the marshy earth. He picked up the wires.

"Hold on," Father John shouted. It took all of his breath. He gasped for more air. "This isn't what Wovoka wants."

"What!" The Indian looked up. "What right you got, talk about Wovoka. What'd you know?"

"I know what Wovoka preached to the Ghost Dancers. Live a good life, live in peace."

"Yeah? Well, that changed after the soldiers came and killed Big Foot's people, dumped the bodies in a trench, the last believers. Nothing but filth, those white troops. Earth's gonna be cleansed of filth in the regeneration. Wovoka give Orlando the instructions on what to do."

"No, you're wrong." Father John raised himself against the pain until he was sitting upright. He wrapped an arm around his ribs and fought for another gulp of air. "Wovoka was a holy man. He knew about the massacres that had happened before, but he still preached peace. He never wanted innocent people to die."

"Shut up." The Indian bent over the wires.

"You dynamite the dam," Father John managed, "and hundreds of people will die. Innocent people, Martin. Both Indians and whites. I don't think you want to kill innocent people. You could've shot Vicky, but you didn't. Who killed the officer up there?" Father John tilted his head toward the top of the dam. "It was He-Dog, wasn't it?"

The Indian glanced between the wires and the battery. "Righteous people gonna live in the new world, soon's the flood's gone and the earth's clean. Orlando's gonna come back. He's gonna bring Wovoka."

"Wovoka will condemn you," Father John said. The pain ratcheted through his voice.

The Indian threw his shoulders back and shouted. "You don't know what you're talking about."

Father John could hear the break in the man's voice, like a spidery crack in glass. He started to his feet, coughing with the effort, aware of He-Dog crashing back through the willows.

From somewhere in the darkness came the faint wail of a siren.

"Clock's set," He-Dog shouted. He held the rifle low along his thigh and bent his head in the direction of the siren. "Fix the battery. Let's get outta here."

"Think of Wovoka, Martin." Father John was almost upright now. He dug his boots hard into the soggy ground to steady himself. "You blow up the dam, Wovoka won't want you with him. You'll be an outcast. You'll be alone."

"Shut up, white man!" He-Dog's voice sounded like the howl of a wild animal. He raised the rifle and hunched forward, a slow, deliberate motion. His top lip rolled back; the scar pulled taut across his cheek.

Father John had a sense of time collapsing around him, compressed into a finite moment of consciousness.

"Drop the gun!" Vicky stood up in the willows, pointing a long-nosed handgun at Roy He-Dog. "Now," she yelled, moving forward and planting her feet apart. "I'll shoot you."

Father John kept his gaze on the gun in her hands. She must have climbed back up the road. He could still see the gun inside the officer's holster. Now she held it steady, not more than three feet away from the back of the Indian's head.

He-Dog reached down and set the rifle in the mud.

The next thing Father John saw was Martin Crow Elk lurching sideways, pulling the wires toward the battery. Father John leapt forward and crashed against the Indian, knocking him to the ground. He rolled over, grabbing his stiff leg and sobbing.

Father John took hold of the wires and, stumbling to keep his balance, ground them beneath his boots until they disappeared into the mud. Then he picked up the battery and hurled it as hard as he could in the direction of the creek, grunting out loud with the pain that seared his ribs.

He walked over and unpeeled Vicky's fingers from the gun. The sirens were coming closer, a distinct, sharp sound that banked against the concrete dam.

He-Dog stood motionless. "You're gonna pay, white

man," he said. "You and this white woman that used to be Indian are gonna pay. You got no right . . ."

"Get down." Father John waved the gun.

The Indian shot him a look of hatred, then began folding himself downward. Onto his knees, his hands. Finally he stretched out, the side of his face against the mud.

Father John picked up the rifle. Then he slipped the officer's pistol into the back of his belt.

He went over to Vicky and slipped his arm around her shoulders. "It's over," he said.

She slumped toward him, as if she'd finally understood what she was staring at: Crow Elk sprawled on the ground, still grasping his leg. He was sobbing quietly, a kind of relief in the sound. He-Dog lay on the ground as still as stone.

"I saw two men wading across the creek," Vicky said, her voice choked with tears. "I was so afraid for you. I ran up the road to the officer's body and . . ."

"I know," Father John said. She was shaking beneath his arm.

It was then that Father John heard the low rumble of an engine kicking over. Then, headlights flayed the darkness on the other side of the creek. There was the sound of tires skidding in gravel. He saw a dark pickup plunging up a track at the far side of the dam. The pickup reached the top of the ridge, then taillights winked up at the sky as the truck dipped south, toward the reservation.

He sensed Vicky tense next to him. "There were others," she cried. "They're getting away."

"The police'll be here any minute. They'll stop them." He hoped that was true. "We'll wait."

•　•　•

Vicky listened to the tires humming on the asphalt. A soothing sound, she thought. She lay her head against the back of the seat and watched the stripe of orange light widening in the sky. John was quiet beside her, lost in his own thoughts, she guessed, his gaze locked on the road moving toward them.

It hadn't been a long wait at the dam. Ten minutes at most before the sound of sirens had filled the air and headlights shone through the pines. And then, crouching shadows darted toward the spillway, like troops moving into a village occupied by the enemy, flashlight beams bouncing in the air. One officer had reached the spillway and started inside, moving through a bubble of light. Other officers materialized on the slope above.

"Drop the rifle and raise your hands."

She'd watched Father John lay the rifle on the ground and lift his arms before putting her own hands into the air. The officers were swarming around He-Dog and Crow Elk.

"Father John!" An officer stepped past the others and shone a flashlight toward them. The light had blinded her a moment.

"You wanna tell me what the hell went on around here?" He threw a glance back at the officers handcuffing the two Indians, then holstered his own gun.

Vicky remembered sinking down into the willows, grasping at the stalks for balance, and all the while, John's voice above her, explaining, explaining. After a while—time had lost meaning—she realized that Gianelli's white Blazer and a line of Fremont County sheriff's cars were parked near the spillway. The explanations had started again and—odd, when she thought about it now—she'd been riveted by the way Gianelli's thick fingers had maneuvered a pen across a tiny pad in his fleshy palm.

At some point, John O'Malley had leaned over, taken her arm, and guided her to her feet. One of the sheriff's deputies would retrieve her Bronco and bring it to Lander tomorrow, he'd told her. He was going to take her home.

Now John O'Malley's voice floated through the quiet. Was she all right? He must have asked before, because he wanted to know if she was *sure*. In the dim light of the dashboard, she could see the concern in the set of his shoulders, the tight curve of his hand on the wheel. She assured him that she was fine.

"It takes a while for shock to wear off." He reached over and touched her hand, keeping his eyes on the road.

"I would have killed them," she said after a moment.

"But you didn't."

The small space, the close air, the priest a few inches away: she felt as if she were in the confessional. "You don't understand. I *wanted* to kill them for what they'd done to Ben."

He didn't respond. The trees passing her window stood out in relief against the pale early-morning light. She was thinking that he wouldn't want anything more to do with her, now that he'd seen the shadows of her life.

"There will be a reckoning, Vicky," he said finally. "He-Dog and Crow Elk will be looking at charges of murder, and Gianelli will probably come up with a lot of other charges. They'll spend the rest of their lives in prison."

"What about the guards in the other truck?" None of the officers had mentioned the other truck.

"They'll find them. Every officer in the county's looking for them. They'll be held accountable."

"And Orlando? What about his accountability? He escaped. He's dead."

"He'll answer to God."

Vicky turned to the window and combed her fingers through her hair. Outside the pines were changing from black to dark green. John O'Malley was a priest. He believed in justice, if not in this world, then in the next. A powerful reason to believe in an afterlife, she thought, since there was seldom justice here. She found herself straining to believe along with him. Justice had to exist somewhere.

The pickup took the curve into the northern reaches of Lander. The street lamps along the curbs looked yellow and faded in the early light. There was a sense of unreality to the brick bungalows, the parked cars, the store fronts that reflected the glow of headlights as they passed. Other headlights blinked in the opposite direction, then turned at an intersection, leaving them moving alone through a shadow world.

They turned into a parking space in front of her building and stopped at the double glass doors. She could see the lobby, dimly lit and one-dimensional, like a photo.

She struggled to hide the tremor that pulsed through her. It was over, she told herself. Ben's killers were in custody. The guards in the truck would be arrested. Orlando was dead. *Over.* The tremor remained, as if her body refused to accept the reality.

John got out and walked around the front. She could see that his shirt was caked with mud, and dried mud clung to his jeans.

Her door opened. "I'll walk you in."

She slid out beside him and started up the walk, her legs wobbly beneath her. He reached past and opened the glass door. They took the stairs to the second floor in silence.

In silence, down the corridor past the closed doors with brass numbers high in the center, 4B, 3B, 2B.

Vicky stopped in front of 1B and fumbled in her jeans pocket for the slim key. "I can put on some coffee," she said, but she knew, even before he began shaking his head, that he would decline.

"It's almost morning. I have to take the six o'clock Mass."

She turned toward him. "You came after me. Thank you."

"Aunt Rose was worried about you." He paused. "So was I."

Auntie, she thought. The old woman had probably been awake all night, pacing the floor, worrying about her. She had to call Aunt Rose right away.

Vicky was about to thank him again when he placed both arms around her and drew her to him. She allowed herself to relax in his strength a moment and to savor the feeling of being at home.

"It'll take time to get over Ben's death, Vicky," he said, releasing her. She felt suddenly adrift again, on her own.

"If you ever want to talk, you know where I'll be," he was saying. In any case"—trying for a smile now that she sensed was hard and off the mark somehow—"I'll be here for a while."

She understood. John O'Malley was only at St. Francis Mission for a while.

Vicky watched him walk back down the corridor and disappear behind the door to the stairs. Then she inserted the key in the lock and grasped the knob. It didn't move. She jiggled the key again. This time the knob turned, and she realized that she'd locked the door on the first try, which meant it had been unlocked. Curious, she thought, as she stepped into the living room and closed the door behind her. She always locked her door in town.

The apartment was still. The shadows of the furniture—sofa, chairs, desk, bookcases—stood out against the dim light glowing through the windows.

A musky odor, like the odor of a wild animal, hit her. And something else—the faintest noise of a breath stifled in mid-gasp. For a moment, she didn't move. Then she stepped to the table lamp and turned on the switch.

The lamp burst into life and the shadows retreated to the edges of the room. On her left, in front of the bookcase, stood a small, pretty girl, with darting black eyes and black hair that hung in tangled ropes over the shoulders of her white gown. A red crescent moon leaped out from the bright blue stripe painted on the front. The skirt was splashed with mud. In an instant, Vicky knew that it was Janis Beaver, aiming a rifle at her heart.

‹ 33 ›

"**G**et ready to die, bitch."

The girl raised the barrel until Vicky could see the notches of the rifling. The picture came to her with great clarity now, as if the scene were playing out in front of her. It was Janis who had driven the truck up to the ridge on the other side of the creek. Janis who had guarded the dam while the two men set the dynamite. Janis—my God, it must have been the girl—who had shot the officer.

"Why didn't you shoot me at the dam?" Vicky felt completely focused and calm. Survival was all that mattered. Everything else faded into the shadows at the periphery of the room. She had to keep the girl talking and watch for the chance to distract her.

"Why, Janis?" she pushed on. "You must've had a clear shot."

Confusion. Regret. A mixture of emotions came into the narrow, finely formed face. "You think I didn't wanna kill you and that priest, after I seen what you did to He-Dog and Crow Elk? Everything was ready; the new world would've been here by now. We was almost to the top of the ridge, and the dam was supposed to blow. But nothing happened. So He-Dog says, something must've went wrong, and he and Crow Elk drove back down. Good thing I decided to go down there after them, else I wouldn't've seen what happened. But I seen how you and that nosey priest ruined everything. I heard the sirens coming and got out of there."

She stopped a moment. A look of wonder came into her eyes. "All them cop cars racing up to Bull Lake," she said, "and they never seen me pulled over in the trees. After they went by, I drove back to the res, and all the way, I said to myself, they're gonna pay. The ex-wife of Ben Holden and that priest, they're both gotta pay."

"How did you know where I live?" Vicky tossed out the question. *Talk. Talk.* A moment's distraction was all she needed. She kept her eyes on the girl, but her gaze was taking in everything in the space between them: the sofa, the little table with the brass lamp, the light glowing through the white shade. There was no weapon, nothing she might grab and fling.

"Know where you live?" Janis repeated. "It didn't take a law degree. Your auntie, she talks about you all the time. She must've told me two, three times about your new apartment. I seen your name on the mailboxes downstairs."

"I locked my door this morning."

"No kidding." The girl was enjoying this, playing with her.

"Don't need a law degree for that either," Janis said. "Just some wire and a plastic card I found in the glove compartment. Worked just fine."

"You're very clever."

This seemed to please the girl. She gave a smile of acknowledgment, then lifted the rifle a couple inches, her finger curled around the trigger. From somewhere outside came the sound of an engine turning over, and Vicky realized John O'Malley was pulling out of the parking space. She was alone. *Hi sei ci nihi.* She would die here, alone. Just as Ben had died out on Rendezvous Road alone.

"Ready to join your ex?" Janis rolled her head and emitted an eery sound, somewhere between a laugh and a wail. "Oh, he was something else, your ex. 'Need some help, ma'am?' A real gentleman. Never even seen the pistol. Never knew what hit him."

Vicky felt her muscles seize and turn to stone. Her breath came in a sob. She'd gotten it all wrong. It wasn't the Lakotas who had followed Ben to Rendezvous Road. It was Janis Beaver.

She was alone with Ben's killer.

Her mouth was dry. Her tongue felt swollen. She stumbled with the words: "Why, Janis? Why did Orlando leave the killing to you? First Dean, right? Then, Ben." It was making sense. Janis was the one who had taken the twenty-two from Aunt Rose's house. She had used the gun to kill both Dean and Ben. "Why did you have to do the dirty work? Wasn't Orlando man enough?"

Janis rocked backward, an agitated, defensive motion. "Dean wouldn't listen. Kept trying to get me to come with him. Said all kinds of lies about Orlando. How he was a phoney. The messiah, a phoney! I covered my ears. Don't tell me filth, I said. But he kept saying phoney, phoney, phoney. Then he went snooping around the ranch and came back to the tipi shouting how the crazy guards must've stolen dynamite from the Arapaho Ranch and what the hell did they think they was gonna do? He guessed everything. He heard what Orlando said about the old world getting cleaned, and he knew all about the dam. He was going to stop the great event."

The rifle tilted toward the floor, almost as if the girl had forgotten about it. Vicky reached for the lamp, all of her energy focused on the switch. *She had to turn off the light.*

"Stop!" The rifle jerked upward. The girl seemed to muster her forces, remembering her intention. "I said, don't move."

Vicky stood very still, one hand still outstretched. She was barely aware of the soft orange light creeping through the window. It would be daylight soon. People would be up and about. Doors slamming, footsteps pounding down the corridor, car engines turning over outside, all the ordinary sounds of life that might distract the girl. She had to keep her talking!

"I think you're lying," Vicky said. "Dean was shot in the mountains west of Fort Washakie, miles from the shadow ranch."

The girl's chest started to quiver, and a low rumbling noise, like a stifled laugh, came out of her throat. "Orlando said, if you love me, you gotta take care of the problem. I went to Lander Sunday after Dean left. Found him outside his office. Told him I'd changed my mind; it was just gonna be me and him. Oh, he bought it, all right. We drove up to this real peaceful place. It was a good place for him to die."

Her body was shaking now, her head bobbing back and forth. "The problem was taken care of, everything was gonna be fine, like Orlando wanted. Then next day Ben Holden shows up and tells He-Dog and Crow Elk to turn over the dynamite, or he was going to the FBI. When he left, Or-

lando said, 'You know what to do, Janis, if you love me.'
He knew I loved him. So I followed Holden down to Lander
and waited 'til he come outta the restaurant. I followed him
to Rendezvous Road. I passed his truck, then stopped. I
figured he wouldn't think anything about stopping for a
woman with car trouble. Now you're gonna die, just like he
did."

Janis raised the rifle and hunched her shoulders over the
barrel.

"Janis," Vicky shouted. "Orlando's here!"

"He'll come back with the ancestors."

"He's here now, Janis. He's bringing the ancestors now!
Look!" Vicky threw both hands toward the orange glow in
the window.

Janis stood very still, some argument playing out behind
the black, fixated eyes. Then she rolled her head toward the
window.

Vicky lunged for the cord and yanked it out of the socket.
The lamp skittered over the table and crashed onto the floor.
Except for the orange glow, the room was swallowed in
shadows.

"You tricked me!" It was a howling noise, the cry of a
trapped animal.

Vicky dropped down next to the sofa and crouched at the
end, her heart thudding in her ears. She could hear the girl
moving toward her, then she caught a glimpse of the dark
figure passing the window.

She inched toward the coffee table and stopped, all of her
senses on alert. Janis was heading toward the table. One step,
two steps. Vicky held her breath. One more step, and she
could maneuver herself behind the girl, throw her weight
against her, grab the gun.

The air exploded.

The sound of a gunshot bounced around the walls and furniture. Vicky drew herself in and huddled close to the carpet. She stopped her breath. The rifle fired again and again. A whizzing sound passed over her head, followed by the thuds of bullets breaking plaster and splintering wood. Then another shot, and she felt something sharp, like a knife, slice across her shoulder. She winced with the pain and jabbed her fist into her mouth to stop the scream welling in her throat. Something wet and sticky was trickling down her arm. She could smell her own blood. She pulled herself into a tight stillness. *The mountain lion is still*—her grandfather's voice in her head—*it waits for its enemy to come.*

From far away came the sounds of footsteps hammering and men shouting. A pale morning light had begun to seep across the room. Vicky felt the slight displacement in the air, like the displacement when a bird flaps past, and she realized the girl had moved along the coffee table and was standing a few feet away, aiming the rifle down at her.

"Vicky!" A voice in the corridor, and someone pounding on the door. Janis flinched, and in that nanosecond, Vicky flung herself upright at the girl. Then they were falling together against the hard edge and the leg of the coffee table. Vicky was aware of the rifle skittering across the carpet and the pain that locked her left arm. She jammed her right elbow into Janis Beaver's chest as they hit the floor together. The girl was coughing and spitting. Vicky felt the sharp nails raking her face.

From behind came the noise of the door slammed back against the wall and someone shouting—John O'Malley's voice!—"Vicky! Vicky!"

She was aware of people pouring around them. Someone

started pulling her upright, away from the screaming girl crawling toward the rifle. And then the rifle was snatched away, and she realized a large man had grabbed the girl, lifted her to her feet, and was pinning her arms to her sides.

And John O'Malley was helping her to her feet.

The ceiling light came on. The coffee table and sofa, the rest of the room swam around her. She grabbed a fistful of John O'Malley's shirt to steady herself. The girl had started screaming obscenities, kicking out at the man trying to hold her. Another man had picked up the rifle and stepped back. Others—who were they? neighbors?—burst through the door, shouting: "What's going on? Anybody hurt?"

She could see the crowd in the corridor—women with disheveled hair and sleepy eyes, robes flung over night-gowns, a man in a white T-shirt and boxer shorts.

Father John was leading her over to a chair. She sank into the cushion, aware of his finger tracing her shoulder. Her blood felt warm and sticky on her arm. "You've been hit. Were you hit anywhere else?"

She shook her head. People were filling up the room.

Father John made his way through the crowd. Vicky watched him pick up the phone from the floor next to the desk and tap the keys. There had been a shooting, he said into the mouthpiece. Send an ambulance and the police. Over the sound of his voice, she could hear the sirens in the distance.

He disappeared into the kitchen a moment, then he was back, pushing through the crowd that stood in silence, frozen in shock. He dropped down on the armrest and set a cold towel against her shoulder. Her skin went numb; the pain began to subside.

"You came back," she whispered. "I heard you drive away, but you came back."

"I spotted a black truck parked down the street," he said. "I thought I'd better check and make sure you were okay."

They were quiet a moment. Then Vicky said, "She killed Ben."

Father John didn't say anything. The sirens blared from the street below, then cut off. Red, blue, and yellow lights flashed across the window.

Janis was still now. She looked like dead weight in the large man's arms, black hair wet and matted against the narrow face. The sirens cut off, and in another moment the building vibrated with the crash of footsteps in the corridor.

‹ 34 ›

Vicky stood at the window over the kitchen sink and marveled at how time always slipped into a slower rhythm at Aunt Rose's house. In the brush shade outside, Susan was working her way around the table, arranging plates, knives, forks, napkins. Lucas sat across from Aunt Rose, giving the old woman his full attention. She was telling a story, her hands darting like birds between them, her face lit with pride, the same pride, Vicky thought, that the grandmothers in the Old Time took in the young warriors.

Aunt Rose must have finished the story, because Lucas threw back his head and laughed into the sky. Vicky felt a stab of pain. Everything about her son—the tall, muscular body; the handsome, golden-brown face and black agate eyes; even his laugh—was so like his father's.

She turned back to the counter and began mixing the potato salad. Her arm was still stiff and sore, but the bullet had only grazed her shoulder. There was still a bluish-red mark that looked like a burn.

A warm fug of onion and pepper odors filled the air. Grease popped from the frying chicken. This would be their last dinner together, she was thinking. Lucas, Susan, Aunt Rose, almost everyone she loved. Tomorrow, the kids would leave.

They'd been with Aunt Rose almost a week. Susan and Lucas had canceled their plans to leave last Friday. She was grateful. She could never have asked them to stay, not when they had begged her to stay all those years ago—two black-haired children with large, sad eyes—and she had driven away, promising to make things right one day. A promise she had never kept.

It had been a hectic week. The phone had rung almost nonstop, until Aunt Rose had pulled the plug and created blissful silence. Reporters and TV crews had knocked on the door, but Aunt Rose had told them to go away. Vicky had made trip after trip—half a dozen-trips—to Fort Washakie and Lander for interviews with the police and Gianelli, going over the same details and dodging reporters in the hallways. When she finally fell into bed at night, her head spun with the details, and she found herself sitting upright, hugging her pillow and staring into the darkness, trying to wrap her mind around the fact that Ben was gone.

Tomorrow, after the kids left, she would return to her own apartment, her own office. Normal life. Norm Weedly had called. The JBC had agreed to hear her arguments for filing a federal lawsuit. She intended to do her best to convince them to go forward. The people deserved clean water.

Vicky finished the potato salad and started to arrange the fried chicken on a platter. The screen door opened. Susan stepped inside and leaned against the counter. Her face was flushed with the sun, her hair shone.

How she loved this girl that she had lost, Vicky thought. It was like an arrow lodged in her heart. A couple of nights ago, they'd sat on the bed and talked a little before Susan had darted away. But it was a start, Vicky felt certain. A small step toward finding her daughter again.

"It's not the same here without Dad," Susan said, so much sadness in her tone that Vicky dropped the tongs she'd been using, crossed the little kitchen, and took her daughter in her arms.

"I know you miss him," Vicky said, running one hand along Susan's silky hair. The faint smell of shampoo mingled with the humid, spicy odors that filled the kitchen. She didn't know what else to say. That *she* also missed Ben? In a way, it would be the truth. He'd been endlessly patient, tolerant, and accepting with the kids, and she was grateful for that, even though he had never been that way with her. It was as if Susan and Lucas were always more than he felt he deserved, and she was never enough. He had stayed close to the kids. *That* was the memory of Ben she would hold on to. The other memories, she would let go.

The screen door banged open, punctuating Aunt Rose's voice: "Got some company." She stood on the stoop and held the door back. "Bring out another plate."

Susan pulled away and started rummaging in the cabinets. "Just like Aunt Rose to find somebody in need of dinner," she said. She was smiling.

John O'Malley, Vicky thought, aware of the pure, glad rush moving through her. She'd caught sight of him at the interviews, but he'd been questioned in one room, she in another. She'd wanted to thank him again for coming back to the apartment. If he hadn't called her name and knocked when he did . . . All week, she'd been trying to block the thought of what would have happened.

She handed Susan the bowl of potato salad, then picked

up the platter of chicken and, backing through the screen door, followed her daughter outside. Halfway across the yard, she stopped. The man in the brush shade—hands jammed into the pockets of his khaki trousers, dark blue polo shirt outlining the muscles across his back—was Adam Lone Eagle. Chatting and laughing with Lucas, as if they were old friends. In a way, they were, she guessed. Lucas had gone to Lander with her for the interviews, and Adam had been there. They had seemed to hit it off.

"Vicky!" The lawyer looked around, then walked over. "Let me give you a hand," he said, taking the chicken platter.

"You fry this chicken?" There was approval in the sideways glance he gave her as they stepped into the shade. He set the platter on the table.

"Nice to see you, Adam." She tried to keep the disappointment out of her voice. If John O'Malley hadn't come to her, well, tomorrow, she resolved, she would go to him. There was so much that had been left unsaid between them.

"Sit down. Eat, eat." Aunt Rose dropped into the webbed folding chair at the end of the table. "Give thanks to the Creator," she said when everyone was seated. "We have good food to sustain our lives, a good house to shelter us. We been blessed with the good people the Creator sent us." She paused. Lucas and Susan both bowed their heads, taking a moment, Vicky knew, to absorb again the reality of their father's death.

"So now we eat," Aunt Rose said. An order meant to be obeyed, just as her own grandmothers and great-grandmothers had been obeyed when they ordered their families and visitors to eat. No one left an Arapaho village hungry. She passed the chicken and motioned for Susan to start the potato salad.

The polite preliminaries took up most of the meal: the hot weather, the powwow next week, the new convenience store about to open. Adam Lone Eagle was observing the Arapaho tradition, Vicky knew. He understood it wasn't yet the time to discuss what they all knew had brought him here.

After Lucas had delivered mugs of steaming coffee, and she and Susan had distributed the rhubarb pie that Susan had baked that afternoon, and the sky had softened with the sun edging below the mountains, the Lakota cleared his throat. Everyone else became quiet. The breeze clattered softly on the brush walls.

"I met with Gianelli and the U.S. attorney this afternoon. Janis Beaver has confessed to the murders of both Dean Little Horse and . . ." He hesitated. "Ben," he said softly. "The grand jury has indicted her on two counts of first-degree homicide. He-Dog and Crow Elk are looking at twenty-six counts of attempting to assist a suicide; conspiracy to commit murder; conspiracy to destroy public property; theft of an explosive substance . . ." He threw up his hands, as if the list were too long to enumerate.

Aunt Rose shook her head. "The shadow dancers went wrong," she said. "Lost their way. Wovoka never preached the stuff Orlando preached. Orlando got it all wrong. Too bad. He could've been good for the people, brought us closer together, given us back some of the old way."

"Unfortunately, the followers believed in him," Adam said. "They found his website on the Internet and came here to be saved. There's no evidence they were coerced into taking drugs. They all told the same story. They had a final celebration, worked themselves into a frenzy, then took the drugs so they could join the ancestors coming after the flood. Orlando had the same intention. But he'd been taking the drugs so long, he knew he had to take more than usual. Before he swallowed the pills, he'd ordered He-Dog and Crow Elk to blow up the dam. Afterward, they were supposed to return to the shadow ranch, take the drugs themselves, and wait for the ancestors."

Adam took a long sip from his mug, working out something else in his mind. Finally he said, "Orlando could count on the two Lakotas to blow up the dam. He understood that . . ." He paused again and gazed out over the yard. "We have an old wound that still festers, an old grudge that was never settled."

"Wounded Knee," Vicky heard herself saying. In the man's expression, she glimpsed the kind of sorrow that her own people carried through the years, like a bundle of broken arrows that had belonged to the ancestors.

Adam nodded. "Orlando knew how to use the massacre. He preached about how the soldiers had killed Big Foot's band and stopped the Ghost Dance before the new world could arrive. He convinced the followers that no one could be allowed to stand in the way of the new world this time. Not Dean Little Horse or Ben Holden. He even sent He-Dog and Crow Elk to St. Francis Mission to warn away Father O'Malley. Those Indians would've killed him, if they'd seen him."

He paused. "You're lucky, Vicky, that they didn't kill you."

Susan gasped. "No more risks, Mom. Promise you won't take any more risks."

Lucas leaned toward her and thumped the table. "We

don't want to worry about you all the time." He hesitated. "The way Dad did."

A new kind of quiet, uncomfortable and heavy, gripped the brush shade a moment before Vicky said, "Believe me, I prefer a nice, quiet, normal life." She glanced around the table, and beyond to the expanse of open land lying hot and quiet under the red-flamed sky. This was normal, she thought.

"I like the same kind of life," Adam said, and she realized that, for the last several moments, he had not taken his eyes from her.

The phone rang again—at least the tenth call this morning, Father John guessed. He looked up from the notes he was making for tonight's parish council meeting. The click-click sound of Father George's computer keys down the hall punctuated an aria from *Falstaff* that emanated softly from the tape player on the bookshelf behind him. Yesterday, both he and Father George had said the funeral Mass for Dean Little Horse. They'd blessed the young man's grave in the mission cemetery.

His assistant was a hard worker, he had to admit. The man had practically run the mission by himself all week.

Father John was tempted to let the phone ring. Gianelli or Banner wanting to talk to him again, another reporter wanting an interview.

Finally he reached over and lifted the receiver. There was always the chance the caller was someone in need of a priest.

"Father O'Malley," he said.

An unfamiliar voice sounded on the other end, a reporter from a newspaper in the Midwest somewhere. Would he answer a few questions about the shadow dance cult? Did all those people intend to commit suicide?

No, they had not intended to commit suicide. Not exactly. It was complicated. They'd believed they were going to the ancestors and would return immediately to a new and better world. He said he'd already given a statement to the press that explained everything. Why couldn't they get it? He had no other comment.

He hung up. It was the last thing he'd needed, after the board of directors meeting last weekend, for his name to be splashed across the national news: JESUIT PRIEST INTERVENES IN MASS SUICIDE. The Provincial was not pleased. Two minutes after CNN had broken the story, the phone had rung, and Father John had known, before he'd answered, who was on the other end.

"My God, John, what is going on out there?" Father Bill Rutherford, an old friend from seminary days, two young men full of promise, great things ahead, which had been true in Rutherford's case.

Father John had started to explain, but the Provincial had interrupted.

"Am I clear on this? The board of directors is attempting to ascertain whether the society should continue to support St. Francis Mission, and you leave the meeting to go to a place called the shadow ranch, where there are one dead man and twenty-six unconscious people. Then you drive to a dam that's about to be blown up?"

He was clear, Father John said. Then he said that he didn't regret what he'd done. There was every chance several of the dancers would have died if the medics hadn't gotten there when they did. Several were still at Riverton Memorial, although most of the dancers, according to the moccasin telegraph, had left the reservation and gone back to wherever they'd come from.

The line had gone quiet for a moment. "Yes, it was fortunate you arrived in time," Father Rutherford said, a quieter tone, less agitated, the tone of the priest, not the administrator. Then, the administrator again:. "CNN says you and that woman lawyer are heroes. You placed your own lives in danger. I'd hoped you wouldn't continue making a practice of this kind of activity. Surely the police can handle such emergencies."

Of course, Father John had said. No, he didn't plan to make a practice of this kind of activity.

"Good. I'm glad to hear it." The Provincial didn't sound reassured. Then—a lighter tone—he said: "I don't want to turn on the TV and see your Irish face on the national news again."

His Irish face had been on the national news for six days, a burden, he imagined, that the Provincial was clenching his teeth and trying to bear, just as he was. Especially since his name was continually linked with Vicky's.

He hadn't been able to stop thinking about her. He'd tried calling her at Aunt Rose's, and finally given up. They must have unplugged the phone. Why wouldn't they? He wished he could do the same. He'd passed her in the halls at the interviews, asked how her shoulder was. He'd been relieved when she waved her arm and assured him she was fine. But she'd looked fatigued and tense, with bluish scratches on her face and dark circles rimming her eyes, as if she hadn't been sleeping. He probably looked the same, he thought. He hadn't been sleeping either.

He'd gone back to his notes when he heard the sound of a vehicle turning onto Circle Drive, then the motor cutting off. His fingers tightened around the pen at the thought of another reporter poking his head through the door. He'd get rid of him as fast as possible.

A moment passed before he heard the footsteps on the concrete steps and the swoosh of the front door opening and closing. He recognized the footsteps crossing the corridor and got to his feet just as Vicky appeared in the doorway.

"How are you?" he said. She looked more rested, more the way she'd looked the first time she'd appeared in his doorway, except that now she wore jeans and a white shirt.

"That's what I came to ask you." She stepped inside and dropped into one of the side chairs.

"Your shoulder?" He walked around the desk and sat against the edge.

"The only part of me that isn't brown," she said. "It's red and blue."

He tried to push away the thought that had nagged him all week: The bullet that grazed her shoulder had come within inches of her head. *Her head.*

"I never got the chance to thank you again for coming back to the apartment," she said. "You got there just in time."

Thank God, he was thinking.

The clacking of computer keys floated from the rear office. Then Vicky smiled, as if a new thought had pushed to the forefront of her mind. "What about the mission?"

"Why do I get the idea you already know?"

She shrugged. "The moccasin telegraph is a wonder of technology. It continues to operate even with the phone unplugged. I heard how the pickups and cars were parked all the way out to Seventeen-Mile Road, how Eagle Hall was jam packed and people stood outside, chanting and praying, how speaker after speaker got up and told the board they had no business closing the mission. And Amos spoke for thirty minutes. In Arapaho!" She threw back her head and laughed. "I wish I could have seen the board members' faces. They must have felt like the cavalry surrounded by Indians."

He laughed with her. "The board left first thing the next morning."

"I hear the mission stays," she said.

"That was the consensus before the board left."

"I'm glad, John." She got up, walked past him to the window, and stared quietly outside a moment. "My family doesn't want me taking any more risks."

"Smart people, your family." Father John paused. The Provincial didn't want him taking risks either, and he had promised to try to refrain. But he would go, he knew. He would always go if someone needed him. And so would Vicky. They were alike, he thought.

She turned toward him. The sun glinted in her hair. "John," she said, "there's so much I want to say to you."

He felt his heart knock against his ribs. "Don't, Vicky," he said. "Don't say anything."

She was shaking her head. "Ben and his family were right, you know. For a long time, I'd been hoping . . ."

He put up his hand to stop her, but she went on.

"But I understand now. This is your place. This is where you belong." She lifted both arms toward the mission and beyond, and he knew that she was not referring only to the place, but to what he was, a priest. "But this is also where I belong. It's my land, my place. I can't keep going to Denver. I can't run away from this place again, but the thing is, I don't think I can stop loving you."

"Oh, Vicky, don't." He shook his head. "Don't love me."

He would never stop loving her. "There will be someone—"

She cut in and hurried on, as if she were delivering a speech she'd memorized. "The fact is, we're both here, and I want us to be friends, John. I really need you to be my friend, but I have to make room in my life for something else."

She pivoted around and looked out the window. He walked over and placed his arm around her. "You deserve to be happy," he said. She seemed small next to him, and he could smell the faint odor of sage in her hair. Outside the sky was blue and clear as glass. A crow was circling above the cottonwoods. Walks-On lay on his side in the sun in front of the residence. All the buildings looked peaceful, rooted to the earth.

She was right. This was his place, this was where he could be the priest he wanted to be. Still, he felt as if something hard had been laid on his heart.

"I want you to be happy, Vicky," he said, letting her go.

She was quiet a moment, her gaze fixed on the mission grounds beyond the window. Finally she said, "It's like the new world that Wovoka promised would come someday. The mission is beautiful and peaceful. The ancestors left this for us, like a sign, something to strive for and hope for. No wonder the people turned out for the board meeting. It wouldn't be the same here without this place."

"You sound like the pastor."

She laughed, and there was something free and light in the sound of her voice that made him glad.

"Oh, no," she said. "There's only one pastor at St. Francis Mission, John O'Malley."